Healing H

Willowbrook, Volume 1

Kerry Kennedy

Published by Kerry Kennedy, 2024.

ISBN 9798224061495

First Edition

Also by Kerry Kennedy

Willowbrook
Healing Hearts

Standalone
Santa Fe Billionaire

Table of Contents

Other Books by The Author

Dakota a steamy, suspense, crime-thriller
Who's Watching Who a tense and gripping psychological thriller.
The Sound, an edge-of-your-seat horror
Jimmy Choos to Cleaning Loos, a rom-com for all lovers of Jenny Colgan, Sophie Kinsella and Carole Matthews.

Meet Me In Casablanca a heart-warming billionaire romance
Santa Fe Billionaire an enemies to lovers, close proximity romance

Children's Books
Boris Flies to the Moon
Boris Vuela a la Luna a bilingual children's book
Boris Meets Father Christmas
Little Miss Daisy the Strawberry
Audio Books
Boris Flies to the Moon
Boris Meets Father Christmas
Who's Watching Who a tense and gripping psychological thriller.
Coming in 2024 to Audio
Dakota & Meet Me In Casablanca
Wattpad Stories & Goodnovel Books
Healing Hearts Book 1 in the Willowbrook Series
Cuffing The Law Book2 in the Willowbrook Series
Love at Lazy Duke's Book2 in the Willowbrook Series
Santa Fe Billionaire
Ice Bound Hearts
Crushing On My Bad Boy Billionaire Best Friend
Ice Hockey Stud and His Best Friend's Sister Book1 in the Minnesota Ice Series
Puck Love Reunited Book 2 in the Minnesota Ice Series
Ice Bound Hearts

9

Coming Soon:
Isadora in L.A. /Shopaholic in L.A.
(Sequel to Jimmy Choos to Cleaning Loos)
The sequel to Jimmy Choos to Cleaning Loos. A romantic comedy. Gerard has a new announcement, that they are moving to Los Angeles. Will Isadora be receptive now that she has finally come to terms with life in the quaint and rural village in the heart of Catalonia. What can possibly go wrong in L.A?
When Ellie decides that she wants to earn her own money and becomes a personal shopper to some of the largest names in Hollywood.

The Baker's Boys
Book 1 in the Richendale Series
When Troy and Bradley meet for the first time, it's insta-attraction only Troy is married to Mel. As they navigate their feelings for one another and fight against the tide that takes them, these two need to manage their relationship in such a way as not to hurt the ones they love in the small town of Richendale. It's not easy living in a small town as Troy and Bradley discover, but they have to fight for the love that fills their hearts.

The Nearly Broken Wedding
(Sequel to The Baker's Boys Book2 of the Richendale Series
Richendale is about to have the wedding of the year when Jed and Melissa finally decide to tie the knot. Then Jed's ex-fiancée arrives on the scene and things start to go horribly wrong. Will Jed and Melissa manage to get to the aisle and pledge their vows to one another? Read this delightful romantic comedy, the sequel to The Baker's Boys as we continue where we left off. Guest appearances from Violet, Troy and Bradley as their love continues to grow and a new baby is on board. A delightful small-town romance.

Saving My Baby
The year is 2073 and things have changed. With the world at risk the government in one country, England has decided that action is required.

Many laws have been passed. One being that every household can only have one child or face being locked away in a camp and their child killed. Harsh sanctions are imposed to keep the child and human count down. One young mother accidentally falls pregnant with her second child and has a fight on her hands to
try to get the baby out of the country. It's tough as border control means nobody goes out or comes in. Can she save herself, her husband and her baby from a fate that means death?
A gripping and harrowing thriller set to make you turn the pages and binge read.

Dedication

To all the guys and girls who have loved each other forever, where life may have got in the way and time took you apart and to finding each other again xoxo

To all my readers, without you none of this would be possible. Thank you.

To my wonderful and amazing man, Craig for always giving me the time and space to write and for supporting me with my endeavors.

To all the bookstagrammers and booktokers out there, who always provide me with amazing feedback and take the time to read and review my books, a huge thank you for all your support.

To the writing community on Twitter and LinkedIn who provide endless amount of support, it's an honor to be part of the communities. Thank you so much.

To my parents who would have been so proud of me, I miss you both always.

Chapter 1

"That'll be sixty-five dollars ma'am." Says Bob whose name I can now see on his name badge firmly fixed to his yellow shirt with the company logo on it.

"Thanks, Bob." I take my card out of my purse and hold it over the card reader.

"Now you have a good day ma'am and drive safe." He beams at me. I could pinch his cheeks, he's adorable. All ruddy faced and at least sixty years of age. I bet he has a Mrs Bob at home who bakes him cherry pie on a weekly basis and ensures her husband never goes without his hot pot or roast on a Sunday.

That pulls at my heart and all of a sudden, I feel a sense of longing, emptiness and engulfing loneliness. Only, this was the life I thought I was going to be having back in Michigan.

Dragging my feet, not something I usually do only I'm not in a rush to get back to Willowbrook, it's a case of necessity more than anything else. I get to my car, open the driver's side and scoot into my seat. Hook my seatbelt on, turn over the engine and start to ease the car out of the garage.

I contemplate whether to drive the next four hours or to find a place to stay in West Virginia. Stopping in Columbus had been an option but to be honest, I wanted to give myself a lot more distance between what I had called home and where I'm heading.

Life can really suck sometimes, and today it sucks a whole lot and then some.

Some love song is playing on the radio. That's the last thing I want to listen to. Some mushy clap trap that only saddens me more. Instead, I press the button on my steering wheel, the one that controls the radio and search desperately for a different channel. There's a talk show, some heavy rock, country music and a gospel channel. Country is out, that's all about heartache, sorrow or falling love with your childhood sweetheart.

Well love has let me down in a big way. Let's say that again. Love. Has. Let. Me. Down. That and Miles. Yes, Miles. Let me tell you a bit about him. As much as I want to hate him I can't. He stole my heart ten years ago when I moved to Michigan at the age of twenty-five. I'd just graduated from med school and done my internship and was assigned my first placement in Michigan State hospital. Was that a big deal? You want to bet it was. A huge big deal. Especially since I was still so young, but I was an outstanding student and worked hard to succeed.

Being a doctor is all I wanted to do from the young age of five. My favourite game to play with Ali was doctors and nurses. My parents even bought me the whole white coat, stethoscope, watch. You get the picture. Ali bless her, had to be the patient. Always. She would have bandages around her arms, slings with the pretence she had a broken arm. I tried to make a cast once but the less said about that the better.

I digress. I was talking about Miles. My heart lurches, it feels as if it is about to drive its way out of my mouth. My stomach gnarls, I'm in physical pain. It hurts so damn much that tears begin to roll down my face.

Instead of taking in the scenery around me, the trees ranging from firs and pines to oaks I'm driving along almost ugly crying with a snotty nose. And I don't have any tissues. Who has a breakup and doesn't have tissues on them? Me that's who.

Instead, I use the back of my right hand to wipe them away and sniff loudly for all the gunk that is dribbling from my nose. We've all done that ugly crying thing, right?

On my first day at Michigan State, I was so nervous that I'd forget everything I'd been taught. My stomach was in knots, my hands were sweaty, and I wanted to run back out the sliding glass doors. Only I couldn't. Saving lives, making people feel better, putting them on the track of health and happiness, that was all I wanted to do. So, there I found myself with first day jitters standing in the reception area of ward 9 waiting for someone to come and take me under their wing.

And who was that? You've got it. Miles. I swear the first time I set eyes on him I almost swooned. You see he's tall, sandy coloured hair and pale blue eyes. If I had to compare him to someone, I'd go for an early Robert Redford kind of look.

"Hey, you must be Sage." He extended his hand. I noticed the long fingers as they made contact with mine as we shook hands and felt an electric shock right though my arm into my chest. I knew then that I was going to be in trouble.

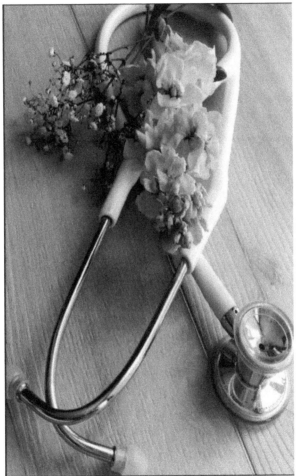

Chapter 2

S*age*
    I wake to my alarm going off, it's practically still night time as I reach for my mobile and swipe to turn the noise off. It's just five a.m and I hardly

slept last night thinking about Miles and what we had, my job at Michigan State and the life we shared.

All those dinner parties, all the theatre events, galas and functions. I miss everything so much and even though I should be bitter and twisted that Miles ended our long-term relationship, I'm hurting too much that I feel physically in pain and sick.

I groan, wishing I had just turned the alarm notification off. It's not like I have anything to get up. I've only got a few more hours to drive to Willowbrook where my parents and my sister, Ali will be waiting for me. I'm hoping my mother hasn't gone all out and decided to invite the whole town.

Laying with my arms behind my head in the darkness tears slide slowly down my face. This time three weeks ago I had no idea my life was about to change. None. Zilch. Only it did and it has left me speechless. How can you possibly carry on when the man of your life for the past ten years tells you he's taken a new role, a fellowship? Which of course is admirable and I know this is what Miles was always working towards. Only I didn't expect him to tell me he was going to London.

There was no discussion and I think if I'm being perfectly honest this is what hurts the most. It's tearing me apart. The fact that he just announced it over dinner one night. A special dinner, the dinner I thought he was going to propose to me during. How stupid and wrong could I have been?

There we were, seated in a romantic corner of the best restaurant in Michigan, The Ocean Prime with its elegant blue seating, round white damask table coverings, the best crystal and cutlery enjoying a glass of champagne. I'd worn my elegant full length black dress, Audrey Hepburn style and yes with the pearls. All I lacked was the long cigarette holder and the tiara. I'd done my make-up all smoky eyes and luscious red lips, and as we sipped our champagne and chatted about our days, my breath kept catching in my throat. Butterflies were swarming my stomach. The expectation of his proposal was killing me.

Now, I feel like such an idiot. We hadn't exactly discussed marriage, not openly like adults that we were. Sure we'd touched on the general stuff like yes we'd like to be married, yes we'd like to have kids. Preferably two you know the ideal, one boy and one girl. You get the picture. How we'd make our money move to the country side or buy a house on the lake and live happily ever after. Okay, so now the tears are rolling down my cheeks. I remove my left arm and wipe my face with my left hand. I'm stripped bare, torn up and seriously ugly crying.

Why can't I just be mad at him? Why can't I truly hate him? Because I still love Miles. I think perhaps I always will. My chest hurts like I can't breathe. There has only been one other person in my life and that was when I was about fifteen. I dated Logan during school and we split up when I decided I wanted to go to college elsewhere and follow my dream of being a doctor in a bit city. Logan didn't want to move, he didn't want to go out into the big world. Not back then, who knows where in the world he is now. Probably snapped up by some gorgeous woman with a couple of kids in tow. My life, how I thought it would be.

I met Miles and he took me under his wing from day one when I joined Michigan State. He was pretty damn difficult to resist and with his boyish charm and good looks, he had me pretty hooked from the start. It didn't bother me that every nurse practically in the hospital, male and female I hasten to add were after a piece of him. He was everyone's favourite, handsome doctor. Corny but true. Oh, so true. I exhale.

Anyway, I digress. Dinner. Ocean Prime restaurant. The best in Michigan, the most romantic restaurant where couples become engaged, proposals happen every day as couples look adoringly into one another's eyes. A bit like I was looking into Miles' eyes.

"I've got something exciting to say." He told me. I took another sip of champagne thinking, this is it. It's really going to happen. I'm going to be married. I had already visualized my wedding gown, a delicate ivory Vera Wang with kitten heel shoes. Bridesmaids in jade green straight dresses with fitted bodices. My hair would be up in a French twist with blush miniature roses threaded through. I was smiling from ear to ear, I could feel how my eyes were dancing and sparkling. Of course, the amount of champagne I was knocking back probably helped.

I reached my left hand out to his right hand across the table, in readiness for the Tiffany ring to be placed on my finger.

"I've been accepted." I narrowed my eyes wondering what the word accepted actually had to do with a marriage proposal. Perhaps my ears needed cleaning out. "To the Royal Marsden in London. Can you believe it? It's been my dream."

His dream, since when? I can't ever recall him telling me he wanted to go to London for his oncology fellowship and there he was sitting across me not evening touching my hand, which I quickly withdraw as if it's been scalded with boiling water and place it in my lap. I was dumbfounded.

My eyes cast downwards taking in the sea bass sitting untouched on my plate, dressed perfectly with broccoli, pearly onion and potato puree. Good job I hadn't touched it otherwise I'd probably have heaved it all up at his words.

"Say something." Miles encouraged me. Like what? What does he want me to say? He's made a life changing decision without even talking to me about it. Not even hinted it to me. I felt dizzy and faint. My breathing was shallow, my chest tight.

"Sage." Miles leant forward. "Are you okay?"

I cleared my throat. "London. Fellowship. Oncology." I stammered. "When did you decide this? We've not ever discussed this and why can't you go to one of the main hospitals here. Why London? Miles, you do realize I can't just give up my career in medicine and follow you." I gulped and almost choked on the lump forming in my throat.

"Of course, Sage. I wouldn't expect you to give up your life. I know you love it here, this was your dream. Only it's not my dream."

I interrupt him. "But it was your dream. You told me when we first met all those years ago. You told me you'd always wanted to work out of Michigan State like your father." Bewildered doesn't cover the turmoil my mind was in.

"Once it was, for sure. I'm not denying that. But I've moved on and I want more. I want to be a specialist and I want to travel. I've achieved what my father achieved, I have followed in his footsteps. Now it's time for me to branch out and I know I'll make a brilliant oncologist specialist."

"I don't disagree, Miles. I know you will but what about us?" I realize I sounded upset, I was clutching on to straws. He had that look he gets when he's made his mind up and is focused on an end goal.

"Why didn't you discuss it with me?" My voice is just a whisper, the last thing I want to do is draw attention to us both whilst my life is shattering into pieces.

"I knew you would try to fight it and dissuade me." He pushes his own plate slightly away and clasps his hands in front of him, resting them on the table. Would I have done? Yes, probably.

"But no notice, Miles. You can't just walk away from ten years together. You simply can't." And now as I lay here in the early hours of the morning crying like a goddamn baby, I wish I'd stood up that evening and punched him right in the face for being deceitful and arrogant instead of whimpering like a dog and hurting inside like my heart was torn apart, thrown to the ground and stomped all over.

"We could do long distance?" Ever the hopeful person me.

"I don't think it will work, Sage. Not with your schedule at the hospital and me doing a fellowship. We wouldn't see each other and this way we're not trying to hold on to something."

"Some things are worth holding onto, Miles." Least way, that is how I felt. Clearly the man I'd spent the last ten years with, didn't feel at all the same way. That is such a kick in the teeth. Your gut feels like it's gripped by a vice, you can't break, suffocation almost consumes you.

And as if that wasn't bad enough, I was totally unaware I had more bad news to come.

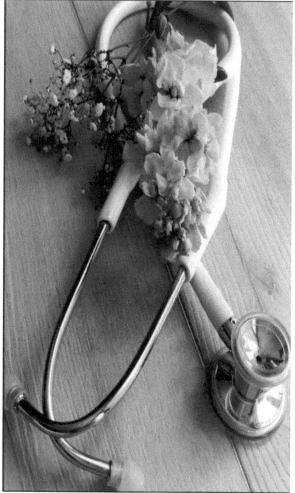

Chapter 3

S*age*
    There isn't anything I can do now but haul my ass out of bed and start to get ready to check out of this small motel and head over to

Willowbrook. I stopped off at the Mineral Springs Motel which is nestled amongst the mountains and forest land on the banks of the Elk river. It's a stunning location but then to be honest, anywhere in this part of the US is. It feels as if I am close to home. Which strictly speaking I am.

It's not that I'm dreading going home. Okay, maybe a bit. The last thing on my agenda was having to move back in with my parents until I have enough money behind me to rent a room somewhere or a small house in Willowbrook. But they're kind of hard to find and I did try. So the last option was asking my parents if I could have my old room back.

"Of course you can, honey. You don't even have to ask. It's just as it was when you left." My mom had said when I phoned her a couple of weeks ago. The excitement in her voice was sweet but in my heart I just wanted my life to stay as it was. You know the life with Miles, the life at Michigan State, not a massive distance away in Virginia. Back home. In my old room.

As I get ready and throw some things in my overnight bag, I groan just thinking about how my room back home will be. It'll have all my stuff in it from when I was a kid. I try not to think about it and sweep the room with my eyes to make sure I've not left my book on the bedside that I read last night. I have my mobile in my back pocket of my faded black jeans that have rips on the thighs and the shin from being worn so much.

I tie my hair up into a ponytail not even bothering to brush it, after all who have I got to make a good impression for? Nobody. Exactly. That's my point. Make-up is not on my mind nor is having a shower. I had one last night and I can take a long soak in the bath at my parent's home. It should only take me another couple of hours to get there. Last night I was just too tired and emotionally drained to carry on.

The sun is rising and across the trees I can see the promise of a beautiful day heading our way, even if it is going to be blazing hot. The mornings are gorgeous as are the sunsets. I'd love to stay and just take all of my surroundings in but then I guess I'll have plenty of time to do that when I get back to my hometown since I haven't secured another position yet either.

So, you may be wondering what happened with my job at Medical State. Cut backs. That's what happened. Although I have a sneaky suspicion that since Miles was leaving and he was the senior doctor there, a decision was made to let me go. Perhaps I'm being a bit dramatic and having an over-active imagination also doesn't serve me well. Paranoia perhaps. I shrug my shoulders, none of that matters anymore.

I'm here now without a job, without a boyfriend who I thought was going to be my fiancé and I'm just lost. Totally, utterly lost. I feel bereft, empty, hollow and my eyes I know without having to bother looking in a mirror are sunken with dark circles. I've also lost some weight. That's what a break up will do to you. It leaves you a complete wreck if you're not expecting it and you're not the one who instigated it.

I'm trying so hard not to think about Miles and the fact that he will be on his way to London now, if he hasn't already left. After the night in the restaurant I was so shell shocked that I just got up and left. He didn't call after me he simply let me go. Looking back, he was more than likely trying to avoid any sort of embarrassment and conflict in the heart of a busy restaurant.

We hardly spoke for a couple of days, besides our shifts meant that we were like ships passing in the night. We hardly saw each other and at the hospital we didn't bump into each other. Personally, I think he was avoiding me and I definitely was avoiding him. In hindsight I think I thought that by ignoring him the situation wouldn't be actually happening. Only it was and after three nights when we were both back at the apartment, Miles made a point of stopping me during my dinner.

"I'm really sorry, Sage. I never wanted to hurt you." Jeez, don't you just hate it when they say that. If I hadn't been so darn hungry he'd have been wearing my plate of spaghetti and tuna. "It's just something I have always wanted to do. I should have discussed it with you, I know that only." He stopped and ran his fingers through his hair. I wish I didn't love him so much, I wish I could hate him and despise him but I couldn't. My heart was breaking literally in two. I pushed my plate away from me, I wasn't hungry anymore.

"Yes, Miles. You should have done. How am I supposed to have known this. At least if you had of discussed it with me, perhaps I could have thought about. I may have decided to give London a go too." I left it unsaid *unless of course you don't actually want me to go with you.* Suppose he didn't ever intend for me to go. Suppose our relationship had run its course, in his mind anyway. Certainly not in mine. I'll never know the real reason.

I'm in the car and take a last look at the cabin I stayed in for the night, turn on the ignition and make my way out of the motel car park and head onto the I-64 towards home. I should arrive at my parent's house for around half ten.

Dolly Parton's *I will always love you* plays on the radio and my eyes fill with fresh tears. Seriously, how many tears can one person shed? My stomach knots. AGAIN. The pain sears through my chest and if wasn't for the fact that I'm a qualified doctor, I'd think I was having a heart attack and about to die.

Chapter 4

S*age*

"She's here, oh look she's finally arrived." My mom is screeching, any louder and she'll be notifying the neighbourhood. Honestly, anyone would think I've never been home since I left for Michigan. Perhaps I haven't been home as often as I should have. The usual Christmas, Thanksgiving, my parents birthdays and the odd visit here and there. That's at least four times a year.

Well I guess mom's would like you around all the time if they could. Dads too. There she is standing on her wrap around porch waving even though I'm only a few paces away from her. She looks amazing in a pinstriped fitted dress with a white collar and heels.

My mother is always dressed like something out of a 1950's movie set. Glamorous is her middle name, it comes from all the years she worked in an office for a very sophisticated, rich man. Her ex-boss owns half of Willowbrook and is now the mayor. Mom doesn't work anymore, she took early retirement and enjoys ladies lunches with her good friends, sits on various committees and does an awful lot of work at the hospice as an administrator volunteering.

Her auburn hair is perfectly styled in a very sharp bob and her green eyes are like emeralds. There is no doubt about it, my mother could easily have been a model in her day. She's petite in every way and when dad comes to stand next to her, he literally dwarfs her with his six foot, two inch frame. He places an arm around my mom's waist and kisses her on the head. It's adorable. They are adorable. Again, my heart pangs – this is how I saw myself being with Miles when we grew older and into our early sixties.

Mom wriggles free and comes dashing down the three steps from the wrap around and with open arms almost crushes me to her bosom. Suffocating, a little, but you can't help love my mother. She's always been there for dad, Ali and myself. She is the backbone of our family and even though she worked long hours as a private assistant for Christopher the now mayor, mom never let anything slip in the house.

Dad has his own business, he's an architect and a damn good one. He's won all sorts of prizes and awards. Though he is in his sixties there is no stopping this man.

"Welcome home, darling." Mom says as she unfolds me from her embrace and links her left arm into my right arm. "Just drop your bag, dad will come and get it." She whooshes my holdall onto the floor from my hand and starts marching me into the house.

We go up the steps and then cross the threshold into my parents warm and welcoming home with its ash wood flooring throughout the downstairs, a large open space where there sits an open fireplace in the lounge area, two Tiffany blue sofas facing each other and floor to ceiling windows. The magnificent beams look like they've recently been oiled and I can smell something delicious in the kitchen.

"I've made pancakes, your favourite." Mom leads me straight to the kitchen area where a long island with a beech wood top divides the space between the two areas. Dad is following behind with my bag. I unhook myself from my mother and turn.

"Hey pop." He pulls me to him and gives me a huge teddy bear hug. Every girl needs a *dad hug* every now and again, today I definitely do.

"Hey sweetheart. It's good to see you. Come on let's get a coffee inside you and you can tell us all about it properly." Coffee, now that sounds like a mighty fine idea. I drove the last two hours straight through not stopping for anything. The aroma of roasted coffee beans meet my nostrils and I literally can feel myself salivating. Did I forget to mention, I'm a caffeine junkie? Something Miles never understood. He would berate me about it all the time, being a green tea lover himself. Never could stand that stuff. Yuck.

Mom busies herself filling mugs up with coffee then turns to the hob to make the pancakes. There is maple syrup, a bowl of fresh blueberries and a bowl of strawberries on the island along with my favourite filler, Nutella chocolate spread. My stomach growls, yep it's hungry alright.

"I don't really feel like talking about it much to be honest." I say as I perch myself on one of the high stools at the island and rest my chin in my hands. The coffee arrives right in front of me, I take a sip. Jeez that's damn hot.

"That's okay, lovely. Take your time. We don't need all the details. We're just so happy you're home, back here with us." Mom looks like she's having all her Christmases at once, her favourite time of the year. Her eyes are lit up and even though she knows I'm hurting inside, her happiness is evident that her eldest daughter is back home in the fold.

"Is Ali at work?" I ask glancing around. There are canvas family pictures on every wall, some in black and white of the two of us when we were children, at our graduations, our proms. It's a history of our lives. There is definitely a cosy vibe in our parent's home. The colour scheme is relaxing with white washed walls and soft furnishings in my mom's all-time favourite, Tiffany blue.

"Yes, she said she'd pop in after work to catch up with you, unless you want to head over to her office and have lunch with her. Ali wasn't entirely sure what time you'd be here. She said that your messaging was a bit, shall we say non-existent."

"Yeah, sorry about that. I haven't felt much like communicating." I finish my coffee and start tucking into the pancakes, after of course I've lavished them with enough chocolate spread to keep me sweet for weeks. Oh, being a doctor and giving out advice then not taking it yourself could be call hypocritical. I can live with that.

"That's understandable, love. Head over to see her if you can." Dad says. "Right ladies, I have work to do, it won't get done on its own." He excuses himself from the island and heads across the living area space, through a set of double doors to where his office is. I love dad's office, it's close to a library, like me, he is an avid reader.

"I'll think about it. Maybe I'll just head to my room after breakfast, Mom and start looking for a new job."

"Right you are love. Of course. But in all honesty, Sage darling you really should take some time for yourself. Going through a break up after so many years and losing your job, both in the same week is a lot to take on board. Don't rush into anything just yet. Promise me."

Well I can't make my mom a promise. All I know is that my savings will only go so far and I am definitely, no matter how much I love my parents – not staying at home for the rest of my life. So, basically I need a job and a good paying job. I'll start with looking at the closest city hospitals and that way I can also make sure I don't end up staying in Willowbrook. It's beautiful don't get me wrong, we're right by the mountains and the forest, we have everything we need but it's just a bit too tight knit for me.

I need to get to the closest big city with a hospital that needs a doctor of my calibre stat.

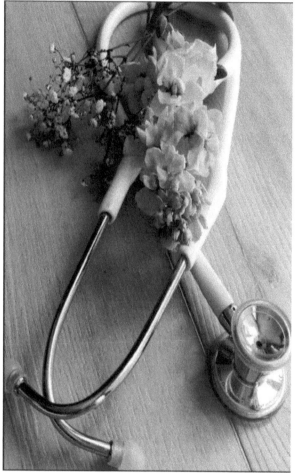

Chapter 5

L*ogan*
      I'm having a totally rubbish morning. First, my dog, Hector an Airedale terrier decided he was going to run after some rabbits on our walk this morning. We headed off early, seven in the morning as we usually do.

Behind my log cabin here in the foot of the hills in Virginia is a trail. You can hike for miles along it and up into the mountains. Hector and I always take the same walk every morning and it always takes us thirty minutes. This is the allotted time for a morning walk, before I have to shower, make and eat breakfast and run him over to Daisy, my sister in Willowbrook.

Not this morning. No. This morning, Hector decided that chasing rabbits was the best thing ever and when I called him he continued to chase them. All I could make out was a wagging tail and his hind sticking in the air. He knows better and usually is not so disobedient. What could I do? Eventually he tired of chasing the rabbits that were much quicker than him and came back to me. You'd think he'd at least have had his head hanging down and his tail between his legs. But no. Of course not.

At three years old, Hector still has the puppy quality about him and loves nothing more than to run along the trail, use my sofa back at the cabin as a trampoline and get up to mischief at a drop of a hat. He's my best friend.

After nearly forty minutes we ended up back at my cabin where I slid off my walking boots and wandered inside, naturally he bounded in front of me and straight to his water bowl in the kitchen. I put the coffee on and headed down the hallway to my master bedroom to have a nice shower. To discover that the water was cold. The darn system needs checking again and I don't have the time to do it. Being the only doctor at the medical centre in Willowbrook has me working some long hours when I have house calls to attend too. What we need is some help only nobody seems to work in a small-town practise like Willowbrook.

They all want these high city hospital jobs or centre of city placements. I can't understand this. Who'd want all that noise, pollution, hustle and bustle when you can have a quaint village practise with all the locals coming in, some with absolutely nothing wrong with them at all only being there for a chat. Mr Willis being one of them. That old man is hitting eighty-five this year and loves nothing more than to come in and chat about his arthritis, the weather, what's in the local newspaper and then bid his goodbyes. I make time for the likes of Mr Willis. He's on his own now that his boys have gone off and married and working. One in Boston and one in New York. Sure, they come to visit him frequently, but there's nothing like being there on the doorstep.

Personally, I'd never leave home. I've lived here all my life. Being born in Willowbrook thirty-eight years ago to my proud parents Bert and Ida. Dad's a retired doctor, he used to run the practise and I guess it's fair to say that ever since I was a boy I always wanted to work in his practise. My practise now. My mother Ida was a seamstress and had her own shop on main street where all the locals would come in for alterations, wedding gowns, prom dresses, suits and the like. Daisy my sister runs it now and she's equally as good a seamstress as my mother was.

Daisy looks after Hector during the day for me, he loves to hang around the shop and the customers and the town folk adore him. We have a stipulation not to feed him too many treats, however.

I made a mental note to call Larkin later today to see if he can come out and fix the damn plumbing. Even though it's summer here in Virginia, I still enjoy at least a warm shower in the morning. Not sure how those people do all these ice showers and jumping in ice water, it's definitely not for me.

Upon entering my kitchen I found Hector sitting with egg yolk smeared all over his chops. Egg yolk. Yes folks, that's right. He'd only managed to get to them from the counter top where I'd whisked them before our walk to make breakfast. Needless to say the morning wasn't going quite as planned, with a dog's face to wash, a kitchen floor to mop and breakfast that turned out to be a bowl of sugar puffs in the end, we're running a bit late.

I message Daisy. "Running late, sis."

"No problem." She fires back almost instantly. "Bring him to mine first then we can grab coffee and heaver over to the shop." Thankfully, I don't have any patients until after half past nine so at least I won't be letting anyone down standing outside the practise.

Running my hands through my dark hair, the same hair that could do with a trim I turn around and assess the kitchen. Floor mopped. Tick. Dishes done. Tick. Dog on the lead and seatbelt harness. Tick. Car keys, nope. I search for them in the fruit bowl I always throw them in, moving aside the satsumas and apples to retrieve them.

"C'mon boy. Let's hut." I say as he trots obediently behind me instead of bounding out as usual. At least he respects that eating a man's breakfast ingredients is not acceptable dog behaviour. I ruffle his head once he's jumped into the front seat and make my way towards Daisey's house, all the while thinking I need to extend our reach out for a new doctor to help me.

I have Luke Combs playing, *When It Rains It Pours.* It kind of sums up how I'm feeling right now with one thing and another going on around me. Hector sensing I'm on a bit of a low ebb nudges my arm and rests his head on it. "You're my best pal, do you know that." I tell him and continue to drive along the densely tree lined road towards Willowbrook just ten minutes away.

I pull up in front Daisy's blue and white two up, two down house, with her white wrap around porch and her small garden out front. It's so typically Daisy. Cute and adorable, pots of flowers out front and fairy lights around the porch. She has a couple of tall candles that are planted into the earth and in the pots leading up her porch steps.

"Hey big fella." She comes trotting down from the porch her arms open wide as Hector flings himself towards her.

"Traitor." I mutter.

"Some one's in a good mood. *Again.*" She says with the beamiest smile on her face ever. Daisy always has a smile on her face.

"Time for coffee before you start?" She asks me all the while ruffling up Hector's fur on his head. I take a quick look at my mobile, it's just before nine.

"Sure, I guess I've got time. Let's do it."

She clicks her fingers, Hector breaks into stride next to her and I walk on her opposite side as we make our way down the path and onto main street with all its colourful store fronts. Bluebell diner is right on the corner. Daisy pushes the door open to allow Hector to go in first and I follow behind.

"Hey girl. How ya doin?" Calls out Barb, she owns Bluebell café. Her hair is the reddest red I've ever seen, it can't be natural. Can it?

"Hey Barb. Two black coffees please." Daisy scoots behind one of the tables and takes a seat on one of the blue sofas. Hector lays down by the table as I slide in opposite her.

"You gotta try to cheer up, Logan. It's been a year and that is sufficient time to get over it. Don't you think?" Maybe she's right only I am struggling with getting over it to be quite honest. I wasn't this grumpy before, I used to be upbeat, joke a minute, lively you know a regular happy kind of guy. That was before and this is now.

I look up as Bluebell's diner door chimes. A woman enters, my breath catches.

Chapter 6

L^{*ogan*}
   It can't be, surely it's not? Only, I do not think my eyes are deceiving me. She has the same dark long hair hanging around her shoulders, the same

slender build and well those cheekbones would stand out anywhere. They're model calibre to say the least.

Her eyes make contact with mine. My coffee misses my mouth and ends up dribbling down my chin. "Shit." I mutter and grab a green napkin from the stack in the centre of our table.

"Are you okay?" Daisy asks.

"Yeah, of course." She swings around to see what has caught my eye.

"Holy damn shit." She exhales and whistles. "Never thought I'd see her walking in here again. Not after, you know."

"Me neither but it's her, right?" I ask because I can't believe my eyes.

"It's her." Daisy whispers.

I try not to stare but even after all these years it is pretty damn difficult not to take in her radiating beauty, her skin like ivory and then there's her butt as she walks towards the counter. She nods briefly at me. Right, what did I expect?

"Are you going to say hello?" My sister asks. To be honest I have no idea what I should do right now. Do I say hello? Do I wait for her to take a seat then approach her and say hi? Do I just ignore the fact that Sage has suddenly turned up out of the blue and is now standing at the cake counter chatting away to Barbara who is ecstatic to see her.

"Well what a surprise, lovely. We've not seen you in here for a while. Are you visiting your folks?"

"Er sort of." Replies Sage. If I'm not wrong she sounds a little bit cagey to me, not like she is giving much away. Sure she's visited to see her folks over the last ten years. We know this because her mom tells my mom who tells the rest of the town. However, I've never managed to bump into Sage previously.

Okay, so I'll be upfront and honest. When I hear that Sage is coming back to Willowbrook, I tend to stay locked in my cabin with Hector. We don't venture into the town except for the practise, only because it'd be highly unlikely for the big city hospital doctor to come waltzing in. So, I kind of feel safe by at least going to my place of work.

"Are you staying long dear?" Barb asks.

"Not really." Replies Sage. Funny, she used to be such a chatty thing when we were dating all those years ago. Ten years, that's a long time ago. It makes me feel old even though I'm only thirty-six. A lot has happened since Sage made the decision that small-town living wasn't for her, specifically not here in Willowbrook that's for sure.

Something about needing to spread her wings, needing space, needing time. All those usual things. It left me not knowing whether they were all just excuses to break off our relationship. It cut me to the core her leaving. We had grown up together, we were best friends and then our friendship turned into a relationship and we were inseparable.

I guess people can change and they want different things out of life as they get older. Still, it took everyone by surprise because there had been no talk of leaving Willowbrook in our earlier years, no inference that this town was going to grow to be too small for her.

"Well I can imagine your folks are loving having you back home again dear. Here, you take this slice of apple pie and cream. I'll be right over with your pumpkin spice latte." Barb pushes the plate with the pie on it towards Sage who takes it and turns to the right to take the furthest seat from us.

I know she's seen me. What she can't even acknowledge Daisy and I? That's just damn rude and arrogant. I'm seething inside. The least she could do was actually acknowledge us.

"Looks like someone doesn't want to chat." Daisy does like to state the obvious at the best of times. Hector stirs by the table where he is laying. I know he's getting restless. He wants his walk before snoozing most of the day at Daisy's shop and being fussed over by the patrons.

"Come on, drink up Daisy I want to get out of here. Besides it's nearly time for us to start work for the day." I nudge her leg with me knee under the table. Obligingly, she drinks the last of her coffee and stuffs the piece of blueberry muffin on her plate into her mouth.

I gather Hector's leash and head out the door. If Sage wants to be like that then she can damn well be like that. I'm not going to be the one that goes over and is pleasant. No way. She left.

Hector bounces around outside whilst we wait for Daisy to come through the door. "Can you take him sis, I want to head over to the surgery and get ready for my first patient."

"Sure thing. I'll take him for a walk around the green. Oh good morning Mrs Linton." Daisy waves at the older woman walking towards the diner with her Chihuahua tucked under one arm. They go everywhere together a bit like Hector and I. She's not limping today which is a good sign.

"How's the leg holding up?" I ask her as she approaches us. Mrs Linton fell recently from a ladder whilst she was decorating. We've told her time and time again to let us know and either Daisy or I will come over and help her. But no, she insists on doing it herself. Says it keeps her busy after her husband passed away suddenly of a heart attack.

"It's okay thanks Doc. On the mend." I nod and pass Hector's leash to Daisy to take.

"That's good. Any issues you come see me in the surgery."

"That I will." She smiles, stoops to pat Hector on the head and makes her way into Bluebell's diner.

"Can't stop that one." Daisy says light heartedly. I nod in agreement. "I still think you should have gone to say hello to Sage. It's been *ten years*. It wouldn't have hurt." I don't want to be angry with my sister so I count to ten. The whole damn town knows how much it hurt me when Sage left me. My heart was torn out and it took me a few years to get over her, to stop missing her, to stop feeling like my left arm had been wrenched away from me.

"I can't." I say quietly and begin to walk towards the surgery. I've got a job to do, Daisy has a dog walk to fit in and then open her shop. And as for Sage, well here's to hoping I don't bump into her again. I cannot open up old wounds, not again and not after what I've just gone through the last year.

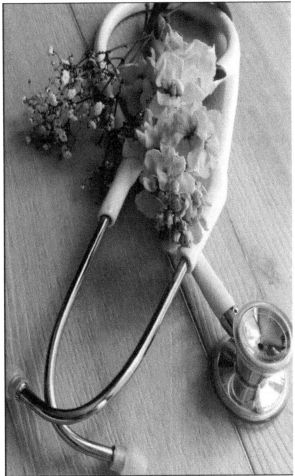

Chapter 7

S *age*
    Damn it, damn it and damn it again. "Here you go, lovely. Not seen
each other in a while have you?" Barb says as she places my pumpkin latte

down in front of me. Nothing goes by the locals in our hometown, hence the reason I want to get out as soon as possible and start living in a city again.

Don't get me wrong, Barbara is wonderful. She's like a second mother and I used to babysit her little ones when I was just a teenager. She always had me in pocket money even though my folks gave me an allowance it didn't cover all the stuff I wanted to buy back then. You know make-up, the latest trend in sneakers and jeans and books. Right, books. My downfall. Thank God for Barbara and her brood of four kids that all needed looking after at some point or other.

Then there was Mr Marshall and his wife Katerina, a Russian lady that caused quite a stir in the neighbourhood according to my mother when she came to live in our small town. I would have been just a kid at the time, only rumour has it that she was some kind of *postal bride*. That was the term back then. It still makes me smile. Anyway, the Marshalls needed their dog Trevor looking after during their holidays so, the gorgeous chocolate Labrador would come and stay with us on the understanding by my parents, that I would be fully responsible for him.

Needless to say I adored having Trevor over. He'd sleep on my bed and snuggle into me with his large head resting on my hip. We were bonded from the moment he was a puppy and the Marshall's let me play with him in their front yard. Special, special doggy. I miss him when I think about him which is right now.

Barb is still standing by the small table I chose to sit at. Yes, the one right at the back. The one that was furthest from Logan and Daisy. I suppose I was being a bit childish. The least I could have done was say hi to him and Daisy. It's not like Daisy has done anything wrong. It's not like Logan did anything wrong either, other than chose not to come to Michigan with me and work at State hospital there. He could have, he'd easily have got in. But oh no, he decided he didn't want to leave this damn small-town and where he'd lived all his life.

What was I supposed to do? I had dreams. B.I.G. dreams not staying in the same town I was born and raised in. Fat lot of good that all did me as I'm sitting here in Bluebell diner with Barb hanging around looking for a bit of gossip bless her.

I don't suppose a lot goes on around here to be honest. "Sorry, Barb. Miles away. What did you say?" I stumble for time to construct a response. One that isn't full of bitterness and anger at Logan for choosing his hometown instead of me. It broke my heart. It shattered it into pieces, my world felt as if it was collapsing around me. The darkness took over my days and it was an effort to focus on packing my stuff up let alone getting out of bed to get showered, dressed and participate in life.

"I was saying, it's been a while since you've seen each other."

"Yes, I guess it has been."

"*Ten years.*" Okay so someone has been keeping count. Wow. I just nod.

"Have you come back for him? He's a good man, honey. A definite keeper." She winks. Good Lord, is she trying to match me back with my ex? This town. Honestly. For real?

I don't say anything, what can I say? I still feel upset about it, even though I moved and met Miles and lived with him for about a decade. Perhaps it's because I just saw Logan again and it has dredged up all those emotions from when I was a younger woman.

"Sure that he is." I finally manage to let pass my lips. The diner door chimes and she turns to face it, I look up. Holding my breath hoping it isn't Logan coming back in to say hi or anything else. How am I exactly going to avoid him whilst I'm here? What I need to do is drink this latte and get back to the safety of my room at home and start looking for a role in one of the other city hospitals. There was one I spotted but it was in New York and although I love the hustle and bustle of the city, it's not somewhere I'd consider putting roots down.

"Well good morning, Sheila." Barb is off, another customer, another local. Sheila is the town's hairdresser and beauty therapist and came to Willowbrook when I was about fifteen. What is wrong with these people I wonder? Whoever comes tends to stay. It's nice and all, sure. We're nestled with forest and mountains surrounding us, we have our own lake and it's a beautiful town. But there is a big world out there.

Knocking back my latte and eating the last of my muffin, I gather up my mobile and head outside thanking Barb on the way out and giving a greeting nod to Sheila. "You must pop in, darling get those ends trimmed."

I'm gobsmacked since recently I paid sixty dollars for a trim back in Michigan. There's nothing wrong with my ends. The audacity.

"For sure. Maybe." I say and get out as fast as I can. Split ends indeed.

I slap my hand to my forehead as I see Daisy not far away on the other side of the street with Hector trotting by her side. He's one handsome dog and I want to run over and bear hug him. I don't. That would mean starting up conversation, asking how she is, her asking how I am. Her asking if I intend to meet up with Logan. I shudder. I can't go there.

It's going to be a challenge to lock myself away until I can get a new position somewhere else. In the meantime I'm going to be wary every time I set out of my parent's house. Not a nice feeling.

Daisy hasn't spotted me, she's busy chatting away to Hector, like having a proper conversation. I have to admit it's pretty cute. Daisy is cute and we always got along when we were younger. I feel like the bitch from hell by trying to slip away without her realizing I'm standing right across from her.

The other snag I've got is that to get back home, I need to go past the one and only doctor's practice in the town. That's right. The very same one that belongs to Logan now. My mother filled me in on the fact that his father retired and handed the reins over. Let's hope I don't need a doctor anytime during my stay here. If I do, I'm getting my dad to drive me straight to the Centra Lynchburg General which his way out of the way. There is no chance in hell that I would let Logan start inspecting me and touching me with those hands of his. I'd rather shrivel up first.

Daisy continues to walk along until she reaches her shop a little way down. It is so perfectly Daisy-like. The outside is painted baby blue with daisies painted on either side of the large glass door. They surround the entire door and the window frames which are old-fashioned bowed windows. There are flower boxes hanging at the bottom of them, a few terracotta pots by the door hosting shrubs and colourful flowers. Mom had many an item made in the shop by Logan and Daisy's mom, in fact my prom dress was made by her. A beautiful lemon creation, straight and off the shoulder, it skimmed just above my ankles. Logan brought me a stunning matching corsage. The only hint he had of the dress was the colour. It was a top secret mission that we kept from him. I wore my hair up in a classic high ponytail.

Right just stop thinking about Logan and the damn prom already. Jeez it was over years ago. Pack it in. I admonish myself. It's hard to forget.

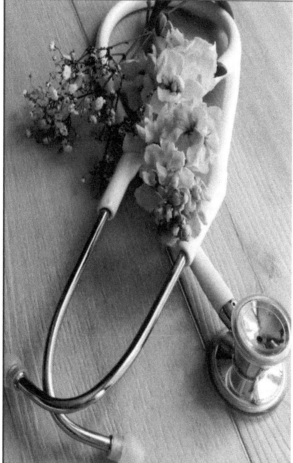

Chapter 8

L*ogan*
I don't know how I feel? Part of me wanted to approach Sage and to be close to her. She was my best friend and my girlfriend after all. If it hadn't been for her choices to go to Michigan State to prove herself, we'd still have

been together. Surely? My heart did leap at the sight of her, she's still trim. I bet she still runs early mornings and does hot yoga. That was her favourite. She said it grounded her and kept her balanced. I could tell just from looking at her as she came into the diner that those legs are still getting a regular workout. Her butt is still high. Why am I thinking about her butt? I shouldn't be thinking about that right now.

I'm supposed to still be pissed off at her for choosing a bit city life over me. Naturally, I don't see that any of that was my fault. I wanted to stay here. It was always in the pipeline that I would take over the town medical practice from dad when he retired. Besides, I love Willowbrook. I love the people even if they can be a bit nosey and in your face at times. That's part of the charm. We all know when somebody needs help and always there to lend a helping hand.

I love our Spring, Summer, Fall and Winter festivals. I'm always in charge of the productions with the headmaster of Willowbrook junior school, Mrs Winters. Together we always manage for the kids to put on a good show. Fall will be here soon and we're already having committee meetings for the Fall theatre production.

My mind wanders as I walk to the practice of whether Sage has been happy and *why* she is back here in Willowbrook. It's not like I've ever seen her around before when apparently, she's been visiting with her folks. Nothing gets passed my mother's radar, she and Sage's mother are tight. Guessing that's how the two of us became best friends too.

Unless I've just been fantastic at not bumping into her. Like I said before, I tend to stay at the cabin with Hector. Some rifts are so hard to overcome and coming face to face with Sage has always been one of them. She ripped me to the core when she made the decision to leave. I could have gone with her, the opportunity was there for me. We would have practised medicine together in the State hospital in Michigan.

I wonder how life would have been if we had. I envisage us having married, had kids and the white picket fence. And that there is exactly it. Working in a bit city hospital wouldn't have allowed all that romance. We'd have been working flat out, fourteen hour days and then some, being on call and too exhausted from flat out days.

There would have been no babies and white picket fences. We were young, just in our twenties. Life was ahead of us, okay it still is just because I'm getting closer to forty than thirty doesn't change that. I am, starkly aware, however, that I ought to get a wriggle on if I want to find *the* one. I thought it was Sage back then and I daresay she thought it was me. So why the hell did she leave me? I don't see the viewpoint of why didn't I go with her. Surely if I'd loved her enough I would have done?

I approach my practice. Mr Hendricks is standing outside waiting. He taps his local newspaper to his leg. I check my watch and see that I'm still good for time. Some of my patients are a little less patience than others.

"Good morning, Mr Hendricks." I say as I amble up beside him to the brick medical centre. It's not changed since the days my father ran it, except for a lick of white paint on the window frames and some fresh olive green paint on the sturdy wooden door.

"Doc. You're late." He says sternly. It's always the same conversation when he has a morning appointment. You can take the military out of the man but you can't take the man out of the military. To make a point I lift my left arm up and stare down at my watch. I look up at him squarely.

"No, Sir. It's only just coming up to twenty-five minutes past the hour." I smile. He doesn't. Mr Hendricks likes to pretend he is still a general with his stern face, bushy moustache and ram-rod straight back. He humpfs at me.

I unlock the door and it whooshes open. "Come on in then." I say. My assistant Eliza hasn't arrived yet. She'll be here very soon with some nice strong coffee and the maple doughnuts I especially like from Dookie-Dooks Doughnut place here in town. My favourite are the cherry glazed flavour. And thinking of her she pulls up in her beaten up station wagon. That woman needs a new ride.

"Morning y'all." She hollers as if she's standing in the park trying to reach an audience a mile away. Brash, loud but damn good at her job.

"Is that necessary to be so loud?" Asks Mr Hendricks. I can sense he has the extra grumps on this morning. I smile and go and help her with the coffees.

"I bought your favourite, cheery glazed." She holds the white bag up with DDD's red logo on the outside.

"You're a good woman, Eliza. If you weren't already married I'd have to slip a ring on that finger of yours." She giggles like a teenager even though she is the same age roughly as me.

"Oh, Doc. You are such a flirt." I make my way across the wooden floored hallway down the corridor to my office door. I love seeing my name in gold letters embossed on the obscure glass. It makes me realise how hard I worked to get her. All the years of study, the exams, the whole nine yards. It's a dream to be able to help people, whether it's with their physical issues, mental or emotional. We have so many support groups running from the practice that it could make your head spin. Eliza is the one who keeps everything going, she coordinates nurses, speakers, therapists, events, my schedule, manages the phone and just about everything else.

Mr Hendricks takes a seat in the comfortable high backed, brown leather chair in front of my rectangular office desk. The office is old-fashioned it could easily pass for something out of the 1800's with its dark book cases, antique office table, the high-winged chair.

"How is the wrist holding up?" I ask him as I place my mobile down on the desk and switch my computer on. Usually I am a lot more organized before my patients arrived and earlier. Having seen Sage this morning threw me a bit and instead of coming the direct route, I chose to go via main street which can add an extra ten minutes to my time.

"It's fine. I told you there was nothing to worry about." Mm I think. He's nearly seventy, fell off a stepladder decorating which he shouldn't have been doing in the first place and it had a nasty fracture. It's good to see the cast has been removed.

"Well let's just take a look." I say as he reluctantly holds up his right hand.

"It's perfectly fine, Doc."

"It's looking good I have to agree. I think there should be no more getting up on ladders though for you. Why don't you ask one of your lads to come over and help you with that kind of stuff? You should be..." He cuts me off abruptly.

"What sitting at home with a tv dinner on my lap watching some awful gameshow or other. I don't think so, Doc. You youngsters have no idea about gumption and resilience." He grumbles clearly annoyed at my inference. I have to respect that their generation it would seem are a lot tougher than we give them credit for.

"Not exactly, exercise is important and I'm pleased to see you on your daily walk. Keep that up." He grumbles again. "I'd like you to have some physiotherapy for a few weeks. Eliza can fix you up a time with Lynn when she's back from vacation."

"Doesn't need physio nonsense, I'll be cutting my wood for winter soon that'll be physio enough." He sounds quite annoyed. I have to refrain from smiling. My own father would be no different.

"Well, I don't think you ought to be cutting up wood fire, Mr Hendricks. How about we book the sessions in with Anne and you speak with your two boys and get them over to start stocking you up. It's going to be another cold one for sure."

He mutters as he stands, clearly our visit is over. I bid him goodbye, he doesn't acknowledge me or turn back. I already know I've probably upset him for the rest of the day with all the talk about physio. He'll be heading over to the Bluebell diner for his usual muffin, he likes the custard variety and his black as black coffee that you can stand a spoon up in.

I check my schedule on the computer, it's back to back patients until one when I can get a break for lunch. I'll head over to Daisy to check in on her and take Hector for a nice walk. By the look of it, I can be finished today by four. I'm looking forward to running later in the woods with Hector.

And so I settle myself in the for the day. My next patient is Rosanne Burton. She's nineteen and wants to talk about contraception. It makes me think back to myself at that age and talking with Sage about the very same subject. What is it with me today? I can't get my mind off that damn woman.

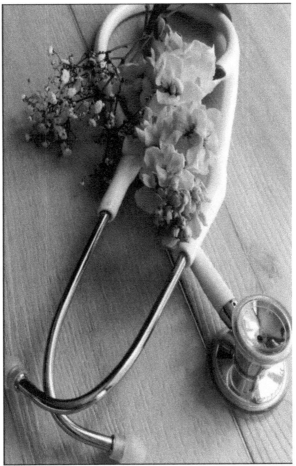

Chapter 9

S *age*
    I'm feeling hot under the collar. I'm not happy that my day started with seeing Logan at the Bluebell Diner. It's not the way I wanted my day to start that's for sure. I wanted a nice cup of coffee, a special muffin that only

Debs can make and to scroll through openings at the close by main hospitals. Even though I don't want to stay in Willowbrook, I think I'd like to be closer to my folks than I have been. Missing them wasn't great and being back home again even just for the night has made me realise that life is too short to push family away. My folks are so happy to see me and I'm looking forward to meeting up with Ali a bit later today.

I didn't feel much like visiting her yesterday but she's over the moon I'm back. She's already suggested we go to the Lazy Duke bar tonight. Am I ready to go back in time and see all the people I used to hang around with in school? It could be awkward, it's always awkward in a small town when you're the one that left. Do I even want to go out? There'll be no getting out of it, Ali is too excited for us to have some proper girl-sister time. There's no way I am going to let her down.

So, here I am on my walk back home, standing right outside the medical practice where I know Logan is working inside. It was never a secret that he wanted to take over from his dad one day. I know via my mother that his dad has retired and it's all Logan's now. It hasn't changed much, I can see there is fresh paint on the woodwork and the door is no longer navy blue but olive green instead. I love that colour. I wonder if Logan painted it this colour specially because he knew how much I loved it.

Oh for goodness sake, Sage get over yourself. Why would he paint an old wooden door the colour you love? You left him, you didn't want to stay. Remember? Yeah, that's right. I didn't want to stay. That isn't to say I didn't want to be with Logan but it wasn't going to work and I had it in me to cut all ties only because I thought it would save us pain and heartache in the long run.

Neither one of us was going to change our dream. He wasn't ever going to leave Willowbrook and I wasn't ever going to stay. There's nothing going to change my mind about that either. "In need of the doc are you, lovely?" It's Mrs Sanderson, like most of the town folk she's in her late sixties, very red out of the bottle dyed hair that looks like it would befit a poodle more than a human. I suppress the desire to giggle, she hasn't changed a bit in all the years. Still with her rouged red cheeks and severe dark eyeliner. This woman hasn't come out of the sixties or seventies yet. And I'll let you into a secret, don't ever divulge anything to her. She is quicker than a strong Wi-Fi connection. It'll be all over Willowbrook quicker than you can say Wi-Fi.

"Not really, just looking." She nods like she knows something I don't.

"All that love longing is it my dear?" I'm stumped for anything to say. Right. The whole town knows the passion and love that Logan and I shared, only not quite enough to keep me here or him coming with me. Really I want to tell her to mind her own business but a leopard never changes its spots and neither will Mrs Sanderson.

Instead, I turn and carry on walking in the direction of my parent's home. I pass Threads a fabric store, not one that can rival Daisy's vintage sewing shop. It looks new to me. I wonder when it opened. After that comes Candy Cane Lane Sweets and Treats. It sounds magical and was one of the places I'd be found spending some of my pocket money. In the vintage style window are displays of old sweet jars with screw on tops, inside housing sweets of all colours. It still looks just as pretty at it always has.

A young woman is sweeping outside the front, her hair is long and auburn with amazing waves. She turns as she hears me approach. "Oh my god, Sage." She cries out and places the brush against the red painted door. "It's been forever." Before I know it she's hugging me. "You haven't changed a bit." I almost feel suffocated in her embrace.

"Hi Milly." I say. Taken aback by her show of affection. I suppose it's kind of nice to be made welcome. Only I'm really not used to it. As you can imagine in a big place like Michigan it isn't the norm for people to throw themselves at you. "You look so good." I say, she releases me. Phew.

"How long are you here for? We sure have missed you." I can imagine. Milly and I used to play together as kids, we were the nerdy geeks who read most of the time, loved science and math class and were swats at school. I'm surprised she's stayed and is working her parent's store.

"Not sure to be honest. I'm in between work placements." A little white lie never hurt anyone, right? "Staying back with my folks until I move on."

"Ah, it'll be a shame for you not to stay here and be back home with the rest of us. Oh, do you remember all those fun filled days, running around with our hair flying in the wind, all those books we'd read and digested? The hours we'd spend under the old chestnut tree in Brewer's park." She's gushing. Yes, actually gushing like she's not spoken to anyone in a long while.

"I do." I'm almost amused by her enthusiasm at seeing me. It's sort of cute.

"We'll have to grab a coffee soon and catch up. Have you seen Logan already?" And there you go, everyone is straight into the whole Logan-Sage thing. IT'S BEEN TEN YEARS. TEN YEARS.

"Coffee would be nice, let's catch up at Bluebell's another day." I give her a very quick hug back and start walking away. The last thing I need reminding of is Logan. Time has moved on, I moved on. I met Miles and we had a good relationship. Okay, so I have to realise that in a good relationship the guy usually communicates about what his intentions are, not just suddenly telling you he's off to do a fellowship on a different continent. My blood is surging and I'm so mad at my current situation. Stuck here in Willowbrook, no job, no guy and having to face my ex.

Chapter 10

S *age*
    "Did you have a nice time out, lovely?" My mom asks as I walk up the path between the flower beds and manicured lawn on either side. She's

smiling that bright cheery smile of hers which I know the garden brings on, it's her pride and joy.

"It was okay." I mumble and make my way towards her.

"Well, did you meet anyone?" Now I know that lilting sounds means *did you meet Logan*. She's very obvious sometimes. I bet she'd love nothing more for me to start dating Logan again, get married, have the house with the white picket fence and give her some grandchildren.

"He was at Bluebell diner, yes." Her smile broadens, I knew it would. Her eyes are sparkling like I've announced we secretly eloped, got married and made that first grandchild for her. Mom places her garden fork down, wipes her hands on her apron and looks at me.

"And, did you catch up? That's so wonderful." Erg. It wasn't so wonderful for me, and by the look of it, not for him either. He didn't even bother to say hello. Actually nor did Daisy which was a little strange considering we'd always got on so well. I guess she's aligning with her brother on the *do not talk to Sage* program.

"No, Mom. We didn't catch up. I'm going into make a herbal tea. Do you want anything?" I don't mean to sound so grumpy but truly I am. I can't help it. I'm still hurting so badly from the split with Miles that it sometimes feels as if my heart will stop beating. I've had a missed call from him that I ought to respond to. It's not like we said we'd never speak to each other again. Only, right now I'm not ready to talk with him. It hurts like a knife being driven through my heart. I might go for a run later this evening when it's cooler. Here in Virginia in the summer it can be excruciatingly hot.

"Oh, that's a shame. Be nice to see you two kids get back together." There you have it, no beating around the bush with my mother. She says what she wants, when she wants.

"If you're forgetting, Mom let me just remind you that he *chose* not to come to Michigan with me." She frowns. Here comes the slant on that.

"I don't think it was quite like that, sweetheart. He didn't want to leave here and you did. It's not as if the two of you couldn't have had a long-distance relationship and figured it out from there. A lot of couples do that you know." I groan and clench my fists because I do not want to hear it. She carries on, "and it *was* your choice to end the relationship. That poor boy, he was a wreck." I'm almost spitting feathers, I can feel myself getting angry and the colour flushing up my neck and into my face.

I love my mom, but right now I just want her to stop talking about Logan and what I did. I count to ten, release my clenched fists and stretch my fingers out. "I *know* that, Mom. But it was pointless. Neither one of us was prepared to budge. I didn't see the point. And whilst I'm at it, don't you think my heart broke that day too?" I dash inside the house leaving my mother looking somewhat bewildered. Shit. I shouldn't have lost it with her, my mom is the best and she doesn't deserve a woman being angry with her because of her own stupid decisions she made a decade ago.

Forgoing the herbal tea, I stomp up the stairs as loudly as I can. Yes, very immature I know but sometimes it's called for no matter how old you are. Fling open my bedroom door and literally throw myself on the bed. It bounces from my full body weight hitting it like a tonne of bricks. I lay my head on my arms folded in front of me and start to cry.

I'm crying because maybe I did make the wrong decision back then. Seeing Logan has stirred up a hornet's nest inside my mind, one that I'd like to quell with a fire extinguisher to the head. I'm crying because Miles, who I do still love and I split up. Why do I have to have so much hurt going on right now? Why can't my life be going in the right direction? It was as far as I'm concerned, perfect until just recently.

Blubbering and ugly crying doesn't suit me but I continue. "Darling." My mother says softly from the doorway. "Hush. It's going to be alright." She comes in and sits down on the bed beside me and rubs my back like she used to when I was a child and upset about something. Usually Logan chatting to another girl at school when we were friends and I fancied him. Or if Lisa L a girl a year older than me was picking on me. She picked on everyone the spiteful, nasty bully. I hope she's gone and got herself pregnant with at least ten kids who have snotty, runny noses. Too much for a thirty something year old to think? Okay, probably but I'm crying over everything now and I just can't stop.

"Look, I'll go and make you some nice herbal tea, sweetheart. Why don't you get a book to read and forget about everything for a while. It's going to take time, these things do. Life can be really hard and all the days seem grey, then one morning you will wake up and it will all feel like sunshine and shooting stars."

I love her for trying but it certainly doesn't feel like that will happen for me for a very long time. How long does it take to get over a broken heart anyway? And on top of everything else, I'm supposed to be going out with Ali tonight to The Lazy Duke bar. Great, my eyes will be red, puffy and I'll look like a boxer has taken me out in broad daylight. I blubber some more.

Mom rubs my back, "there, there." It doesn't make me feel any better.

"I just wanted what you and dad have, Mom. That's all. You know I thought I had it with Miles. I really did." I sit up, rest my head on her shoulder and allow my mother to pull me tightly into her. It feels comforting and my tears begin to ease off. For now.

Chapter 11

L*ogan*
   It's been a long day, I'm ready for my run with Hector after I collect him from Daisy then I think I'll head over to Lazy Duke's later for a few beers. I'm not much of a drinker, usually I have a couple then switch to water

with lemon or lime in it. Also, I have to drive back to my cabin even though I could walk the three miles.

Krissy has just left, she's been having trouble conceiving and I feel for her and Trevor. It's been a couple of years now but we've got the IV treatment programme starting for them. Today was more a visit to go through the process with her and confirm to her who she'll be having as her go2 person. I'm keeping everything crossed for them, they're late bloomers Krissy and Trevor now heading into their early forties and desperate to start a family. They run our local garden centre stocked with more ferns and spruces than you can imagine. It's always a joy to go there and pick out a tree for Christmas.

Trevor is the newcomer to Willowbrook and I say that because he's only lived here for nine years. Before that he was in Atlanta working in finance. He met Krissy on a holiday with some friends when they were backpacking a few of the Virginian trails and stopped at the Lazy Duke bar. There she was, story has it. Krissy with her long honey-blonde hair, grey-green eyes and a body that looks like God created it with his own hands. She's always lived here in Willowbrook with her older sister, Anika. Her parents have always run the garden centre, it's been in their family for more than eighty years. Needless to say, the two of them hit it off and after a long-distance relationship, Trevor came to his senses and moved to Willowbrook bringing capital with him to plant into the business. The rest is history.

I forgot to mention that Willowbrook is hard to leave, even if you do – well people always come back. For the most part, people tend not to leave. Take Carol and Iain Bishop, she heads the library and he is our minister. They came on a trip, were welcomed into the community and ended up being transferred. Then there's Lynn now that's a story all of its own. On the run from her violent and abusive ex, she ended up here. Scared, beaten black and blue and only the clothes she wore on her back. My own mother took her in, the poor woman was only twenty-five back then, and now she's thriving and has a baby on the way. Duncan our handy plumber-electrician-do-it-all man around here, took an instant shine to Lynn and made it is job to ensure she felt safe, secure and waited patiently until she was ready to let another man into her life and trust him. It makes me smile when I think about our caring community.

I shake my head as I lock the door of the practice. I'll never really understand how Sage could have decided to leave all of this for a large city like Michigan. Money perhaps? Prestige maybe? Who knows. I guess I'll never find out since I'm doing my damndest to avoid her, only I can't hide out in the cottage all night. Hence I've decided to come back into town and have a drink at Lazy Duke's tonight. There's no way she's going to be there, it never was her favourite place to be. She'd only go if I insisted or her best friend Hazel dragged her along.

Hector goes nuts when he sees me at Daisy's shop. She's slinging her hippie bag over her shoulder and getting to lock up for the day too. "Hey, how was your day?" She asks checking to make sure she's not forgotten anything. A stunning electric blue piece of fabric is draped across her sewing table. "Oh that, it's going to be a prom dress for Annette." She explains.

Annette is the daughter of Michael and Sarah Peterson, he is the manager of our local bank and his wife Sarah is an artist, pretty good one at that. She's had a few exhibitions here and there and has a huge following on social media, apparently.

"Pretty colour." I say as I continue to stroke Hector's head. He's licking my hand and making a huge fuss. God, I love him. He makes my heart swell. I bend down and grab his head with my hands and place kisses on his head and hug him into my chest.

"You're such a soppy thing." Daisy says. "Right, ready. Let's do it."

"By the way, I'm going to Lazy Duke's tonight. You want to join me?"

She thinks about it for a few seconds as we head out the door and she locks up. "Nah, I'm going to finish reading one of my romance books and snuggle up with Gilly." By the way, Gilly is her black and white tuxedo cat. She's four and a very affectionate cat. Hector loves her and you'll often find them curled up together, especially in the winter.

"You do know that real life isn't at all what you read in those books of yours, don't you?" She smiles at me like I'm a Neanderthal.

"It can be, Logan. You're just not looking or willing to share your heart with anyone again. It's buried in there guarded and locked away. You need to start dating again." I scoff. No fucking way. That's definitely not going to happen. First, I lost Sage then my wife Eliza passed away five years into our marriage. The big C got her and no matter how hard she fought to hang on, it wasn't to be. It cuts me like a razor sharp knife to the chest, I drag myself away from thinking about Eliza. My beautiful, strong, kind-hearted Eliza. I draw in some breath.

"I know it still hurts, Logan. It's only been a year but you have to try to get out a bit more. Besides, if I come some girl's going to think I'm your hot date." She punches me playfully on the arm.

"You're not hot, Daisy. In your dreams." I get another punch for that. I guess I deserved it. I know she's my sister and all, but it is fair to say that Daisy is a very beautiful woman. I'm surprised she hasn't been snapped up yet, but I do have a sneaky feeling she's got it bad for our Marshall Dayton. What I want to know is why he hasn't got his shit together and asked Daisy out on a date. I hope it's not because he's scared of me. I mean he is one of my closest friends but I'm not the big brother, ogre type who would go nuts for my friend dating my sister. Daisy deserves a good man and Dayton is one of the best.

Chapter 12

L*ogan*

It's busy tonight in the Lazy Duke. I've been coming here ever since I was allowed out to drink. This place will probably still be standing when I'm dead and buried. It used to belong to Driscoll Duke, and apparently it goes back a couple of hundred years ago from the early days of Willowbrook being discovered. Every new homestead it seems had a salon and this right here where I'm standing is the one for Willowbrook. It's the oldest bar this side of Virginia and serves as a historical foundation for our town, it was erected in 1779 and originally served as a tavern and stagecoach stop for westward bound travellers. I'm a bit of a sucker for history so I could go on and on about it's past.

The Lazy Duke is a two-story log and stone, Colonial style building with walls that are at least two-feet thick and constructed of hand-cut local limestone. The Duke's will always be the owners and right now standing behind the bar is one of my best buddies, Abe. He is a mountain of a man with tattoos running up and down his arms and across his chest. He has warm hazel eyes and dark hair that he wears in a man-bun. His shoulders are broad and his muscles pop and zing just pulling pints. The man works out more than I do and the girls *love* him. He's a gentle-giant standing well over six-two.

There was talk of him going to play football because he is a mean player, only he decided, a bit like me that he didn't want the big life. He stayed put and I'm kind of glad he did. Abe sees me entering the bar and reaches his hand up and waves. "Hey there. Pint?" He shouts out, I nod. I love that when you come in here, your drink is almost ready for you, nice and cold just as I like it. The bar is three deep, it's usually this busy on a Friday night when there it's live music night, which is pretty much every Friday.

I make my way through the people milling around, recognising many of the faces old and young. They clear a path so I can get through, being a doc in a small town is almost like celebrity status. It has its advantages but don't get me wrong, I never play on it. I get a few pats on the back by way of a hello from a couple of the guys and finally reach the bar. Juliette Myers is singing one of her country ballads, her voice is clear and strong as she sings about broken love, second chances and walking hand in hand with the man she loved forever. It pulls at my heart some, having had Sage leave me so young and then my own wife dying not that long ago. Is there such a thing as second chance romance? According to Daisy and her damn books, it's a thing. I'm not so sure. There is no way I am about to open my heart up again. It hurts too much.

"Hey buddy, good to see you." Abe shakes my hand across the bar, finishes pulling my pint then hands it across to me. At the end of the bar I see old man Walker nursing a whisky. He really ought not be drinking the hard stuff, his liver is already shot but some people won't listen. He'll have this one and then make his way back home where his son takes care of him. Lennox gave up working in Denver a few years back to come home and take care of his father when his mother passed away. He's into marketing so it's easy for him to continue working. He often says it was the best thing he ever did, coming back to Willowbrook and starting up on his own. Fair play to him. That's what our community is all about, we take care of our own even the newcomers.

As soon as you set foot in Willowbrook you become family and we keep our family close. It's rare for anyone who comes to leave and I'm convinced it's because they always find that little slice of heaven here in the beautiful small town that is nestled by mountains and forest. "Yeah, I'm good." I say to Abe and take a sip of the ice cold beer. It slides down nicely, just what I need after a busy day in the surgery and seeing Sage this morning.

I can't get her out of my head and it's really starting to irritate me. "You playing tonight?" He asks me. I look down at myself.

"No guitar with me. Didn't realise you'd want me to play." It's fair to say I usually have a couple of pints then get on stage. The locals love their doc up there singing ballads. I do get heckled but it's all just fun. Usually by the females in the bar, all trying to get me to take my clothes off.

"Never stopped you before. We'll slot you on third. Juliette is doing another few tracks then we've got The Virginia's on after then you can go up, but hey bro – keep the pace light tonight. None of that shit that makes them all want to weep." I smile he does have a point. Maybe it's time to give them something a little more up-tempo tonight.

"You got it." I say. Abe is busy and goes off to serve someone else. I lift my glass to old man Walker and turn around to go and find somewhere to sit and then I see her.

Damn it. What the fuck is she doing here? I can't peel my eyes off her, something weird happens to my gut and I feel myself twitch. *You have got to be fucking kidding me.* I've not had a sensation like this since forever. She is *the* last person I want to have this kind of reaction for. Her dress clings to her body like a second skin, the red brings out the colour of the lipstick that glows like a siren on those full, pouting lips of hers. I mean, seriously. WTF?

Next to her is Ali her younger sister, dressed in cut-off denims with frayed edges and rhinestones sewn on them, cowboy boots and a pretty floral shirt. But Sage. She's dressed like she wants it and Big Time. Where has that come from? I've never seen Sage look like this before. Maybe this is what the big city has done to her. Is this how they dress over in Michigan?

My mind is racing, my heart is beating so fast it feels like it has a life of its own and is going to jump right out of my chest at any minute. She looks over and our eyes meet. A second, two seconds, we lock eyes. I stir again in my jeans, they're too tight as it is, I can't get a hard-on standing here in the bar like this. People are going to notice. Sage looks away but not before I see her blush. Ali pushes her along towards the bar on the other side to where I am.

I desperately try to think of a million other things than Sage in that red dress, high-heels that make her legs look like they go for miles and that siren, red lipstick that would look good wrapped around my manhood. Involuntarily I groan quietly. This is real bad.

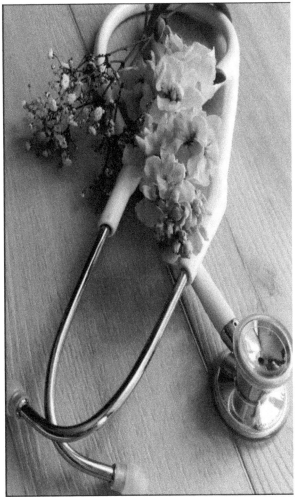

Chapter 13

S^{*age*} I've stopped dead in my tracks, Ali is yanking on my left arm. "What's wrong with you? We'll die of thirst if you don't get a wriggle on."

She's full of good humour and of course I've heard through my mother, yes the local announcement service – that Ali has the hots for one Marshall Dayton. Of course, when I asked her on the way over as we walked, our arms linked together - she flatly denied it.

"Don't be so silly. He's just a friend. Jeez, Sage. We've known each other practically all our lives. What has gotten into you? You go away, come back for all of five minutes and making stuff up."

"I'm going on good authority, Ali. It's okay if you do. He's a great guy and he's seriously good looking with that boyish charm about him. You know, like an early Tom Cruise look." That got me a soft punch to my right arm.

"Behave, first he doesn't look anything like Tom Cruise." She paused and put her hands on her hips and cocked her head. "Okay, maybe a little with his grin, those alluring come to bed eyes and that dark hair."

"There you go, see."

"Still, doesn't mean I fancy him or anything. We see each other at Bluebell's in the morning and have a quick coffee, sometimes he comes over to the library when I'm working to check on things. You know, he's a decent guy and he does have a job to do. You know checking in on us all and making sure we're all safe and sound."

"Nothing much happens in Willowbrook, surprised he doesn't sip coffee all damn day. What is there to do for a Marshall in this tiny town." I said as we neared Lazy Duke's, hearing the noise coming from within. Ali had shrugged her shoulders.

"Damned if I know."

As soon as we stepped inside I knew it was a mistake. It's busy and I don't do really busy not even when I lived back in Michigan. Yeah we went out, Miles and I and sometimes I'd go out with my colleagues or friends but not that often. Honestly, being a doctor in the State hospital left little time for going out. I was mostly shattered, my body ached from tiredness and my eyes felt like lead weights nearly all the time. So, here we are being dragged towards the bar, making our way through groups of people. I look up. My heart misses a beat. Butterflies dance around my stomach and I want to fucking slap myself for having feelings like this, you know like a hormonal teenager.

Least my body has forgotten, I'm in my thirties and it won't be long before I'm a forty year old woman. That gets me like a bee sting to the back of the hand. I'm not married and I don't have children. Of course I wanted all of this with Miles and I'm trying hard not to go back to how I felt last week. I couldn't if I tried because dominating my view is only Logan. All six feet two of him, broad shoulders, muscular arms and I can see the veins in his forearms as he holds his pint in his left hand. Fucking hell. Why does that man have to look like a damn centrefold? I'm guessing he has the perfect man-v too.

"Hey." Ali yanks on me again. Soon I'm not going to have an arm left. She stops pulling and takes one look at me, then the direction I am looking and says, "ahhhh. So *that's* why." Her laughter isn't funny to my ears. Is she kidding me? "You've still got the hots for Logan over there. Damn girl." She blows out a low whistle.

I feel like turning around and leaving the bar immediately. His gaze is intense, he's not letting go of my eyes. My core heats up, the warmth is spreading through my body from the pit of my stomach, intensifying the longer he stares at me. Why can't he just stop? Now I'm wishing I hadn't opted for a dress, least ways not one this short. What on earth was I thinking? It's Lazy Duke's not some high-end restaurant in Michigan. I've seriously got to get back into the habit of living in my jeans and cut-off shorts. Not dresses fitted better to a cocktail party. Oh, the life I had with Miles is so far removed from this godforsaken small-town.

It's me who looks away and starts to turn back towards the door. "Oh no you don't big sis." Ali has me firmly by the left wrist. "You aren't going anywhere lady. You can't avoid him forever and at the moment you don't know how long you're staying for."

"Not for fucking long, I hope." I am not impressed but I do manage to avoid looking at Logan as Ali and I make our way towards the bar where she promptly orders shots of Tequila. Wow, it'll take me all of three shots to be on my butt. I'm not much of a drinker, more of a sipping a glass of wine kind of girl. These days that is. Before when I was with Logan we'd drink like most teenagers did, when allowed that is. A few beers here and there, sometimes we'd sneak a bottle of Tequila into my room when my folks were out of town that sort of thing. Heady days of youth, no hassle, no stress just fun, fun and more fun. I long for those days, to go back in time. Would I have done everything differently? Would I still have left Willowbrook?

I knock the first drink back, sensing that Logan is still looking at me. Why can't he leave already? "And ladies and gentleman," I hear Abe say into the mic where he has taken his place on the stand, "let's give it up for *the one and only, Doc Logan.*" The crowd goes nuts, the girls are wolf whistling, I get that. Even though I'm still mad as hell at Logan for not choosing me back then, I have to admit he is a girl's wet dream. That pisses me off.

And there he is. Up on stage, all that fine prime man and the way his hips narrow and are encased with his long lean legs in those tight jeans, is enough to send my pulse into over-drive. God, I hate my body being a traitor like this. My mouth is dry and I am transfixed, like most of the girls in the bar right now. Except of course Ali, who I notice has left my side. I turn around looking for her and see she's huddled in a corner right by. You guessed it. The Marshall. I told you so!

Logan taps the mic. "Well hi y'all. We've got some old and new tracks today. Before we begin, I'd like to say that this first one is dedicated to someone very special in my life." There are more cheers and some clapping and then he starts to play the guitar. My heart melts, I'm melting at the sound of his fingers strumming away. It takes me back so many years to his bedroom and listening to him play just for me.

He begins to sing, the words come out and as he sings, tears begin to fall down my eyes. It's the first song he ever sang for me by my favourite artist, Dolly P.

If I should stay
Well I would only be in your way
And so I'll go, and yet I know
I'll think of you each step of the way
And I will always love you
I will always love you
Bitter-sweet memories
That's all I'm taking with me
Good-bye, please don't cry
'Cause we both know that I'm not
What you need

But I will always love you
I will always love you
And I hope life, will treat you kind
And I hope that you have all
That you ever dreamed of
Oh I do wish you joy
And I wish you happiness
But above all this
I wish you love
I love you
I will always love you
I, I will always, always love you
I will always love you
I will always love you
I will always love you

I'm a big ugly mess as I stand and listen, my heart feels as if it has shattered all over again.

Chapter 14

L*ogan*
     I can't take my eyes off her, from the moment she stepped into the
bar. Her red, skin-tight dress hugs every curve of her body and her legs, those
damn legs go on for miles. They look toned and slender and sexy as fuck in

those heels she's wearing. I don't care that she looks over dressed like a city slicker here in Lazy Duke's. All I can see is a red hot woman staring right back at me as I play her our song.

The moment I spotted her when she came through the door with her sister Ali, I knew what I was going to sing as my opener. All the anger I was feeling somehow just evaporated and skittled somewhere under a rug. All I could see was her and the memories of when we were young and good together. She looked like a rabbit caught in the headlights when she saw me, it was enough to make me want to smirk but I held it back. I'm not the one who left, but I am the one who wanted her to stay and listen to our song, I want her to know what she could have had.

Jeez, I'm so conflicted with emotion right now. One part of me wants her to be up here and close to me, with her head on my shoulder. Like it was back then when we were teenagers and she'd listen to me playing song after song. Sometimes we'd co-write and I'm saving our next song for my last of the set tonight. That'll make her wonder why she ever left me for some big city, chasing a dream she could easily have had back here in Willowbrook.

If she'd not run to Michigan, we'd have been running dad's practice, now mine – together. It would have both our names on it. Sage and I were a team. We'd always been a team. There wasn't a person here who didn't think we wouldn't get married, have some babies, a yard with a white picket fence. You know, the whole nine yards. It took me by surprise when she started to share her dream with me, she was wild with excitement and I honestly thought for sure, we could make it work long distance. What I wasn't expecting was her to tell me that it was better this way. Better that we ended it whilst we were still young and open to explore other relationships and love. Not to be under the burden of commitment. Shit. Why am I thinking all this crap when I'm up here on stage?

I'm conflicted between being mad at her for all those years ago and wanting her to regret every damn, last minute of the decision she made. I know through my folks that she met someone else, some Miles guy. Another doctor who worked in Michigan State. According to my mother, he has decided to do a fellowship in Europe. London, I think

See, I never would have done that to Sage. Not the beautiful girl I grew up with, the girl that was my best friend. The one whose back I always had. I'd never had let her down. She'd be settled here with me now.

I can see tears streaming down her face. The song has rocked her, it's breaking her heart in pieces. Lost love will do that to you, it only takes a word, a song, a movie that can make it feel as if you lost everything. It'll break your heart leaving you feel bereft. Good. I want her to feel like she lost out. I want her to stay. I want to stop thinking all these damn thoughts. I've got a set to play.

The crowd in the bar clap and holler when I draw the Dolly P song to an end. I get wolf whistles and a bra thrown at me. Yes, that is usual. The locals love me and most of the single women often throw a bra my way. Does it make me blush? Sure does. I have to face ninety percent of them in my surgery over the course of the year. It's pretty hard to remain professional when you know whose bra was thrown in your face on a Friday night.

Sage is wiping her eyes. Ali I can see is still chatting with the Marshall. He's keen on her and I'm guessing any day now they'll probably start dating. I hope so. The Marshal is a good friend of mine, like Abe. We grew up here, went to the same school, graduated together and been through a lot of growing up together. I don't know where I'd be without those two and my sister, Daisy.

Nobody notices but me when Sage puts here drink down on a random table and starts to head out of the bar. Ali doesn't look up from her close chats with the Marshall, the crowd close to the stage definitely don't look up. She's moving quicker than wildfire as her hand reaches door ready to push it open.

Do I want her to go?

Do I want her to stay?

I have no idea what I want anymore. I'm still smarting a decade later and on top of that my heart is in shards from the loss of my beautiful wife, the one woman I couldn't save no matter how hard I tried. I can't allow myself to have any feelings for Sage again. There would be no trust there and besides, I've heard she's only staying temporarily. My heart can't take another relationship, I'm too scared to lose again. It's easier to live alone up in my cabin with Hector.

I seek female company every now and then, but not in this town. Usually, I'll driver over to Coppertown where It's easier to go under the radar. Nobody knows me there and nobody wants anything fro me. I'm just another regular guy hanging in a bar or club. It's not often but when needs must, then they must.

As she leaves, I strum up my guitar and start playing the next track. It's the one we first ever co-wrote. I remember how Sage had lain on my bed with the pad on her lap, her hair in a messy bun scribbling away as I played the chords. It took us a couple of hours but when I played it for her, she cried then too.

Love can only happen once
Don't let it slip through your fingers
Promise you'll never leave me, promise you'll be mine forever.
My heart would simply break in two, if there was no me and you
My heart would never fall again, if there was no me and you

I continue to sing and watch as she ever so slowly turns around. I'm not sure if she's going to stay or if she's going to go. My voice is filled with emotion, damn it. Even I'm choking up.

Chapter 15

S*age*
     I can hardly breathe and my heart is banging so hard against my chest. All my emotions are raging to the fore. It feels like my heart is breaking all over again. How can this be when I moved on? I made a new life, I was

with someone else for almost a decade for Christ's sake. His voice carries towards me as I stand with my hand on the door. Not knowing whether to wait for his set to end and to see him. I can't stand feeling like this.

What's the point in any case? I don't want to stay here? I want another job in a State hospital, it's what I trained for, what I worked so hard for and studied all those years for. Not to end up in some small-town practice. There aren't any jobs anyway, not that I know of.

I can hear the last words of the song, *that* song the one we wrote together. He had been strumming his guitar, we were so young. A different life, just seventeen and I was reading on his bed. I should have been doing my homework but when Logan played his guitar everything else would be forgotten. I'd listened as he began to put words to the music, his eyes on me not on his fingers strumming the chords. On me as always, only ever on me.

Like then, they're tugging at my heart. Part of me wants to run straight up on stage and the other half wants to slap myself for being so ridiculous. I'm angry that I feel this way. I have no right to feel like this. I ended it all those years ago and he cut my heart apart by choosing Willowbrook instead of me.

I let go of the door handle even though I can hear the pain and the longing in his voice. Surely he can't want to be reaching out to me. Can he? Why would he? By the village grapevine aka my mother, he never wanted to see me again. Another reason why whenever I've visited home to see my folks and Ali, I've tended not to venture too far. I'd heard Logan had stayed up on the cabin and only came down to the practice.

So, yes on purpose I have avoided him over the last ten Christmas holidays, Thanksgiving celebrations, coming home for birthdays. Tonight was the first time in all those years of visiting, that I have ever set foot in the Lazy Duke and that was only to keep Ali happy. It would seem she's content by the close proximity she has with the Marshal.

I get my breathing under control and begin to walk further and further away from Logan's voice and pick up speed until I realize I'm actually running. Running as fast as I can away from him. This is pathetic, I'm a grown woman who's experienced life, been round the block a few times not a teenager running away from some guy she kissed and is embarrassed to look in the eye again.

Finally, I stop running. I'm at the park where he and I used to hang. Not a play park with children's swings but a green park. Tall lush trees, the greenest grass you've ever seen and a monument to lives lost. Here we'd sit in the early days and just talk, kiss and cuddle before things became more serious and we moved on covering all the bases. I don't want to think about that right now. I want to understand why I'm so damn conflicted inside and raw with emotion.

Perhaps it's because I've been ditched by Miles for his fellowship. This is how it must have been for Logan all those years ago when I chose my medical profession over a life here with him. Marriage, children, the whole nine yards with the white picket fence. I realize I've been crying and wipe the tears from my eyes as I lower myself to the ground and bring my knees up to my chest and fold my arms around them. I lower my head to rest my forehead on my knees and inhale and exhale deeply. There's no one else around, it's late and dark. It doesn't enter my mind why they still haven't put lighting in the park. It doesn't enter my mind that even though it's been a warm day it's now much cooler and all I am wearing is a short, very tight dress and that my heels are not really made for running.

I just sit there quietly. My phone vibrates. I ignore it. It vibrates persistently. Reaching inside my small bag I can see a missed call from Ali and two voice messages. The instinct to call her back is zero, I'm not feeling talking with anyone right now. But I do read her message.

Hey where did you go? I looked up and couldn't see you. Someone said they saw you run out of the bar. What happened? And answer my calls. I don't know if I should wait for you or head off home alone later.

There's no way I want Ali to walk home on her own, even though Willowbrook is a perfectly safe place, you never know if some weirdo is lurking around.

I couldn't listen to Logan singing our song. Don't walk home alone. See if the Marshal can walk you back. I'm at the park and will make my way back shortly. I just needed to get some air and catch my breath.

I wait for her to reply.

Okay, if you're sure. Be careful xx

I send two kisses back to Ali. There isn't anything I can do about my emotions right now only time is going to figure this out, or a new job in a different State or in the heart of Virginia. It'll take me away from Willowbrook and all the memories. They're too much for me. Being home here is too much for me to take. I knew it wasn't going to be easy but damn it, did Logan have to play those songs? Why couldn't he just have played some new material, it's not like he hasn't got a whole back catalogue of material that doesn't concern me. What the fuck was he playing at? The anger at him burbles up inside my chest. I'm starting to feel it's getting cooler and I know I really shouldn't be out this late on my own.

Standing up I get the distinct impression someone is approaching me. It's a hunch and it makes my skin have goose bumps. A shiver goes up and down my spine. I've braced myself. What am I going to do if there is an attacker? Only scream. Although, I suppose I could take off my four inch stiletto shoes and use them to stab an attacker in the eye.

"Hi." I hear a low and deep voice say. "I thought I'd find you here." I know that voice. I know it so well.

Chapter 16

Logan

How could I let her go? It ripped me singing those songs knowing it would evoke all those memories of our past. Damn it. Why can't I let it go? Perhaps I'm lonely. I know I'm lonely. Anyone who has lost someone they love would be lonely and bereft. Am I looking to fill that void? Should I fill that void? Do I deserve happiness again? According to Daisy, who believes she is the oracle on matters of the heart, yes I do.

I'm not so sure. All I know is that right now I am so damn confused and conflicted. Torn between running off stage to follow Sage out the door after my set and feeling hugely guilty for what feels like deceiving my wife's memory. Oh God. I hate this. I hate it so much but I can't help myself.

There's only one place I know that Sage would have gone to if she hasn't gone back to her folks house. And trust me, I know Sage very well. After spending all our childhood years together, it's like knowing the back of my own hand.

My heart was in my mouth the whole time I was up there singing. My eyes never left hers and I saw the way she looked at me. There was a distinct look of longing in those eyes of hers. Something I've not seen for a while.

She's sitting there right by our tree, nothing but moonlight and stars lighting up the area where she sits. Alone. Small. It takes all my strength not to rush to her and put my arms around her. From the fact that Sage has come to *our* place, I know my songs had an impact on her. I don't even know why I sang them. Out of all the hundreds of songs I know and have written, on my own – I could have played anyone of them. So why the hell did I opt for *our* songs? Why indeed.

"Hi." I say. She doesn't say anything for a while. I bet she's holding her breath. She used to do that frequently when we were younger. Like she's counting to a hundred before saying anything. It's the way she dealt with anything that made her mad. Am I making her mad being here? No doubt. After all she has avoided me for the past ten years. No word of a lie, even when I know she's come back to visit we have never bumped into each other. Sure, I have stayed up at the cabin with Hector but even when I've gone down to the practice I have never laid eyes on Sage. The woman is as covert as a top spy.

Still she does not respond. I'm standing here for what seems like eternity. I cough and shove my hands into my pockets feeling like a complete ass having followed her to our favourite place.

"What do you want?" Sage finally says, her voice is cold. Did I expect open arms and warmth? Er, no. Of course not but still. It makes me shiver.

"I came to see if you were okay." I inch forward to be closer to her. She senses I have moved.

"Just stay where you are. Don't come near me. What the fuck were you thinking up on stage? Why plays those songs? They mean nothing now, Logan. Nothing." Her voice makes me feel like I'm standing naked in a winter's storm. Jeez-us when did she become so *hard and cold*?

This isn't the Sage I knew. The warm, loving and giving woman. The woman who went off to Michigan state and left me with a broken and wounded heart.

"You're right. I shouldn't have done. I'll be off. It was a mistake. A huge mistake. I shouldn't have followed you out here." And it's true, what an idiot. Now I just feel stupid and like a prize jerk. I turn away and begin to walk my head hanging low. Why do I feel like my heart is having a seizure? Why do I feel so empty and hollow, like I'm reliving a decade ago the day she left me and waved goodbye from the back of her parent's car?

That day has scarred me. There was no changing her mind once she had decided she wanted to get out of Willowbrook and live in the bit city. A different state. I mean, she could have gone easily to Virginia. They offered her a position. What was so wrong with Willowbrook? What was so wrong with me that I couldn't get her to stay? The truth. I didn't try hard enough. I loved Sage so damn fucking much that her happiness is all that meant anything to me. There was no way on earth I was going to force her to do something she didn't want to do. Sometimes in life if you love someone you have to let them go, not keep them to become sad and depressed. It had to be her choice, not mine. But. We could have had a long-distance relationship.

I shake my head as I walk and hear her voice, still like steel. "Just stay as far out of my way as possible. I won't be here long. As soon as I get a new job I am out of this damn town." That woman has no heart. She can't have. Still the wanting to get out of Willowbrook.

If I was half a man, I'd turn back to her and wrap my arms around her and bring those angry lips to mine and crush them and draw her breath out of her body and fill it with something warm and heartfelt. I'd sling her over my shoulder and drive her to my cabin and make mad love to her. *Where the fuck has that come from?* I walk faster. I need to get away from Sage. She's dangerous.

I haven't got time to be thinking these thoughts about her. It's the last thing I need. What I need more importantly is to move on with my life, get myself another doctor in the practice since I'm over-stretched as it is with the town folk and those coming in from nearby towns where there is no practice.

"Fine." I shout back at her. "Whatever you want."

"Always having to have the last word eh, Logan." And here we go like old times, she says something, I say something back. Only back then, we'd end up making love after an argument. Not me walking away as if I have daggers being thrown at my back.

"That's right. You got it." I march off as fast as I can with one ear out to hear if she says anything more. There you go, I got the last word in. So childish, so utterly ridiculous but damn it, Sage brings out the very worst in me right now.

I'm going home to my cabin and flinging myself on the bed with Hector. At least he never hurts me or lets me down. As for Sage Bennett oops, Dr Sage Bennett – let's get it right, she can stay out of my damn way too. The sooner she high tails it out of Willowbrook the better.

Chapter 17

S *age*
 Wow, he always has to have the last word, right? He's always been like that. Stubborn too. I guess when we were younger though it didn't matter. I would just hook up with my best friend or go to the mall shopping.

We wouldn't be off with each other for long and the making up was so much fun. Yeah, let's not think about *that* right now.

I'm way too mad at Logan. And why did he have to come and follow me in any case? So annoying. Like I wasn't pissed off at him before, well now I'm really mad at him.

Even though it is summer here in Virginia it is milder and in this ridiculous short dress – yes, exactly what was I thinking wearing this to the Lazy Duke. I feel like a complete idiot. I'm starting to feel the chill, it must be close to ten p.m. Time to go back to my folks, I hope they don't ask me about my evening and they're in bed already.

Mom and dad usually hit the hay around this time. Dad is an early riser even though he's pretty much retired he loves to get up early and potter around. He's one of the last people I know who still reads a good old fashioned newspaper. He'll take a nice cup of coffee up to mom and when I used to live at home, he'd always bring me one up to. The thought of a nice coffee first thing tomorrow morning does bring a small smile to my face. Only a small one though after Logan coming to find me.

It's quiet when I get in. Ali has messaged again to see if I'm okay. I've told her of course I am but I refrained from telling her about Logan coming to find me. She's only going to try and play match-maker and he is *the last* person I want to be with. In fact I don't want to be with anybody right now. It still upsets me that Miles decided to head off to London without so much as batting an eyelid about the fact that we'd been together for ten years. **Ten. Whole. Years**

My feet feel so much better now that I've slipped my high heels off and the floor feels warm underfoot. "Hey there, Honey did you have a good evening?" Shit. My mother's voice scared the hell out of me.

"What are you still doing up?" I make my way into the kitchen. "And why are you sitting in the dark?"

"I was waiting up for you of course."

"Mom, I'm way passed thirty, you don't need to wait up for me. I'm not a young child anymore and in the dark, seriously?" She lets out a low giggle.

"There's something very peaceful about sitting in the kitchen in the dark and just listening to the house. I find it therapeutic." Well, that just sounds like nonsense to me but each to their own.

Instead, I put the light on and turn the know to adjust the brightness so as not to completely blind my mother. "There that's better." I say and pull a chair out next to her around the square, distressed pine table. It's homely and I recall doing a lot of homework here in this kitchen. With Logan. Damn it. I can't get that man off my mind.

"It was okay, Mom. Ali has a crush on Marshal Deacon. It's cute. Do you think they'll get together?" Mom gets up and reaches in the fridge for a large carton of milk, then a cupboard near the stove for a tub of dark chocolate powder. Mmm, I love my Mom's homemade hot chocolate.

"Well they've been chatting for many years and I know she really likes him. I hope so, Darling. He is a good man, so kind and generous. I think he's just a bit shy."

"It's not the eighteen hundreds anymore, she can ask him on a date you know." I place my elbows on the table and rest my chin on my hands whilst mom stirs away on the stove. The smell of hot chocolate begins to fill the kitchen. Lovely.

"I think she'd rather wait for him to ask her. I know Ali isn't exactly backward at coming forward, but she's a bit old fashioned like that. Anyway, enough about Ali. Did you see Logan?" And here we go, how did I know that was coming. My mom never really liked Miles very much, she always said he was a bit stand offish, arrogant and not the right match for me. Well he must have been at some point because I spent ten years of my life with him. And no, I don't consider it a waste of my life or the last ten years. We had some amazing times, I can't simply sweep them under the carpet.

Mom places my mug of hot chocolate in front of me and reaches for the glass vintage jar on the island holding the marshmallows and drops a few in my mug. This is perfect.

"Yes, I saw him. He was playing on stage. And he chose to play some romantic bull..." I stop myself before swearing in front of my mother. "Rubbish all the while looking at me. What's that all about? He can't stand the sight of me since I left him. You'd think he'd get over it."

"Ah, so you were looking at him all the while then, to notice. I mean." Okay, so my mom does have a point. "Time can heal, Sage. Maybe he sees things differently now he's grown up now. Logan is a fine young man, he's head of the practice now which by the way is looking for a new doctor. So whilst you're searching perhaps give it a go." I almost choke. My mother has got to be kidding me right? She knows exactly how much I do not want to be anywhere near Logan.

"Are you okay, Honey. Did I say something?" Like she doesn't know. My mother would love it if I got back together with Logan. She'd paint a white picket fence, start knitting booties for babies, cardigans and matching hats. I place a hand to my forehead. I think I'm getting a fever and need to leave the kitchen immediately before she continues.

"I'm not intending on staying here, Mom. I made it perfectly clear before I arrived this is just a short stop gap. I'm looking for State hospitals to work in not the little practice here in Willowbrook. God help me. I can't see myself dealing with the likes of the old folk in this town or the kids for that matter and as for the gossip mongers, they'd have a field day. Bit City slicker like Sage now down to earth with a bump having to stay here in Willowbrook." I stand up, I'm ready to end the conversation.

"I don't think anyone would see it quite like that, Sage. Everyone would welcome you back with open arms. I don't think you quite realize how much people missed you. I often talk about you and most folk want to know when you're going to come to your senses and move back home for good." Her voice is soft and gentle. I feel mean.

"Night, Mom." I give her hug and kiss on the cheek then extract myself from my mother's tight embrace and head off upstairs shaking my head. I know she and dad would love me to stay here but I can't. I'm not built for this small-town. I never was or why else would I have gone all the way to Michigan? And as for working alongside Logan, I'd rather eat dust. Although on the other hand, I do need a job and I need one asap because there is no way I want to eat too much into my retirement fund or savings.

Needless to say it's going to be another night for me without much sleep as I lay awake thinking about money, being back home in my old bedroom and Logan.

I sigh as I pull the duvet up and over my head, like that's going to stop my mind from whirring.

Chapter 18

S *age*
    Needless to say I had an utter rubbish sleep. My eyelids are heavy and my eyes feel like pins have been stuck in them. I groan as I open my eyes. It's just getting light which means it can only be around six-ish. Aarrgh. It's a

Saturday and I'm wondering what on earth I can do today hanging around her in Willowbrook.

Chances are I'll heave over to Bluebell's diner and grab some pancakes or maybe a muffin. Perhaps both. My stomach begins to grumble as if on cue. If I had a dog I could go out walking with it, that'd be nice. But hell, I think I'll take myself off for a hike after breakfast.

There are some amazing trails. My favourite is the McAfee Knob it's a slow but steady climb with stunning scenery from the Appalachian trail. Logan and I used to go there often when we were younger. It brings back a whole flood of memories that I push to the back of my mind because for today, I seriously am not going there in my head.

The only problem is it's around a four to five mile hike and then back. Not sure I fancy camping out there on my own. I've never done this before. Like I said, it's something Logan and I used to do. It surprises me that all the time I spent outdoors as a kid and teenager seemed to dissipate during my time in Michigan. Not that there aren't scenic treks and the like in Michigan but I never found the time. With a busy schedule at the state hospital and my relationship with Miles, there never seemed to be any time to be able to get outside. Our holidays were usually city breaks something Miles favoured mostly to meet friends and his huge family dotted between Miami, New York, Texas and California. We travelled extensively. But outside trekking, hiking, biking, running – never. Do I miss it? Now I'm back here and it's on my doorstep it hits me just how much I missed it.

Inhaling, I reach my arms over my head and stretch my fingers and toes. I take a few deep in and exhales then swing my arms over and forward to bend at the waist and touch my toes. That feels better, my back has been aching the last few days. I'm thinking it's all the stress coming out.

The house is still as I slip my legs from under the duvet and hang them to the floor and do my neck rolls. I'm not one for dashing straight out of bed, honestly it's not that good for you. It much better to ease yourself into your routine, the body and heart need that little bit of time to adjust to the pace you're going to set for the day.

The early morning sunrise is beautiful as I draw the cream curtains open and look out onto the back where my mother's beautiful garden can be seen. Plants, trees and shrubs adorn the space and beyond that is just large fields that once belonged to her family but had to be sold off to pay for food on the table. Thankfully we still have this gorgeous view and not some housing project go up. I shudder at the thought. This is the view I know and love.

Don't get me wrong, just because it's stunning doesn't mean I don't want out because I do. This is only a short stay until I can get placed in a state hospital.

I slip my feet into my summer slippers and grab my jade kimono robe and throw it over my body and tie it at the waist. Just in case dad is wandering around early, he likes to be up with the birds.

Downstairs I find him sitting at the same table mom and I were at last night having our chat, his glasses with steel rims are practically falling off his nose as he reads the local newspaper. "Good morning, sweetie." He says glancing up and adjusting his glasses.

"Morning, Pop." I place a kiss on his head then head straight over to the coffee machine and pour myself a tall mug of coffee, I add some cinnamon and a bit of vanilla powder. Mmm, it is delicious.

"What are your plans today then?" He asks as he folds the newspaper and places it on the table. Can't tell you the last time I saw anyone reading a newspaper, we're all so damn busy with our mobiles that it makes me smile. In the kitchen with dad, his glasses, the paper on the rustic table – it feels like I've just been transported back in time.

I'm eight years old, long braids, braces and my school pack on ready for dad to walk me to the bus stop before he would drive himself to the office for the day. It even smells the same of roasted coffee and vanilla beans. How simple life was then, being a kid was *the* best. I sigh.

"That's a deep one. What's on your mind this early in the morning?" I move my chair closer to him so I can rest my head on his shoulder. He pats my right hand. "C'mon out with it. You know you can tell your father anything." Which is true, I can. Dad never judges or criticizes me. He is the best.

"Nothing much. Just you know, the break up with Miles. Moving back home. Not having a job, no house. It's just overwhelming, Dad that's all."

"I can see that, Sage. But one thing at a time. Firstly, you're back with us which is wonderful for your mother and I. Secondly, you will find another job wherever you want it to be. Although, naturally we'd love you to be closer to home this time. We miss you, Sage honey." I know they do. And to be honest I could have visited a lot more often than I did, but Miles wanted to always visit his friends and family and well you know exactly how it is, right?

"Thirdly." He continues. "A man will come into your life who will sweep you off your cute little feet. He will be the right man for you, Sage. Not that jumped up sprout who was all too important for his own good. You deserve a man who is going to worship the ground you walk on, who will pull your chair out for you at dinner. His eyes will light up when you walk in the room. His heart will burst out of his chest with pride knowing you are the one on his arm. Mark my words, girl there is someone out there waiting in the wings." I squeeze my dad's arm.

Do you think dad's get a guide book when they have daughters, they learn all the lines and the just the right things to say? Or do you suppose my daddy is just a little bit biased and he still believes in fairy tales? Of course he does. I'm his little girl. And why not believe in fairy tales? After all, mom and dad have been together for over thirty years and every day I see them have a little kiss, dad always pats my mom on her butt. The affection between them hasn't waned and despite some hardships they're still here, under the same roof with two daughters who have always felt safe, secure and loved without conditions.

I gather myself together and take a sip of my delicious coffee. "I was thinking of going to McAfee Knob." I tell dad.

"Along the Appalachian trail? That's some hike. Are you going to camp?"

"Not sure, I'm thinking about it."

"Just be careful and make sure you have the mobile of yours charged up and a battery pack with you just in case. It's a hike and a half that one. You've not been up it for over ten years."

"I know. Maybe I'll go part-way and then drop back down."

"That's a much better idea. I think I'd be happier with that. Unless of course you're giving Logan a shout." Now he's gone and done it. That word that begins with an L. It's all I can do from stopping my coffee coming back out my mouth.

My dad, seriously? I bet my mother's been speaking to him.

I flush. Why am I flushing? It's not even like I am remotely interested in Logan. "*No, dad.* Definitely not with Logan." With that I kiss him again on the top of his head as he wears this crooked little smile. I know that smile.

It's the one that says *we'll see Sage, darling.*

Chapter 19

L*ogan*

    That woman drives me to distraction with her stubborn damn attitude. All I was trying to do was check she was okay. I knew she'd go to our spot. Well you know what, fine damnit. I can do without her attitude, the sooner she disappears to some high-flying medical position in a different state, preferably one the other side of the goddamn country – the better.

Hector is buzzing around waiting for his morning feed. I'm as grouchy as sin having not slept a wink last night. That and the fact that I still haven't found someone to step into the practice to help me out. I need someone else on-board like yesterday. Eliza, my assistant has messaged me to say that one of the Cooper's kids has come down with something and could I run by their house at some point during tomorrow if there's no change. First, I need to get out for my run and exercise, Hector too. He's got way too much energy for my liking this morning. His nose brushes against my legs, I bend forward to ruffle the sprout of curly locks on his head. Reminding myself that he needs to go in for a shave soon. Damn he looks cute when they buzz all his hair off. It's way too hot this time of year for him to still be wearing his winter coat.

"C'mon boy." I hand him a snax treat from the good-treat bag which he can hear rustle from a mile away, I swear he's got some great hearing on him. He can be fast asleep snoring away, but as soon as my hand goes near that bag, he's up and in here like a junkie to weed. I'm wondering what the hell they put in these treats anyway.

He takes it and wolfs it back in one breath then runs to the cabin door. I slip into my trainers quickly tie up the laces and head out the door. Hector bounds in front of me, picks up his stick from last night's walk and brings it to me. I throw it for him and start to run. Nope, if you're wondering, I never do stretches or warm-up before I run. Never have. Never will. Of course, this isn't what I tell my patients, no siree. They all get told about the importance of stretching pre and post session. Don't want any strained muscles and torn ligaments coming into my practice.

The morning air is fresh, I can sense that Fall is coming soon and to be honest I cannot wait. I'm so over summer already. With the global situation, it just seems to me that with each passing summer, the temperatures creep up more and more. The mid-day will be crucifying today for sure. I inhale deeply and intake the fragrance of the pine trees that surround me on the trail that will lead up to my favourite hiking / running trail to McAfee Knob. The view from up there is out of this world, it's a beauty spot amongst beauty spots. It always relaxes me when I'm on top and Hector loves a long hike.

I've got a bladder pack on my back, his collapsible water bowl, some treats and a few protein bars for myself. The aim is to get up and back down before the sun soars down at two in the afternoon.

My pace is steady, I know exactly how fast not to run to ensure I can make the top and get back down. Sage and I used to camp up there when we were teenagers and let me tell you, making out on a blanket on the ground by the campfire, with the stars above you and a glorious full moon, is one of *the* most romantic things you'll ever do. The thought brings a smile to my face, one I quickly remind myself to know off. There's no way I need her intruding my thoughts today, not miss high-o-fucking-mighty. This run is about my headspace, one I'd preferably not have crammed with Sage Bennett. She doesn't get to have head-rent not today.

Hector comes back to me with his stick. "Steady boy, we've got a big hike ahead of us and then some." Of course he just tilts his head, sits at my feet with his tail wagging waiting for the stick to be thrown. He's used to the trail, I do it frequently. At least a couple of times a month. Hector can handle it. I've also got some iced towels from the freezer that I put in last night so I can wipe him down and hang one round his neck when the sun will start to become stronger.

He rushes off for the stick and I beam. I'm so damn proud of him, he makes my heart swell. When they a dog is a man's best friend, you had better believe it because he is my everything. After losing my wife, it broke me in two. I couldn't function then either, a bit like when Sage left me. The only difference was that I'd grown up by some nine to ten years and could handle everything a bit better. It still cuts me raw when I think of her beautiful face, her smile, the way her eyes would light up when I walked in the room. And Hector, well he reminds me of the beautiful times we'd spend walking in the mountains, eating a Bluebell's diner, the moment I brought him home to my wife and she adored him.

He bounds back, I throw again. By the time I get to the top I'm going to be worn out just from throwing the damn stick. "C 'mere." I call for him then whistle. Obediently, Hector comes to me and hands the stick. Since I know the trail pretty well, I leave it on a rock and tell him no. He understands this means end of play time. I'll grab it on the way back down. The last thing I want is a worn out dog who could end up suffering from heat exhaustion.

The trail is all mine this morning and I love that it gives me time to myself. It can get busy being the only doctor in the small-town of Willowbrook. There's never a dull moment, so this free space out in the great outdoors is always refreshing and very welcome.

Then, I see something ahead of me. I squint my eyes to get a better look. It looks like a female from where I'm standing as I stop to take a better look. The shape is way too feminine to be a man. I humpf. I kind of wanted this whole trail to myself today. Selfish, yep. But sometimes you just want to be on your own. You get that right?

Hector walks next to my slow jog, I don't want to run out of steam before we start the slow incline to the top. Drawing closer I can't help but keep my eyes in front of me at the shape, whoever that is has got some long legs on her, they look slender and I bet they're toned too. I can just make the outline of a high and perky butt. Man alive, am I getting a rise in my running shorts? Now is seriously not the time for my hormones to start wanting to get some action. Fuck's sake.

Maybe I should pick my pace up and just get passed her, that way I won't be so damn distracted with that butt moving side to side as she trudges up the start of the incline. Yes, that's what I have to go. Obviously, it's been a while since I've had any action. Perhaps I should drive into Coppertown tonight and see about getting laid.

As I draw closer, I peer some more not in a purvey way. It's just that. Well something gives me the impression that I know that ram-rod straight back, the way those shoulders are squared off, the way that dark, long ponytail is swishing from side to side and those legs. It's all looking a bit familiar to me.

It fucking can't be. She looks round, shocked someone else is on the trail. Hector runs up and starts to sniff her hand. She puts it out and strokes his head, he licks her hand. Fucking traitor. I groan because right here on the path I wanted to claim my own today is only friggin Sage Bennett. Damnit and back some.

Chapter 20

S *age*
    "Well hello little fella. Aren't you cute." I have no idea who the dog belongs to as it snuffles my hand. The owner must be somewhere around. The dog seems quite taken with my scent because now he's licking me. How

adorable. I'm thinking I'd love a dog but with a crazy schedule if I can get back into a main hospital, it just wouldn't be fair. The poor thing would never see me. That tugs a bit on my heart because I've always loved animals and some kittens and a dog would probably make my empty life complete.

I hear someone call out. "Hector come back now." I turn and am shocked to see Logan is not far behind. Right. Fine. WTF. Why does he have to be up here today of all days? Except us, there is nobody around. This is such a huge bummer. Hector runs off like a good boy that he seems to be, whereas I stand with my mini rucksack on my back, hands on my hips seething.

The anger curses through me like wildfire, I don't even stop to think why I am still so angry after ten years. Come on, surely I would be over it all by now. It's not even like I didn't go off and create a new life, the one I wanted. Big flashy medical career in one of the most respected hospitals in the country. Meeting Miles was also a highlight but let's not think about him right now. The way he landed his bombshell on me, he has been awarded top shelf position in my mind of *the things to forget that aren't worth bothering about anymore*. Needless to say, Miles is permanently on that shelf. Of course, one day I may bring it down and think about it, allow myself to go through all the emotions of a split after being with someone for ten years. But it sure as hell is not happening today.

Besides, I've got more pressing things to worry about right now. Like, why am I getting butterflies in my stomach at the sight of Logan's very toned, muscular tan legs? Oh my word. They are something out of a boxer shorts advertisement. Seriously, I'm almost salivating. The narrow hips they run down from are making me have heart palpitations. This is rather fucking annoying. I do not, do you hear me *do not* want to have this experience over his body. Lusting for my ex is very bad for my mind, body and health.

Shit, there's only two options for me. To carry on up and hope he overtakes me and doesn't say a word, or to go back down. Only I've been trudging for just over two hours and I'm nearly over half-way so the thought of going back down really doesn't appeal to me. From memory, however, we hike at roughly the same pace. Perhaps he's become a serious fast walker.

From the look of the size of his chest and those formed biceps with veins running down his forearms, did I say they were sexy. Well I am telling you those arms are like a girl's wet dream. Several wet dreams. Fuck me, I want to slap myself and then some. Am I blushing? Shit, I am and he's getting closer. Does he have to wear such tight shorts? Now where do I look? Dear God, please help me out here.

Of course God isn't listening to a damn word I'm saying today. Logan is now almost by my side, he has that stupid irresistible lopsided grin on his face with a dimple. It's the one that all the girls swoon over, no wonder they all wanted to clamber on stage the other night at Lazy Duke's. And I have to point out most of them are either with someone or married. I can only imagine the line of girls and women who have fake illnesses just to get an appointment at his practice?

What I need to be wearing now is a suit of anti-Logan-awareness-armour. My heart is beating so fast and my mouth has gone so dry, it's the kind of stuff you read about in one of those Melanie Harlow, Lauren Asher, Elle Kennedy books. But for real? Me, here. Him. Holy cow.

"Hiking?" He raises his dark eyebrows and I notice his long black eyelashes that frame those gorgeous warm eyes of his.

"Bit obvious isn't it?" I snap back. I mean, what else would I be doing out here? Ballroom dancing. I'm dressed in combat shorts, hiking boots and socks and a vest tee. Yeah, see it looks exactly like I'm hiking. Dumb ass question in my opinion.

"I guess. Are you enjoying it? I imagine you've not been up here for some time. Like *ten* years."

"Jeez-us, have you been counting." I humpf. Stick my fingers through the straps of the back pack and carry on trudging. I'm seriously not in the mood for idle conversation with Logan today. Although, I have to admit his dog, Hector is simply adorable as he bounces around in front snuffling away at the ground.

"Nope. Just saying."

"Well can't you say it somewhere else?"

"Only one track." I sideways glance at him, he is definitely smirking like he's enjoying winding me up. Dick-prick. I feel almost breathless and I can assure you it's not from over exertion. Nope. It's his scent as it floats past my nostrils, a heady mix of man-sweat with citrus. I'm pretty sure he is still wearing the same fragrance he did as a teenager.

"Walk ahead of me then. You look fit enough to run the whole damn way." I tell him, wishing I hadn't given him some kind of back handed compliment. Slapping myself springs to mind right now.

"Nah, I like this pace." I so want to stamp my feet and push him over and off the trail. I'm imagining him toppling over and falling a good hundred feet or more. Perhaps not the best thing to do, it's not like I actually want to cause him any harm. I just don't want him to be hiking up with me for the next two and a half hours.

"Hear you're looking for a job." He says. "What happened in Michigan?"

"You're a bit nosey aren't you? It's none of your business, Logan. Besides I'm sure my mother had told your mother everything and you're on top of the latest hot news spreading around Willowbrook." I huff again.

"There's a lot of huffing going on over there. You sure you're up to this walk? You want me to check your chest out?" He sniggers. I flame red. My right palm is itching to slap his face actually. "Maybe you ought to go back down if it's too much for you. You know, being a city girl an' all now."

"You are pissing me off, Logan. Firstly, I am not unfit I run every day I'll have you now. This is a walk in the park." Before I can finish he rudely interrupts me.

"So, what's with all the heavy breathing. Oh, you're one of them." Hector comes back, sniffs my boots then runs off again. Oh the simple life of being a dog, right? I stop and turn to look at him, controlling myself from going into a full-on rage

"One of them, what?"

"You *like* me."

"You have got to be fucking kidding me. Are you for real? What happened to the nice, silently confident Logan I knew?"

He is laughing, it's deep and throaty. Damn it, this man has more sex appeal in his right pinkie finger than a hundred men put together. Make that a thousand men. It's really frustrating because I just want to slap and push him. I am annoyed with myself for having this insta-attraction. Everything is buzzing around inside me like crazy, my stomach is experiencing some kind of warm flush creeping all the way up through my stomach.

"Admit it, you're attracted to me." I balk and laugh. Shit he is for real. This is hilarious.

"Listen, Logan. Please don't ever compare me to those bra-throwing, hip grinding women who throw themselves at you. I am definitely not one of them and nor will I ever be. Now go on about your hike and leave me on mine."

"No can do. What if you trip and twist your ankle? You shouldn't be up here alone on your own." I sigh now in full exasperation mode.

"I'm a big girl now, Logan and I hope you're not being sexist assuming a woman can't go out and hike on her own. Because that would be a real shit show." I continue to walk.

He follows. "No, wasn't implying that. Was just saying. Ordinarily, it is safer to hike in pairs."

"Well I really don't want your company."

"Mine specifically or in general no company." Is this man ever going to get the message?

"I. Don't. Want. Your. Company." With that I march off as fast as I can possibly get my legs to go. Hector undecided starts to run between the two of us. If I wasn't so damn annoyed with Logan and myself, I'd think this was all really funny. But I am mad. Mad as hell.

"I'll race you to the top then Miss Fitty." He gives out a low rumbling, throaty laugh. "We'll see how fit you are compared to a good old fashioned country boy like me." And off he strides with those impossibly long, toned legs of his with tattoos running up them. Now I've got a great view of his high, tight butt and let me tell you, if I wasn't so angry with him, I'd sure like to cup it in my hands and see what else he's got tucked in those shorts.

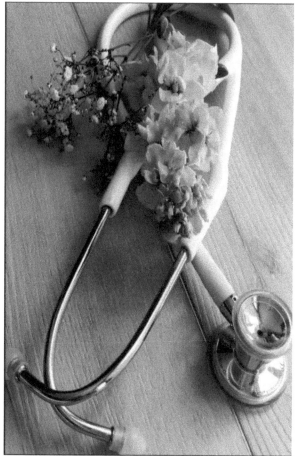

Chapter 21

L*ogan*
  Well I see that Sage has no intention of making up. Not that I particularly want to make up, but hell we're both on the same trail here and Hector is taking a shine to her. The pull of her is like a magnet, one that I'd rather not be experiencing of her right now. She looks so damn fine with

those long legs of hers and her face is still as pretty as a picture. Time has
stood her well, and I can honestly say that she doesn't look much older than
she did ten years ago.

"We're stuck on this trail together, Sage. We may as well at least try to
be friendly to one another. I'm for sure not going down." I tell her standing
my ground. She is doing a lot of huffing and puffing which is amusing me.
I know how stubborn she can be and right now she's being more stubborn
than a goddamn mule.

"Fine. Can't you just jog on ahead. You've got long legs and you were
practically running up here to be able to catch me up." Voice full of
indignation. It's all I can do to stop myself from laughing.

"I could. But I'm not going to." I tell her whilst I reach down and throw
a random stick for Hector. He runs off with a wagging tail, if only life was as
simple as keeping a dog happy.

"Oh, for goodness sake, just go on ahead already. I don't feel like being
nice to you. What happened ten years ago has happened. I can't change that
and nor can you. Let's just keep to our own paths and try not to coincide with
each other." She marches on, I get a nice bird's eye view of that tight butt of
hers. I can see she must do a lot of working out. You don't get a butt like that
by sitting around, plus the miles she must walk in a day in the state hospital
would rack up.

"No, we can't change anything, Sage. You're right. We can, however, act
like grown-ups that we are. Don't you think?" I am hoping she does because
as much as I don't want to be on side with her, I can't helping wanting to be at
the same time. I need to have a talk with myself about this. Those old wounds
may be exactly that, but they still feel like they were only caused a short while
ago. When Sage left my heart was torn wide open. Hell, I was about to ask
her to marry me. It takes a while to get over that and ten years doesn't even
come close. The love for her then was so fierce, I'd have walked over coals for
her, I'd have walked to the end of the country if she'd have asked me. Now
I find myself conflicted between wanting to stride off and leave her being a
downright grouch or staying by her side and trying to make conversation. Do
I want to continue avoiding her?

Willowbrook is such a small community and if she's staying a while, we're
sure to keep bumping into each other. Surely it's better to make the effort

than having to keep trying to avoid one another. It's not as if I can hole myself up in the cabin for the duration of her stay.

She doesn't say anything and carries on walking. My stride matches hers and we fall into a silence the atmosphere heavy. Damn it, why did she even have to be on my walk this morning? All I wanted was peace and quiet not to be torn between trying to stay out of her hair and wanting to stop the stubborn woman and kiss her so hard, to let her know just what she has been missing.

Right, I need to stop all thoughts of kissing Sage Bennett. It's mucking with my head. "How long you planning on staying in any case?" She shrugs her shoulders, I can't help checking out her ass. Again. So shoot me, I'm a guy and we can't not notice these things. I'm sure she's checked me out, unless of course she's made of stone. That brings a wry smile to my face.

"I don't know. I want out as fast as I can. I'm looking for another position." And out of nowhere come the words I wish I could have trapped in my mouth.

"There's a position at the practice. I need someone desperately, I'm over-run at the moment. Now that we're covering a couple of the nearby towns." She stops and turns to glare at me.

Her eyes are blazing. Whoa. "Work with you? At the practice? Dear God. Help me. You are out of your goddamn mind." I'm not going to lie, seeing Sage in one of her special tantrums and being mad is as sexy as hell. It makes me laugh, it's deep and throaty. Her eyebrows raise.

"I don't recall anything being so funny, Logan." She huffs again and I laugh some more. Hector brings his stick and drops it at her feet. Of course she has to bend down and wow what a view. Her butt is amazing, I'd love to be pulling it on to my lap. Holy shit. *That's enough of that, you don't even like her anymore.* Or do I?

"Stop checking my ass out, Logan. And no. I will not come and work with you. I'd rather eat my savings and be penniless."

"C'mon now buttercup, you don't mean that." And she stops again, places her hands on her hips.

"Don't call me that, again. That was then and now is now. Just shut up if you haven't got anything decent to say."

"What's wrong with buttercup. That's your nickname."

"It's not my fucking nickname anymore, Logan. I'm sure as hell not calling you stud-a-million ever again." Now I really can't stop laughing, it's full on belly laughing. Hector sits and moves his head from side to side. I don't recall the last time I laughed out loud like this.

"Oh, I'm sure you will one day, Sage." She goes a pretty shade of red but that glare in her eyes, it's cutting right though me like a laser. Why am I even saying this? What is going on with me?

"You have got to be kidding me, Logan. Never."

"Well buttercup." I get another glare, I swear she wants to punch me in the face right now. Maybe I deserve it, but seriously she's a little firecracker when she gets going and I love it. Did I really just say that? Shoot. "The offer is still there. I need some help. You need a job. It can be an interim thing for you. That way you don't need to eat into your savings."

We trudge some more in silence. I take in the magnificent trees that stand all around us, the sky is clear blue and the sun is beating down. We'll need to pick our pace up if we're going to beat the worst of the heat, that's for sure. Sage will know this. The years we've walked this trail are ingrained in us forever. The days we'd spend laying on blankets outside our tent at the top, chatting, making out and laughing. Days that were so simple and uncomplicated. Until Sage got in her head that she wanted more than Willowbrook and more than me.

Then I heard she met some guy, Miles and well – I never went after her. Sure, I'd thought about it. How could I not? She was my sweetheart, I had the ring from my grandma Ivy in my pocket the day I went over to see Sage, to take her to the movies. Only it never happened. She was so excited that she had been accepted to Michigan State. Her smile lit up her face, her eyes danced and that damn happiness of hers. I couldn't steal it away. It broke my heart and then some that day, the ring burnt a hole in my jeans pocket and I wanted to break down and cry in front of her. I wanted to beg her not to go, to stay with me here in Willowbrook.

We would get a house together, work together at the practice, have kids and a pick-up truck. The American dream. I've still got the ring. Funny, I never gave it to the woman I did actually marry. In my heart it will always be Sage's.

Chapter 22

S*age*
   He is just getting on my nerves now, being this close to me. I am not
sure what irritates me more, the fact that he thinks I'm going to call him
stud-a-million again, which by the way is *never* going to happen, or the fact

that I still find him so irresistibly attractive. God, I wish I could just fall off the mountain already.

And as for working with him in the practice, I hate that idea. Can you imagine being in such close proximity to one another? Ugh, it makes me shudder. For a start I don't think I can even trust my own senses being around him. Also, I don't plan on sticking around Willowbrook so there is no point allowing anything I feel or this ridiculous attraction to take hold. No. I need to be firm. I need to stand my ground and when I get back home to my folks, I am going to slap myself left, right and centre. That should knock any of these thoughts out of my head.

Yet, I can't help noticing him by myside with this long muscular legs striding away. He's keeping to my pace another thing that is irking me. Can't he just walk faster? I can even smell his citrus and musky fragrance, of course it's masculine just like every inch of him. His jaw is strong and square and that damn stubble is doing weird stuff to my insides. My fingers are literally itching to reach out and touch him. I clench my fists. No way. Absolutely not.

"So, how are you finding it being back?" Is he talking to me again? Honestly, hasn't he got the hint?

"It's only been a couple of days. But already I can feel everybody nosing around. If someone asks me again, how long I'm staying for I'm going to start charging them." He chuckles. Damn it. It's deep and throaty. I have a vivid flashback of him between my legs when were younger and the sound he used to make when I'd come right into his mouth. Holy Mother. Please throw my off this mountain right now.

"Well, it is a rarity to see you around. I can't remember the last time I saw you at Bluebell's. Also, Daisy will probably try to get you to go out with her and catch up. I know she has missed you. You kind of left in a hurry." His voice tails off like a whisper, it cuts my heart. I did leave in a hurry. Everything was so exciting back then, there was a big world out of Willowbrook waiting for me. I didn't stop and think, I wanted to grab it. Never in a million years did I imagine that Logan wanted to stay. Sure, I knew his dad's practice would be his one day but at eighteen what do you really know? It seemed like it would be forever away. I carry on walking lost in my own thoughts. It would be nice to hook up with Daisy but not if it brings me closer to Logan. The man needs a warning sign on his head.

Don't get too close, you'll fall in love with me.

"Are you going to at least think about the practice? On a serious note, Sage I need someone to help out and you're a good doctor. You needn't get attached, it's just a job offer not a marriage proposal." I am trying my best to ignore him. It's really difficult since part of me wants to just feel his arms feel around me again, the other part wants to slap him hard for being so damn gorgeous and sexy. I wonder how many other women he has been with other than his wife?.

His wife. That makes me feel jealous inside, the one who finally claimed him, the one he spooned with every night, the one he said the words *I love you*, too. The woman he laughed and cried with, the one person who was his world. Shit, how can I even feel jealous of a woman who has recently passed away and what must he be going through?

The least I can do is be civil surely, only I am struggling with that. Why can't I simply not feel knotted up around him? Why can't I let the past be the past? I hate this internal conflict, it's eating me alive. What I need is to get out of town fast, maybe I could rent somewhere in Coppertown and get out of Willowbrook.

"Logan, I don't think it would work. I don't want to be anywhere near you."

"You're so stubborn, Sage. You always have been. What's the problem? Frightened my animal magnetism will draw you in to my bed again?" Right? He is so not funny. What he deserves is a slap.

"You need to get over yourself, Logan. I told you. If you were the last man alive I'd not be jumping in your bed at night to get warm. So take that and shove it wear the sun doesn't shine."

I huff off, now he's just made me madder than hell all over again. For a smart man he says some dumb rubbish.

"Hot headed still. I love that you haven't changed a bit, Sage Bennett." My name on his tongue, oh how it rolls and sounds so sexy.

"Well don't get loving anything else about me, Logan. We were over a long time ago, you know when you didn't want to be with me. You chose this godforsaken town over me. Over our relationship." I bite back at the words that want to fly off my tongue but think better of it. No need to be an ultra bitch. We've still got an hour hike to get through and then back down.

Hector is walking slowly in front of us and I am wondering if the heat is getting to him. Maybe Logan should take him back down and leave me to my hike. I need headspace, time to think.

"I think you'll find I loved you both. Willowbrook and you, Sage. You gave me an ultimatum – your or my life here. You knew from the beginning of time, I'd be taking over dad's practice."

"Doesn't mean you couldn't have come back to it. Hell, maybe we would have come back together." I bite back furious at him. Perhaps it's all the years of it being bottled up coming to the fore, that and Miles being a super asshole.

"What's happened has gone, Sage. We're adults for goodness sake, let's start acting like it. You are more stubborn that an ass. You need a job, I need a doctor. Let's just make this work and if you prefer I can work a different shift to you. There's no problem with you working mornings and I work afternoons."

"Nope, I'd rather not work mornings."

"Ah, so you are considering it then?"

"I didn't say that did I?"

"That's settled then. I will do the mornings and you can come and fill in during the afternoon. That gives me the afternoon's free to do all the other stuff that needs doing. Great, you can start on Monday."

"Not likely."

"Stubborn. Just you wait Sage, you'll be begging me for a job in a few weeks' time along with a place in my bed. Trust me, I know you."

Jeez-us, is he for real? I am spitting feathers right now, I am so ready to pull his tongue right out of his goddamn mouth.

"Ha. You have got to be kidding me. You take yourself and your britches off to Coppertown and find some other woman to lay with. That should take your dick out of the conversation." Oh. My. God. His laugh is so loud, so deep and throaty it knocks me off guard and sends fluttering butterflies through my stomach.

A place in his bed. He is the biggest joker I've come across.

Chapter 23

L*ogan*

    I am hopeful that Sage is going to come and help me out at the practice. The split shifts can work because let's face it, all my joking around about her getting back into my bed – I seriously need some help. I am overrun with patients at the moment.

The rest of the hike up has been pretty silent, I know when to stop pushing it and by her tone and her manner, kind of seemed like the best way to be. After all, I don't want to push her in the opposite direction and well, Sage does have a habit of running the other way.

I'm only hoping that she gives Willowbrook another go because it's a stunning part of the world to live here in Virginia. Our town folk are always on hand if you need anything, the community is close and most of us have lived here all our lives. It's a real place to call home, not like a large city where I can only imagine you are just another body, another number.

Hector has slowed down and is now more or less heeling by my side. The right thing to do would be to march on up to the top, we're only twenty minutes away at the pace we are walking. Together we walk in silence, except for the sound of leaves under our hiking boots and the odd twig breaking underfoot. The birds are singing and the sky is cloudless blue, it's beautiful, serene and just what is needed after a busy week.

It'll soon be autumn, my favourite time of the year here in Virginia when all the leaves change and we are graced with oranges, browns and startling reds. Especially stunning is the Northern red oak. I inhale deeply the air filling my lungs and I couldn't think of anything better. Other than of course feeling Sage's body against mine once again.

I'm wondering how I have gone from not wanting anything to do with her to suddenly wanting the warmth of her body flush up against mine. Maybe it's the close proximity, the missing her for so long. Life is too short to keep holding a grudge against someone and I have grown up. I'm no longer that young adult who thought his life had collapsed who went on a serial dating rampage to forget her until later in my twenties when I met my wife. I had a nickname that took me a long time to shrug off and I'm not proud of it. *Manwhore*. Yes, that is exactly what they called me and trust me there were no shortage of girls and women who wanted to be with me. I shake my head, was that really who I was during that phase? It makes me shudder but at least I never hurt anyone. They all knew the rules, hook-up only - nothing more.

"Ouch. Shit." Sage's voice brings me out of my thoughts, she has stumbled to the ground.

"Are you okay? What's going on?" I ask her now kneeling down beside her. The smell of lemons and coconut fills my nostrils. Her face is contorted like she is in pain.

"I think I've just sprained my ankle. It's painful."

"Let me take a look." Hector sits obediently then lays down bored with us stopping.

"I'm a doctor, Logan I do not need your help now get your hands off my leg. Right now." She is actually yelling at me. Damn this woman. She needs to be put across my knee and spanked. The wilfulness of her is still inside her.

"For goodness sake, Sage let me take a look. Why do you have to be so damn hot-headed all the time?" She huffs and leans back on her hands and raises her left leg.

"Well just don't start touching my legs, it is *only* the ankle." She is so full of indignation that I am fighting hard not to laugh and chuckle at her. Her lips are full and pouty, what they need is kissing long and hard. That'd take some frigidity out of her. I know what else would make her not be such a wound up tight ass. But I keep that to myself as I take a look at her ankle.

"Yep, it's sprained. We're near the top. Do you think you can make it to the top? Bryce's cabin is up there we can stay there the night and rest it. Tomorrow I can organise for the crew to come and lift you down. We've got not signal unless you've got a sat phone."

"Forget it. I am not spending the night in Bryce's cabin with you. Are you fucking kidding me right now? It's a one bed shack with just a small table and a chair. Oh and a fireplace. I am not sharing a bed with you Logan." I have to fight with myself not to pull her to me and kiss the breath out of her lungs. She is so damn adorable and sexy at the same time when she is this mad. Man alive. I can feel something weird happening to me. The question is, do I go with it or fight it?

Chapter 24

S *age*
    "You're going to have to run down, Logan." I say pointedly avoiding the fact that he is now so close to me that all I can do is remind myself he is not what I want. His intoxicating smell is hitting me right in the clit. The

cinnamon notes not wasted on any inch of my body. His rugged face sporting some shadow and bristle makes my hands want to reach out and stroke it. Good Lord.

The way he is intently looking down at my ankle and probing it trying not to hurt me, makes me want his fingers to travel further up my leg. Holy Shit. The look on his face is concern and I know he has gone into full doctor mode. Good. Because I need him to stop talking about me getting back in his bed. Although, I have to admit I am getting strong flashbacks of being in bed with Logan. I feel myself heating up and hope he hasn't noticed as he brings his eyes up to mine. I can only imagine my pupils have dilated and my blushing is a huge giveaway. Don't you just hate it when your body deceives you like a traitor?

"You don't have much of a choice to be honest, Sage. You're going to have to stay in Bryce's cabin until I can get some help. If you put pressure on it, you'll be off it an awful lot longer than you want to be." He says matter of factly. And of course I know he is absolutely right. I sigh.

Hector is lying down beside Logan's booted feet like the obedient dog that he is. His big brown puppy-dog eyes are watching as Logan's strong hands assess the damage. This is so damn inconvenient. A nice gentle morning walk was all I wanted and to get to the top for the view across the town of Willowbrook and further in the distance to the forests of West Virginia and the peaks. Alas, now I sit here with his hands roaming freely over my ankle and his touch is like velvet.

"You have to go back down, Logan and get some help. For sure I can stay at Bryce's but all your talk about sharing a bed is never going to happen. When are you going to get that through your thick skull? Besides, my folks will start getting worried if I'm not back later today. You know what they'll be like. A search party will be out and that's just wasting valuable resources. You know the marshal will get on it if they go to him about me being missing." He chuckles because he does of course know what my folks can be like.

The last time I went missing was when I was seventeen. It wasn't as if I had literally fallen off the face of the earth. No. Logan and I had driven off to a spot between Coppertown and Willowbrook, there's a clearing where you can park up and hook onto the bonnet and just gaze up at the stars and the moon. That night is exactly where I was with my guy, making out and having wild fun. Only, the next minute we're both dazzled by strong headlights practically blinding us and the marshal's voice of the time, hollering out both our names. Shocking especially since my panties were already moved to one side and Logan had two fingers inside me. I groan now as I think about it. We had to beg him not to let my parents know what exactly was going on.

Thankfully, Marshal Clint had seen a thing or two in his day and Logan and I were not the first kids he'd ever come across in the middle of a making out session.

"Yeah, I know what they can be like. Do you remember when Marshal Clint found us?" He chuckles, it's deep and throaty. His eyes light up. I know what it's like to fall right into those damn warm, sexy eyes of his. *It's not going to happen, Sage. Get back with the programme.* My warning stands no chance against his touch, his throaty chuckle or his eyes caressing every part of me right now.

"Do not remind me." I pause, my mouth is dry. His head is not that far away – how easy it would be to kiss him. *Holy shit girl. Stop it right now.* Lusting after Logan is so bad. Instead I find my voice. "So, it's settled. You'll go on down and get some help. You can leave Hector with me if you like, I wouldn't mind the company." Hector lifts his head at the sound of his name. I'm hoping Logan says yes and that he leaves him with me. Though I know it's perfectly safe up here, there is no telling how long Logan will be in getting me some help. Usually, the rescue team is pretty quick which I know from experience since I was volunteer for a while back when I was a student.

"Let's get you up to the cabin. I know you don't want to even touch me right now, Sage but unfortunately you're going to have to allow me to pick you up and carry you." I balk at the idea.

"Any excuse right? I am pretty sure I can manage the last couple of hundred meters. Do not put another hand on me."

"Fine, have it your way but don't grumble about the pain. Why you gotta be so damn stubborn all the time is beyond me. Can't you accept a little help every now and then? I'm only offering to make it easier for you. Don't flatter yourself that the minute I get you in the barn, I'll be tearing your clothes off and making wild, passionate love to you." He is angry with me now, I can tell the way his eyes darken and how he is now standing with both hands on his hips and his feet hip width apart. There is definitely something quite sexy about Logan when he's mad. Am I going insane thinking like this? I feel like I am. The thought of him throwing me on the cabin's single bed and tearing my clothes off like a wild man causes a stir in my lower region, I try to squeeze my legs together. He raises his eyebrows but thankfully says nothing.

"Alright, already have it your damn way." I huff and puff like a five year old not a thirty-something year woman. We're all entitled to a little huffy puffy moment, right? And with one sweep I am up in his strong arms, my legs over his left arm. His smell fills my nostrils. Instinctively, I want to nestle my face into his neck and smell him some more. Crazy moment. So damn crazy. He makes me feel as light as a feather with those biceps of his popping his tattoos.

Holy shit, I could be heading for a whole big bag of trouble here.

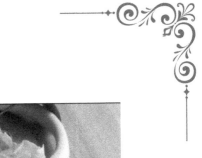

Chapter 25

S*age*
    Logan has gone down the mountain, I estimate, with the legs he has on him and his faster than my pace, that he will get to the bottom in a couple of hours. There will still be plenty of daylight and the rescue team can come

and get me. Hector has gone down with him, after some deliberation we decided that there would be plenty of light still for him to get down and for the team to come and get me.

Thank God. Not that there is anything wrong with Bryce's cabin but you know, who wants to be stuck in a tiny cabin with just one single rickety old bed, a table that has seen better days and the only chair in the place that now just has three instead of four legs? At least there has been no vandalism, it's just tarnished with age. It's not quite like the cabin was many years ago when Logan and I would come up here, the nights we've spent on our own with the small open fire going on chillier evenings, nestled in the single bed and making out like there was no tomorrow.

Despite the throbbing and pain searing through my ankle, it does make me sigh. Life was pretty perfect back then, just him and me, our school days although all those exams and the hard work I had to put in for studies to get my grades for med school, those I do not miss. Not one iota.

All in all, I think I've got at least a five hour wait on my hands and only a few granola bars, some chocolate and a bit of fruit to keep me company. I hobble over to the single porcelain sink that has seen better days and try the tap for running water. It works, well after some weird noises and a bit of clanking – the water spurted out and thankfully, I can get enough of the natural mountain water to replenish my drink bottle.

There's nothing much I can do except lay on the bed and rest my ankle to keep any pressure of it until the team can come and get me. What a drama. I'm angry with myself for spraining it and also that I found Logan so damn irresistible. That cannot happen, no way not under any circumstances. The past is where is should stay, right in the past. I do not want to go back there and besides, like I keep banging on about – I am definitely going to get a placement at a large State hospital. Although preferably one a little closer to home this time. It's good to see my parents and even though I don't want to be actually back in my childhood bedroom, it's still nice to be around them. I missed them both.

My mind wanders to Logan and his sincerity talking about the position he needs filling at the practice. Let's face it, I need some money in the interim period. I can't just stay at my folks house as nice as it is and I love them, which I truly do. But eventually I want my own place to rent until a placement for another hospital turns up. Who knew it would turn out to be this difficult? Surely hospitals are always on the lookout for new doctors and specialists? I humpf and fold my hands behind my head. No point looking at my mobile again since there is a distinct lack of signal up here.

All I can do is look at the beams on the ceiling of this tiny cabin noticing all the cobwebs and no doubt spiders lurking to fall on my face. Ugh. The thought makes me shudder.

The practice. Can I work closely with Logan? Would it actually work doing different shifts? I mean, it certainly has its positive elements. For a start it's within walking distance of my folks house and Bluebell's diner. That is very important since she makes *the* best coffee and blueberry pancakes I have ever tasted. Secondly, it'd mean I wouldn't have to dip into my savings. Thirdly, err there is no third. It has two positives.

Right, then negatives.

I don't want to be in close proximity to Logan

I don't want to get too close to the locals

I'm not intending on staying in Willowbrook. Ever.

Okay, so it's only three to two. But there must be a whole host of other reasons since my instinct is telling me not to work alongside Logan. Sooner or later we'll get entangled and embroiled in each other's lives. Maybe what is scaring me the most is this damn annoying attraction I am having for him when really I'm still smarting. I'm not even going to go there with why after a decade I am still not over it. It's not like I care about Logan anymore, it's not like I didn't go off and have a great life. So, what is my damn problem?

I'll have to make a decision soon though, only my savings are not going to last too long if I don't get anything asap.

What seems like an eternity later, I do hear the whirring and loud noise of the helicopter. There is a clearing not too far behind the cabin and I guess this is where they'll put down. I'm mortified and embarrassed to have them come out to rescue me, it's just the pits.

Before too long someone knocks on the cabin door. "Are you in there?" I hear the gruff sound of a man's voice.

"Yep, it's open come on in."

The door opens and in walks a large and very tall man dressed in the orange squad protective clothing. He must be sweating buckets in this heat. "Hi there. Heard you had an accident Dr Bennett." And so formal.

"Yeah, sprained the ankle and can't get down on it."

"Right, well don't worry, we'll have you lifted out of here in a few minutes. Dr Logan said he's already inspected you so we don't need to do all of that." He comes towards me. I recognise his face as that of Samuel Jordan, a guy who went to the same school as us. Wow. He was such a ditz at school and a real trouble maker and yet here he is, serving the community.

"Samuel, oh my gosh. I can't believe it's you." I push myself up to a seated position.

"I know, right? Not many people thought I'd make to a real job. Especially not with a drunk for a father and me being Willowbrook's very own bad boy. Got myself sorted out, went to college and here I am. Never looked back." His green eyes are quite attractive as is his dark beard. Come to think of it, he is very good looking in a rugged kind of way. Not that he's doing it for me like Logan did earlier but hell he could be a welcome distraction at some point. Don't tut. A girl's got to keep her options open. Just because I've split from Miles, I can assure you I do not intend to be celibate.

Samuel puts his rather fine arms around me and lifts me up as if I am as light as a feather. "I don't think we need to put you on a stretcher do we Dr Bennett?" I shake my head.

"You can drop the Dr, Samuel. Just call me Sage. I'm impressed you made it through college. Couldn't have been easy for you at all." And I am. He came from the roughest end of town with a father who drank from morning until night causing his mother to flit on him and his little sister, Naomi when they were still young. The marshal had to come and speak to Samuel and be called out for all sorts of misdemeanours. It was a surprise that he never got locked away.

He smells of apples, I bet it's his shampoo as it fills my nostrils. Who doesn't love that smell? His eyes twinkle. "There's nothing of you." He smirks. I bet he is enjoying having me in his arms, it brings a smile to my mouth. Easily he carries me through the small cabin door minding to duck and not hit his head on the low beam.

Within a few minutes he has me in the back of the helicopter and the engine is fired up by his pilot, a blonde man with grey eyes who appears to be older. "Thanks so much for coming all the way up here to get me." I tell him once I am fastened and secured in.

"No problem, that's what we're here for." Mr Pilot says as Samuel positions himself up front. Up in the air I look down at the majestic sight of the Virginian mountains below with the trees starting their slow change in readiness for Fall. I can see the lake in the distance. It sure is pretty and peaceful.

Remind me again, why don't I want to stay?

Chapter 26

L*ogan*
   I have checked with the crew and they have assured me that Dr Sage Bennett is in fact nicely tucked up back at her parents' house. I let out a sigh

of relief. They have been extremely responsive and I make a note to ensure I buy Samuel a beer at some point.

Hector has fallen fast asleep outside the cabin under one of his favourite trees, I can hear him snoring from where I am sitting on my bench outside on the porch. It's been quite a day and to be honest I am spent from running back down the mountain in the blazing heat. But now it's nearly seven in the evening and the sky has started it's magical prowess changing gradually from dusk to an awaiting dark night with a sky full of stars.

Sitting out here on my own with Hector is as peaceful as it gets and I relish it. Sage is, however playing on my mind. I wonder if she'll get off her stubborn high horse streak and fill the position at the practice. I couldn't think of anyone I'd trust more to work alongside me. Even if it appears it's only going to be a while.

Hector's legs move in rapid succession as he lays on the floor. I whistle a few times to bring him out of his dream. He grunts and carries on snoring. To be that damn dog would be a mighty fine thing.

I need to shower and consider going over to Lazy Duke's. Being a Saturday I would ordinarily play a set. A car engine breaks the silence I was enjoying.

"What you up to, loner?" It's my sister as cheery as ever. Her hair tied up in a high pony and wearing shorts that are so short, my immediate reaction is to send her home to get changed. Daisy will be Daisy and has a mind of her own.

"Not much, enjoying the peace and quiet until you turned up." I tell her and smile. Daisy makes her way over and sits beside me on the bench.

"Heard you ran up against a bit of trouble on the trail." She looks intently at me. I know what she is trying to do. Get some gossip but there ain't none to tell. Not right now anyway but I'm working on it. Despite the fact that it was the last thing on my mind only yesterday.

"Not really. Just a hike like any other time." She raises her eyebrows and shuffles her cowboy clad feet on the ground in front of her.

"Not what I heard."

"Really? Well, I can assure you miss Nosey there ain't no gossip from just Hector and I on a trail walk. The poor fella is out with the fairies."

"Oh, come off of it, Logan. The helicopter went up today and the whole town knows it was for Sage." That's not going to please her one little bit. I can't wait for that fallout to happen. I can only imagine Sage is now spitting feathers that the entire population of Willowbrook knows she was airlifted back home. Lordy, Lordy. Glad I'm sitting up here by my cabin and not in the house with her and the folks. It brings a slight smile to my face.

"Rumour has it, you and Sage were out walking together." Daisy crosses her arms in front of her chest. I laugh. "What's so funny hey, Logan? Is it true? Have you two started to kiss and make-up?" Now my younger sister is clapping her hands together like a five year old.

"No, we have not kissed and made-up. Honestly, Daisy I think you've got the wrong end of the stick here."

She shrugs. "Well Deb's says that Samuel had to go pick her up after you just left her up on top of the mountain." I raise my eyebrows, any more and they'd be touching my hairline.

"He said what?" God, the rumour mill has been working over-time. Clearly. "I did no such thing."

"Ah, so you were up there and out walking with her then? And, did anything happen?" I scrunch my eyes together. "You know," she continues. "Like anything romantic. Tell me you kissed her." Jeez. My sister sure has an overactive imagination.

"I did not kiss Sage, okay. And I did not leave her on top of a goddamn mountain. We agreed I would run down for help so neither one of us had to be close to the other stuck in Bryce's cabin." I huff and fold my arms in front of my chest. "Now why don't you hurry on back to town and put the record straight miss gossipmonger. Whilst you're at it, you best go home and put some pants on. Catch your death dressed like that." Daisy sticks her tongue out at me, I so want to pull it right out of her mouth. Some things never change.

"You are such an old wart, you know that Logan. Besides, I'm off to Lazy Duke's tonight and shouldn't you be playing? To be clear then, you were a fool and didn't make a move on Sage?"

Exasperation hits me, "I told you already now zip it and get out of here. I've a shower to have and get my ass over to the bar." I do not tell her that I have offered Sage a job at the practice. It'd be round Willowbrook in seconds and by the end of the Chinese whispers, story would have it that I'm putting a ring on her goddamn finger.

Yep, that's what it's like living in a small town. You only have to look twice at a girl and they've married you off, bought you the house with the white picket fence and started to name your babies and their babies. If I wasn't so hacked off that they're saying I abandoned Sage up on the mountain, it'd make me smile.

"Suit yourself big bro. You best be playing some happy-clappy music tonight, none of that love sick nonsense you played the other night. I may just pay Sage a visit myself and see if she fancies hobbling over with me."

"You will do no such thing, Daisy. Stop meddling in business that is nothing to do with you. By the way, how is Marshal Deacon doing?" At least Daisy has the decency to blush, she crosses her arms in front of her chest and cocks her head to one side.

"Well that's just none of your business, Logan. But rest assured. When he puts a ring on *my* finger, I'm going to be shouting it from the tree tops." Her face lights up and her smile couldn't be wider. I sure hope it works out for her, only they're taking it so slow over the years that they haven't even got to the date stage. I could be ninety at this rate before I see any nieces or nephews coming my way and I kind of am really looking forward to that.

With that Miss-Gossip-Pants stands up and nods her head at me. "Catch you at the bar later."

."Get changed first, Daisy." My voice is stern. She flips her finger at me. Nice, real damn nice. Since when did she become so goddamn stubborn. I think it's the water round these parts, it's not just Sage but it's Daisy too.

I stroke my chin feeling the stubble. Should I shave it? Nah, it'll do for tonight besides the ladies love it. One lady in particular – even though I know she'll be safely tucked up on her bed tonight or on her parent's sofa.

As I go back inside I whistle for Hector, he gets up and shakes himself then saunters over to me. We head inside the cabin together. I'll have a shower, feed us both then head over to the bar. I wonder if I ought to go and pay Bennett a visit. Hector whines. "You're right boy, she'd probably send me off with a flea in my ear."

I stroke the smattering of curls on his head and feed him. Tonight would definitely not be a good night to go and visit Sage Bennett. It does bring a smile to my face, however, imaging just how mad she is right now. She always was a firecracker and so damn hot when she was angry.

My dick pulses. I rearrange myself and chastise myself for even having these thoughts, but you know. What can I say? For some unknown reason, my feelings are coming to the fore. Now all I have to do, is convince her.

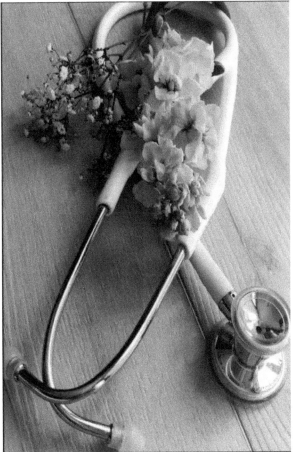

Chapter 27

S*age*
     Well this is a whole bunch of fun, not. Sitting on my mom's floral
sofa – honestly it's been the same since I was growing up. It's cute and all but
I think my folks home could do with a bit of modernization or color change.
What was I saying? Sitting on my mom's sofa with my leg resting on two

patchwork pillows. Those actually make me smile because I remember mom and I making them together for my sewing class project when I was about eleven or twelve.

The class had to come up with something seasonal, it was Fall running into Thanksgiving and these ones are squares with a turkey on, pumpkin pie, leaves in russet orange, greens, reds. For a kid, I think they turned out pretty good.

"Now, Honey keep that leg up and don't move. If you need anything I will get it for you." She places a glass of milk on the low coffee table in front of the sofa. Milk? I need wine or whiskey or something with alcohol in it to allow me to forget that a crew had to come and lift me off a simple trail. I'll never live this town. Ever.

"Now, should we get Dr Logan to come and take a look at it?" I swear I am going to launch myself off this sofa quicker than a nuclear missile any moment.

Through gritted teeth I manage to stay civil. "Not necessary, Mom. He took a look up on the mountain."

"Ah, but that was a few hours ago, dear. Perhaps we should give him a call and get him round again." Did she just wink at me? Did my own mother put Logan's name and wink in one sentence? She did. Jeeeeez-us. I throw my head back on the navy scatter cushions has propping me up with.

"Mom, *I am a doctor*. Just want to point that out to you. I do not need Logan over to take a look at my ankle. It's a sprain it will be perfectly fine. Besides, I can't be laying around here all afternoon. It'll drive me insane."

"Nonsense darling." Mom comes and sits down next to me and takes my left hand in both hers. "What you need is some soothing. I hear he has very special bedside manners." I swear to god, I am going to scream. My mother it would seem, is trying to play matchmaker only it isn't going to work. It was bad enough when he was checking it out up on the goddamn mountain, his closeness was turning me inside out and upside down. No way is he coming to my folks house to check in on me.

"Look, I think the best thing is I go up to my room and get some rest."

"Don't be like that sweetheart. You can stay down here and I will keep you company." Her face is all smiles and shining eyes. I actually think my mother is enjoying having me on this damn sofa like some kind of sick child.

"Oh, by the way. I forgot to mention that I have invited Logan and his folks over for Thanksgiving dinner." Choke me now someone, please before I do something irrational like gag my own mother. I slap my right hand to my head and feel my heart racing. Never mind the damn ankle being sprained, I think I'm going to die of a heart attack.

Logan. His folks. Thanksgiving dinner. All here. In this house. I have got to get out before that happens, we're not too far away from the holidays. Okay, I am probably over panicking because we've only just started to get into Fall and my mother does begin to plan for it, in February. I kid you not, she starts planning early perhaps not February but you get what I mean. I'm sure your mom is the same.

"I won't be here." Where did that come from? I haven't got anything secure but there is a handy motel over in Coppertown. I can check myself in there if I haven't secured anything in a state hospital by then.

Her face drops and she squeezes my hand a little tighter. "Nonsense, of course you're going to be here. It's unlikely you'll get a new position in the next five weeks."

"Great, thanks for that Mom. Such confidence in me." I shake my head and stare up at the white painted ceiling and the wood fan light that hangs.

"I didn't quite mean it like that, what I mean is even if you did get a position you wouldn't have to run out on us all so soon. You could choose to start after the holiday." I don't say anything because I have to get out of here. I feel trapped and cramped and I've only been back a couple of days. I daren't even leave the house now because everyone will be talking about how Dr Sage Bennett had to be airlifted from the mountain. Instead I let out a groan.

"There, there." Mom says like I'm some five year old instead of a grown woman in her early thirties struggling with the fact that my ex left me without discussing our future and now I'm in such close proximity to my childhood sweetheart. How did my life get so complicated and confusing?

Miles is how. Bloody Miles. I swear if I see that man again I'll scream. As it is he has reached out a couple of times to let me know that he is getting on well and that he is sorry how things turned out. Like we were only together for six months instead of ten years.

There's a knock on the door. Mom lets go of my hand and smooths down her apron she is still wearing from baking, which by the way the cake smells delicious. I am hoping she's making my favorite red velvet cake. "Hi, how lovely to see you." I hear her voice lifted, that makes me feel on high alert. It's her for special guests voice. "Come on in, she's through there on the sofa." Same voice. Now I feel like getting up and hobbling as fast as I can because I know that tone and it's usually reserved for one person only.

And there you go, yes it was. He stands there taking up the whole doorway with his broad masculine shoulders. A black plain tee on that I can see his tattoos trailing up his arms and peeping out the top of near his neck. Those fine biceps on display as he has his arms folded in front of his chest and those damn narrow hips. My mouth goes dry. He has a smile on his face, that cocky one I want to slap right off.

"Came to check on my patient."

"Oh for fuck's sake. I am not your patient. Just get out. I am perfectly fine."

"No way to talk to your doctor now then is it?" He comes closer.

"I swear if you come anywhere near me I am going to scream."

"Ah, the mistrusting and hostile patient. Don't you worry I've come across all sorts of patients in my time. Go ahead scream, it may even make you feel a bit better." Then I hear him mutter under his breath. Did he really just say what I thought he said? His smile and tilt of his head tells me, that yes he did in fact just say, *I'd like to hear you scream for something else.* I fist my hands.

"Logan, would you like to stay for a nice piece of cake and coffee?" I groan. Is there no stopping my mom? Clearly not.

"Absolutely. Never pass up on one of your cakes." He tells her, all the while his eyes are fixed on mine. My heart is racing, cardiac over load coming on. Logan attack is happening. And there isn't a damn thing I can do about it. Someone please rescue me and quick.

Chapter 28

L*ogan*
    The look on Sage's face is a picture, her jaw is so far open it's almost skimming the floor. I wink at her. She scowls back at me. Her mother brings

me a slice of cake and a nice mug of coffee. It's sure good to be back in this house, it's been an awfully long time.

"You sit down, Logan make yourself at home." She tells me fussing around.

"Thank you. I don't mind if I do." Sage folds her arms across her chest.

"You don't need to be here. Haven't you got better things to do with your evening?"

"Not really, although I am going over to the Lazy Duke later to play a set. You feel up to coming?" I ask her before I take a bite of the delicious cake. It melts in my mouth. Her mother really is the best at baking.

"Oh, Sage what a brilliant idea. You can sit on the sofa they have and prop your foot up there."

"I am not going out mom. Besides, I'd rather chat to Hazel and catch up with her."

"Nonsense, you need to get out a bit more." Her mother says much to Sage's chagrin.

"God help me already. I am not stepping foot in the Lazy Duke. The whole town knows I was airlifted today for an itsy bitsy sprained ankle. I can't be doing with everyone talking to me about it. I'll be the laughing stock."

"I don't think people are laughing, Sage. It could have been an awful lot worse." I say earnestly. There have been some serious accidents up on the trail and only last year a young guy fell off the edge. Thankfully, his fall was braced by the branches of a tree. It saved his life. "Accidents happen." I finish off the cake and drink my coffee. It is getting on and I ought to be making my way to the bar. I've got Hector in the car who will be coming with me. He's a regular there too although he does spend most of his time with Abe's cat, Molly a cute little black and white thing who he rescued from one of his barns out the back.

"I don't care. I'm not going." There you go, she's being her usual stubborn self.

"You're going to have to get out a bit more especially since you don't have anywhere else to go right now." Her mother says who is now seated in a chair opposite me. She winks. I smile. If I didn't know her better, I'd say she is trying to play matchmaker. Who can blame her really. I heard through the mother's grapevine that she didn't care much for that Miles guy much who Sage was shacked up with. Apparently, he wasn't the right man for her daughter.

I daresay she had the whole marriage for Sage and I planned ever since we were about fifteen. I know my mother did and when Sage made her grand decision she was so hurt and disappointed. She wasn't the only one who needed consoling. For a split second anger riles through my body but then I glance over at Sage and am reminded of exactly why I fell in love with her in the first place with her voluminous eyes, dark hair hanging over her shoulders and a the face of a Botticelli. Don't start running away with yourself, I am not saying I am in love with Sage right now, but okay – I sure as hell want to get to know her all over again.

We have got a lot of ground to cover. Ten whole years. Her tastes may have changed. Although I bet she is still nuts for reading those romance books of hers. It makes me smile.

"What are you smiling at? Do you like seeing me in discomfort and why can't you just go away?" I chuckle.

"Sage." Her mother says sternly. "Don't be so rude to Logan. He's come here to see how you are doing and this is how you treat guests? Honestly, we bought you up better than that."

"Tell you what," I begin not about to be deterred. "How about I carry you to my truck and take you to the bar? You'll have a great night. Hazel may even be there with her husband. I know for a fact she has a sitter organized tonight for the kids. Daisy will be there and it'll be great for the three of you to catch up."

"I am not going anywhere in your arms. I'd rather walk on my sprained ankle."

"Great," her mother claps. "So, you will go then. Thank you so much Logan. This one really needs to get out."

I nod my head. Damn, I cannot wait to get her in my arms and feel her heart beating next to mine. Even if it is only for a few brief seconds.

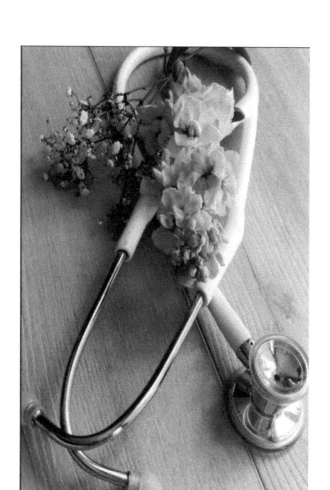

Chapter 29

S*age*
     "Listen, you know I didn't want to come, right? So what is your problem, Logan. Why the hell can't you just let me be?" Even though I'm now sitting in his truck so damn close to him, anger is cursing through my

veins whilst all the while my body is acting like a traitor and raging a war with my head.

His button down plaid shirt hugs him well and I can see a tattoo peeking out from the cuff. It looks like a sword or something. His shadow on his chiselled jaw needs to be caressed, only not by me. *Yeah, keep reminding yourself of that one, Sage.* Damn it to hell and back.

"I do know that, however, you need to get out and mingle a bit more, Sage. Everyone knows you're back in town and you don't want people to begin to turn the other way when they see you in the street. And how would it be if you wanted one of those pumpkin lattes you love so much in Bluebell's diner and everyone plain old ignored you and gave you dagger eyes? Well then how do you suppose you might feel? Then there's Daisy, she's dying to catch up with you. You can't just come lording it back in town because your life has gone to shit and then expect everyone to be nice to you when you're trying your damndest to ignore everyone."

Wow. "Quite some speech, Logan. You ever considered taking up public speaking?" I fold my arms in front of me. He's got my seat so far back that I can stretch my legs out, he's even put two damn checked pillows in the foot well for my ankle to be slightly raised. My question is, how did he know I would come out? I bet he's been talking to my mother. It wouldn't surprise me if she had something to do with it, I mean it's not like a guy goes around in a pick-up truck with homely, cosy cushions in it. Is it now? Exactly my point.

"No need to be so ratty. All I'm saying is that you can't hole yourself up at your folks house. You don't know when you're going to land a new job and right now we're all you've got so suck up and shut up." He keeps his eyes firmly on the road as we head for Lazy Duke's. I could have walked if I hadn't slipped and hurt my ankle. Not only have I had to be airlifted off the mountain, I've also got Logan having to drive me around to a bar that I don't even want to go to. Am I narking? You bet I am.

"I don't need you or anyone, Logan. I'm a grown up woman who has managed to get this far in life. Honestly, you should check yourself out first living up there in that damn cabin of yours like some kind of hermit." There take that with gloves off. And as much as I want to keep my eyes ahead of me, I simply can't. Logan is like a magnet, the force of him unsteadies me as I study him out of the corner of my eye. I'm not giving him the satisfaction of knowing I am checking him out. And why exactly am I doing that? Oh FFS, because I can't help it, alright. Happy?

"Everyone needs someone, Sage. With no job, no man and living back at your folks, personally I'd say you are a prize candidate for needing us all around to help you." He looks so smug that I want to slap him. He turns to face me and his molten eyes make my breath catch. The depth of warmth in them is the same as when he used to look at me when we were together. There is something still in them. This isn't good not by a long shot.

He hits his foot gently on the brake and the truck comes to a stop in front of the bar. "Sit tight and I'll come and get you."

"Oh for god's sake, I am not an invalid. I don't want the whole town talking about me, Logan. Just leave it. I can get out myself. I do not need you to come and get me out of the damn truck." Logan chuckles, it's deep and throaty my girl flower reacts. *Oh for fuck's sake, really?* What a traitorous bitch it is.

"Have it your own way, Sage Bennett. You always were a stubborn filly." Oh piss off is what I'm thinking if you want to know. This was a ridiculous idea but what were my choices. This or sitting at home with my mother clucking around me and singing the praises of Dr friggin Logan. At least here I can go and sit in a corner on one of the sofas and drink as much wine as I can to make me forget what a shit show my life is right now.

"Well, *hello* there." Babs arrives with her husband in tow and just perfect, the town gossip has to see me getting out of Logan's car. Rumour will have it that we're back together and getting hitched next week. I feign a smile.

"Hi Barbara. Good to see you again." I manage to haul myself out of the truck not very graciously but still better than having Logan carry me out. He stands to one side holding the door open for me, his eyes are on me and I feel myself flush.

"You poor thing. I heard you had to be airlifted off the mountain. Are you alright my dear?" And here we go this will be the topic of conversation with the locals all goddamn night. Get me a bottle of wine now please so I can drown myself in it.

"Just a sprained ankle. That's all." I manage to hobble out of the way of the door so Logan can close it behind me. He offers me his right hand, I smack it away. "I've got this." I can tell he's suppressing another one of his chuckles.

"A sprained ankle and all the cost of sending up a helicopter." Mutters her husband. Jerry never was a very friendly kind of chap. *Thanks for that your miserable jerk.*

Barbara nudges him in the ribs. "Oh hush, Jerry. What you say that for? Can't you see the poor thing is in pain. Good you came out though my dear. It's always so nice to see you. We don't often get to see that pretty face of yours when you come to visit. How long did you say you would be staying for?" She knows damn well I've not mentioned any of that. "Your mother told Logan's mom you lost your job and your man. Such a shame." She tuts. I'm flummoxed. Word gets around quick. I've only been back a few days and already everyone knows I have no job, my guy ditched me and I'm living back at my folks.

"Come on. Barbara we'll see you inside. Let's get her in and rested with her leg up." Logan guides me away, I try to shrug his over protective hand off me, yet I can't help feeling a rush go through my entire body at his powerful grip. God help me.

"Of course, absolutely. Let me go ahead and get the door." Barbara says and makes her way to the bar. Jerry follows behind her like an obedient dog, it doesn't take a nuclear physicist to know who wears the britches in that house.

"You can drop the act now, Logan." I say as we walk behind them and struggle free of him.

"No act, darlin'." He says and winks. I swear my legs almost buckle as he winks at me and my breath catches in my throat. My dry throat that is. I sure as hell hope my body doesn't keep playing up like this. I am heading out of Willowbrook at the very first opportunity. Even if it means I have to be a cleaner in a goddamn state hospital.

"Hey guys. Over here." I recognize that voice as Daisy's. She's by the bar standing very close to Marshal Deacon wearing the cutest blue dress with cherries on it. Her long blonde hair is tied at the nape of her neck with tendrils running down each side of her face. She is as pretty as a picture. Her smile is beaming, how can I possibly try to ignore her, again.

Logan steers me in the direction but can see I am struggling and in one swoop I find myself up in his arms, my head automatically rests on his shoulder and I can smell his fragrance and feel his stubble on my head. It feels safe, warm and far too familiar for my liking. I kick my legs out in front of me.

"Make way for the lady." He says out loud and the people in the bar part ways like he is some kind of god. Please someone just kill me now, already. This is mortifying and embarrassing.

He plonks me down on a bar stool and makes sure I am stable. "You idiot there was no need to pick me up. Don't ever touch me again." He throws his head back and laughs.

"Abe, get her some wine make it a large one. She needs thawing out. Sage has got so much ice running through her, she's like the ice queen." What an effing jerk. I kick him in the shin with my good foot. He raises his eyebrows. "Now, now no need to be such a mule. I've got to get ready for my set."

Abe plonks a large glass of red, velvety wine in front of me. "Hey Daisy. How are you?"

"Honey, it's so good to see you. I wanted to say hi the other morning at the diner but you kinda looked so far away. Sorry to hear about your job and your guy. That must have been pretty rough and then almost falling off the mountain. Jeez, you must feel shell shocked." I just nod. What else can I say.

"I didn't almost fall off the mountain, Daisy. I sprained my ankle. Your brother, saviour of all women, has made a mountain out of it all though."

"Sure, you know what Logan's like. But then he's always carried a torch for you." Cringing now. I gulp more of the wine, fuck it, I need to down the glass. It feels warm and soothing as it rolls down my throat. Abe checks if I want another one. I nod. Of course I do. I have to get through the evening with this lot.

"And I hear you're dating the Marshal here." I say smugly.

"Oh, Lordy. We ain't dating Sage." Daisy blushes. I scoff.

"Why ever not? You've both had eyes for one another forever. Isn't it about time?" She blushes even more almost matching the color of the cherries on her dress. Deacon Marshal coughs and sips at his beer.

"Anyway, it's so lovely to see you, Sage. It really is. How about we have a nice coffee and cake at Bluebell's later this week and you can tell me all about Michigan. I'd love to hear about it and what your plans are."

"Sure, no problem. I'm not doing anything you can come get me anytime." Logan comes back to me, now wearing an old looking dark grey tee. I can see the swell of his biceps and the tattoos covering his arms, my eyes appreciate them even though I want to gauge my own eyes out for looking. Heat rapidly rises throughout my body. I squeeze my thighs together.

"Something you like?" He asks.

"Nope. Not really. Get me on the sofa." I say without thinking.

"Darlin' that would be a pleasure." Oh for fuck's sake.

"Forget it, Logan. You've got as much hope as hell freezing over." He goes to pick me up but I swat him on the head. Instead he lets out a low chuckle and rests my right arm on his and allows me to hobble with as much dignity as I can muster towards the sofa that rests against the wood panelled wall on the left. The very one with a bird's eye view of the stage. Funny, I never noticed it being placed there the other night. If I didn't know any better, I'd say someone moved it there specially.

Chapter 30

L*ogan*
        I can't help chuckling because I have never come across another woman like Sage Bennett. She's always been headstrong. There was a time when we went horse riding once when we were teenagers. We'd gone to Montana on a trip when we were seventeen, our first trip away together. The

log cabin we stayed in was perfect situated on a ranch with horses. Of course, the first thing Sage wanted to do was go horse-riding.

"Do you even know how to ride a horse, only I've never seen you do it?" I asked as she unpacked her suitcase. Which I have to say looked like she had packed everything she possessed in it. Me, I travelled light just a rucksack with a spare pair of jeans and some t-shirts.

"Sure, I can ride." Mm I knew that was a little lie because we had been together for a few years by then and we'd never gone riding.

"I don't think you have." I said looking at her suspiciously.

"Sure, I have when I was a kid. My folks took us on a holiday to Texas and I got to ride a horse then." It turned out they had taken her there and she had ridden a horse. ONCE. It's safe to say that Sage Bennett was not a skilled horse woman. Not to be deterred she decided we'd go out riding that afternoon. Our instructor led us round the yard and went through how we had to sit in the saddle how to use the reins and spent two hours with us. My ass was as sore as hell. It wasn't on my agenda to go on a flat trek the next day but oh no, Sage wanted to go. Off we went the following morning, a beautiful fall day in Montana with burnished red leaves on the trees. I tried to tell her that perhaps it wasn't such a good idea to go off on a track on our own and leave the main group at the front. Sage insisted we'd be fine that we were only going to check it out then literally turn back and join the others.

"They'll never know we left the group." She said. And off we went against my better judgement but when Sage wanted something, Sage usually got it and who was I to spoil her fun. At that point I had stars in my eyes for that girl, butter would melt for Sage just by her looking at it. Her horse saw a snake and reared causing Sage to be thrown from it. Thankfully, she didn't break anything or knock her head but she did have a bruised hip for quite some time and her pride was dented.

I look at her now as she sits on the battered leather sofa that yes, I did place in front of the stage. When I am playing up there, I want her to see me. I won't lie, originally when I saw her in Bluebell's diner the other day, I was still angry at her but life is too short to have a grudge and all those feelings I had for her, well let's just say they're back and in full force.

Now, all I have to do is convince her that I am the one she was meant to be with. It's going to take some doing since this lady sure has got a bee in her bonnet and is throwing me daggers right now with her eyes.

Daisy wanders up to her and sits down next to her. Naturally, I can't hear a word they're saying but whatever it is, it causes Sage to laugh. Her whole face lights up, her eyes sparkle and her smile is so wide that I can't help thinking what it'd feel like to have her lips on mine again.

"Ready, Logan?" Abe asks. "Let's get this show on the road. And remember don't be playing those mushy love songs until your second set. The guys want some uplifting stuff today. You hear me?" I grin widely, I have no intention of playing love songs for Sage tonight. Instead, I'm going to rock this house and give everyone a night they'll not forget.

Daisy gets up off the sofa and winks at me. *What is she up to now?* My sister can be a meddle maker at the best of times. Marshal Deacon hands her a glass of red wine, I watch as Daisy blushes then turn my eyes back to Sage who sticks her tongue out at me. I can't help laughing. She balls her fists and throws them down on her thighs.

"It'll be over soon sweetheart and then I'll take you home." I say through the mic. If looks could kill, I'd be a dead man.

"Are you guys back together?" Shouts out Dazel from the bar.

"Not yet." I drawl through the mic. Oh, hush. I know Sage is feeling mortified right now but there's no harm in a bit of fun. Shoot me. This girl needs to be carried home to my cabin, laid on my bed and have a night she'll never forget and I am just the man for her.

"I am going to kill you when I get my hands on you, Logan." She shouts out. I wait for my drummer Tommy to join me on stage, we do a quick couple of minutes warm up and dive straight into some familiar country tracks.

"Anyone have any requests?" I shout out to the bar.

"Yes, These boots are made for walking all over you." Sage shouts out and folds her arms in front of her chest.

"Coming right up for you, darlin'." Tommy and I go straight into the song for her, the words not lost on me. Hell, she's going to take some time to come round to my way of thinking but I'm a man on a mission and this time, I am not letting her go.

I'm going to make it so that Dr Sage Bennett doesn't ever want to leave Willowbrook or me ever again.

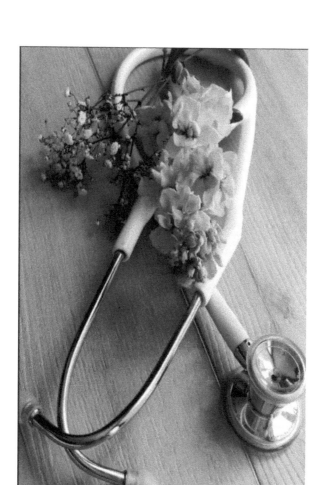

Chapter 31

S *age*
    What can I say? Logan sure can sing, he's always been a great singer and the way his long fingers strum the guitar sends warm shivers up and down my spine. Please don't tell me, I'm having any kind of feelings because I buried them a long time ago, when he chose to stay here.

He finishes and winks. Damn him. He's so sure of himself but it does make me smile because of his gall. My heart flutters even though I want it to be made of stone as far as he is concerned.

The next thing I know he's standing right in front of me with something in his hand. "What are you doing?" I ask him, not before taking in his broad shoulders, those narrow hips and yes, okay so... my eyes did travel to his crotch. Quickly I look back up at his face and notice his shadow on his chin. My breath catches.

"I got you some ice for that ankle."

"Oh, right. Very thoughtful of you."

"I am a doctor. Just looking after my patient.

"I'm not your patient." It feels like we are the only two people in the bar right now, the way he's looking at me with his warm eyes that hold a smile, his crooked grin, his dimple. Lordy, am I having hot flushes? Surely it's not the start of my menopause. *Get a check on yourself Sage.*

Logan kneels down on one leg and gently lifts my resting leg up. He places the pack wrapped in a chequered tea towel underneath. My breath catches again as his fingertips brush my ankle. Butterflies rage in my stomach and a warmth creeps up my body.

"There, that should feel better. You need a tight bandage on that." He tells me, his fingers still resting on my ankle. Why don't I tell him to get them off? Why am I rendered speechless?

"Are you proposing down there?" Daisy says. Where did she come from?

"Are you kidding, this one is like the ice maiden." Logan says. I go to kick him with my leg but the pain from my ankle sears up my lower leg. Damnit.

"Logan, you're such a jerk. Thanks for the ice pack now you can leave me alone. Daisy, I need a ride home." I tell her. She sits down next to me and places her left hand on my right thigh.

"Oh no you don't. I think you've been doing too much running away, Sage. 'Bout time you stuck around. Besides Linnie is playing next and you love her music." It's true, I do love Linnie's music. She has one of the finest female country voices I've heard even better than some of the top music artists out there. Why nobody has snapped her up is beyond me, unless you count Abe. I'm sure there's a story brewing there. My mother told me that she'd seen them on several occasions walking out together. So old fashioned, right? My mother is kind of stuck in some different era than the rest of us.

"I'll stay for her set, then *please* take me home." I am almost begging her.

"No can do, I promised Deacon I'd stay and keep him company." Daisy says a little too smugly for my liking. I narrow my eyes and glare at her. "But Logan here, he'll keep you company then take you home. Now you enjoy the rest of the evening, Sage." And with that she's up and off leaving me with man mountain in front of me, with his feet hip width apart and his crotch practically in my face. I'm all hot and flustered, my throat is dry. I remember only too well how those hips can thrust.

I can feel the damn heat rising up my neck and to my face. "You okay there, Sage? You're looking a bit hot under the collar." I guess it was nice of him to think of me with brining an ice pack. Maybe I could relent some. My mother said something the other day that of course I plain old ignored.

"It's time to let the past be the past, Sage darling. It's no different you having left him all those years ago to what you're going through with that twerp, Miles." She'd said in the kitchen over our pancakes and coffee. And I guess she has a point.

When you're young, however, it's the end of the world, everything is the end of the world from your hair not turning out the right shade, to putting on a single pound, your boyfriend not wanting to come to Michigan with you. It left me unable to think straight. I thought I was his life. Now I'm slowly coming to realize my mother is right. I did exactly to him what Miles has just done to me. I upped and left the only difference is that I *did* discuss it with Logan.

"I'm fine. But could you please take your dick out of my face. It's disturbing me some." He roars out with laughter, it's deep and throaty. Am I seriously getting wet panties over Logan? Please somebody kill me right now. This cannot be happening.

For one, I'm not staying.

For two, I can't go back

For three, I'm sure I'll come up with a reason.

"Alright, darlin'. Let me go and get you some nice warm cider, you know to thaw you out a little. We don't want you to be the ice maiden forever."

God, he thinks he is so funny. I fold my arms in front of me. Warm cider does sound nice though.

"Well hello, Sage. How are you?" Mr Wilkes who runs the hardware store sits down next to me. He hasn't changed a bit since I've been gone, same grey hair, round spectacles, ruddy face. "It's so good to see you around again. And with that nice boy of yours." Shoot me please.

"He's not my boy Mr Wilkes." I am trying to remain polite with a fake smile on my face.

"Nonsense, you two belong together. Damn shame you ran off like you did."

"Excuse me." Now's he has really got me. "I did not run off anywhere. I followed my dream to work in a state hospital. I told him I was going but he chose to stay here."

"Well, you're here now. You can change all of that, the way that lost man looks at you, it's like watching a forlorn kid. I hope you're not going to let him down again, Sage." He gets up and moves over to a nearby table where he joins the older members of Willowbrook. I'm left totally flummoxed. This town, these people. If they all think I have any intentions of getting back with Logan they're hugely mistaken.

"About the practice." Jeez, he gave me a shock. I didn't see Logan coming towards me. He hands me the warm cider mug. "Have you decided?"

"Fine, I'll help but only until I get a better offer in a state hospital." I check myself, did I really just say that? What the hell is wrong with me?

"That would be amazing. Once you get stuck in, trust me, Sage you won't ever want to leave Willowbrook again." He looks hugely confident, as I raise my eyebrows. There must be something in the water they're all drinking. "Look forward to having you on board. We'll get the papers drawn up over the next couple of days, by which time your ankle should be a lot more comfortable and get you all settled in." Logan sits back against the sofa and drapes his left arm across the top. His fingertips graze my shoulder. The warmth, his closeness, his fragrance, his stubble, those eyes. Lord it's intoxicating.

I am going to have to watch it because the last thing I can afford to do is let my traitorous body get the better of me. But damn if he isn't so fine and sexy, then I don't honestly know what is.

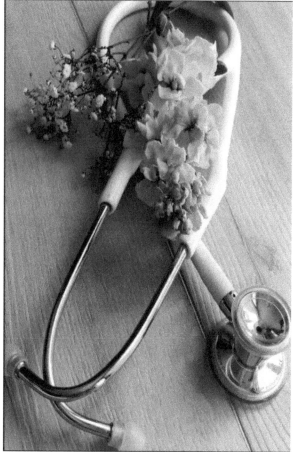

Chapter 32

L*ogan*
    I'm nervous and excited. Having Sage working alongside me is like a dream come true. It's what I always wanted all those years ago. I had hoped back then that she'd forget about her desire to go to Michigan and realize that her heart was here in Willowbrook with me. That I meant more to her

than being a state city hospital doctor. I had our lives mapped out, the practice, the cabin in the woods, marriage, kids. The whole nine yards, only it didn't work out that way but maybe this time it could.

Okay, so I'm running a bit ahead of myself. I have to remember Sage is only coming to work for me until she lands a different job and money can run out quicker than running water. Still, I am happy on this particular Monday just a few days after I took her home from Lazy Duke's.

Her closeness in the car was driving me insane, I could smell her fragrance Coco Chanel – it's always been her favorite. It took all of my strength not to reach out and grab her hand and hold it in mine. Her whole stance was *don't touch me* as we drove in silence to drop her off at her folks house. It did make me smile, the way she sat there like the frigid ice queen. I'm sure going to change all of that if it's the last thing I do and even if it takes me most of my life.

You see, I still love her. It's been buried and it made me sad, angry and bitter until I met my wife who I loved with all my heart. Yet, all of those feelings for Sage have resurfaced like a volcano erupting and there isn't a damn thing I can do about it.

"Good morning, Logan." Eliza is ahead of me this morning as she unlocks the door to the surgery, coffees in one hand, her large red handbag hanging off the other and struggling with the lock. I run up to help her. "I've got it." She says. Glad to see the coffees, since I didn't get much sleep last night thinking about Sage being in the practice with me today. I cannot wait to see her, although I'm expecting her to fall at my feet, hell with her stubbornness, I'm not expecting her to even smile at me or talk to me except where patients are concerned. But.. I am a very patient man and I know I'm going to get her on side.

"We have Dr Sage Bennett joining us shortly." I tell Eliza as she places her bag on the reception desk, hands me a coffee then bustles to her station and starts to switch on her computer.

"I heard. And we sure are excited to have someone in to help you out, Dr Logan. It'll be nice to see you be able to take some time off every once in a while." She smiles brightly. I'm not sure I'll be taking much time off, that'd mean I can't be close to Sage. My focus is on winning that damn woman over. She is going to be the death of me.

Sadie, our nurse comes in all bright and breezy. Her hair is a new shade today – baby pink. It suits her with her dazzling blue eyes. Last week she wore electric blue, glad to see this is a more subtle shade. I also notice that her nose piercing is a tiny stud to match her hair.

"Good morning, guys. It's going to be a bright sun shine filled day." She says full of the joys of the morning. That's Sadie for you, always bright and cheery, always smiling, cracking jokes and being a wise ass mouth. We love her, it's like having a kid sister around. Sometimes I envy her having nothing much to worry about, at twenty-two she lives with her folks here in Willowbrook, goes out to the bar with her girlfriends and hasn't started dating anyone serious. Sadie is living her best life.

"Good morning." Eliza and I say together.

"Someone is a happy young woman this morning." I smile at her. She's infectious. Oh, to be so young again.

"I bet you got laid last night." Eliza remarks drily. I'm guessing having been with her husband for god knows how many years, her sex life is down to once every other week. I chuckle.

"Actually, I had a threesome. You should try it sometime, Eliza. I highly recommend it." Sadie says smugly. I almost choke on my coffee. Way too much information for a me about one of my staff and before nine a.m.

"Er, I'll leave you ladies to your dirty talk and head to my office." And with that I hastily move away from them both.

My office is light and airy, the color scheme is neutral walls with an antique square desk dominating the space. There is the patient bed to the right with a screen that wraps around it. Behind my desk the window is large allowing in much light.

As soon as I step in my office I feel like I'm at home. Sitting here in what used to be my dad's chair gives me a huge sense of pride. To follow in his footsteps and serve our fantastic community is all I've ever wanted to do. And here I am, nearly ten years later keeping the people of Willowbrook healthy as can be, being there for them during loss and grief, offering them someone to talk to about their worries and concerns. We pride ourselves on offering the best we can for them.

"Hear we've got the new doc starting this morning." Sadie says as she pops her head round my door. I nod.

"Dr Sage Bennett will be joining us at nine. We'll do a walk round introduce her to you and Eliza and then she can get stuck in. She's got ten patients today."

"And I hear you used to date her." Nothing is sacred in Willowbrook. "So you guys going to get back together? Cool." I raise my eyebrows.

"As romantic as that would be for you, Sadie, it's not going to happen. This is a professional working relationship."

"*Right. Of course it is.*" She flounces off. I bet the whole town is going to be thinking that Sage and I are going to rekindle our flames. Of course, I want that. I want that woman back in my bed, I want to hear her moaning my name, begging me to touch her. And I better stop right there, I definitely cannot risk having a hard-on in the office just as she's about to walk through the door which, glancing at my large wall clock behind me, will be any minute now.

"Hi." I hear her voice as she stands in my doorway with Eliza beaming next to her. The sight of her literally takes my breath away. Her hair is tied up to a high ponytail, the pale blue summer dress cinches at her tiny waist and flows down to her knees. She looks exactly like she did when she was seventeen and as much as I am fighting it right now, I feel the blood rush to my dick.

Oh God. I am in so much trouble.

Huge fucking trouble.

Chapter 33

S *age*
    I'm not going to lie, this morning had me a bundle of nerves. What the hell was I thinking telling Logan I'd come and work at the practice? I must have had way too much to drink, or maybe it was the touch of his warm, masculine hands on my ankle. Sending electricity through my legs straight to

my damn pussy. Either way, I think I've totally lost the plot but I can't back out now and my mother. Well, let's just say she's already planning the goddamn wedding. Someone needs to rein her in right now.

"Sweetheart, I am so excited you're finally going to be working alongside Logan again. This is the best news I've had in a while." I raise my eyebrows. Can't have much going on in this town then is all I can think.

"It's not a big deal, Mom. Calm down. I'm still leaving town when I get a new position. I need the money otherwise I'll be dipping into my savings and I can't do that. I'll need cash for a deposit on a place when I move out."

"Oh nonsense, darling. Don't be so ridiculous. You'll be staying here in Willowbrook. Mark my words, lovely." She clearly has lost the plot more than I have. Mom starts clearing away the breakfast dishes and loads the washing machine. Then she turns to me at the island and rests her hands on it.

"There are worse men in this life than Dr Logan." She looks so sincere, I want to laugh because there is no way on this earth that I am going to date Logan again. Never. Ever. Sure, we'll probably end up being friendly. Nope, that's too much. Sociable to one another, I have to work with him now that I opened my mouth. And maybe in time, I'll ease off the dagger woman that I know I am being only I can't help it. I wanted him to come with me. Yet I can now see this is no different than Miles telling me he was off to do a fellowship in London. That of course is the rational side of my brain. But my heart is constricted and not allowing any other man in. No fucking way. I am not prepared to go there again. First Logan then Miles. As far as I am concerned this heart is under lock and key and I've thrown the key to it far away.

"Don't start planning any weddings, Mom. It's never going to happen. You know I will be leaving and when I say I'm going to do something, I usually do."

"Ah, but you're more grown up now, honey. You'll see how wonderful this town is and the people. Surely you can't have forgotten how kind everyone is, how we've all got each other's backs?"

"I get that, Mom. But I also know how stifling living in small town can be. Jeez, you can't go to the bathroom without someone knowing."

"I think you're being overly dramatic, Sage." She goes back to loading the dishwasher. I watch her placing things in it and wonder how it must feel to be so content. To have lived somewhere all your life and never wanting to leave it. All her friends are here, most from her childhood, she's only ever been married to my father and in a way I am a little envious. These were all the things I wanted, okay not staying here in Willowbrook but the man, the husband, the kids and of course my big medical career. Being stuck in Willowbrook is not going to give me the career I want.

In any case, I have to get going. It's way too late to back out now and I am a woman of my word. I said I'd be there and I'd help Logan out so that is what I must do.

Standing in his office doorway, I am suddenly swamped with so many emotions, my mind is in shock. This man sure did grow up to be one handsome guy. He's still not shaved and that stubble deserves some fingers to caress it, his mouth is upturned and is he daring to wear a smirk. He winks. With Eliza standing right next to me? Maybe it's some kind of tick, nervous reaction. Surely, he isn't giving me flirty winks in front of his assistant, is he?

"Good morning, Sage." His eyes are twinkling, I know I've made the wrong decision when I start feeling warmth creeping up through my stomach and my legs go weak. His broad frame dominates his room, the tattoos run up his arms and as he plays with the pen in his hand I can see his ropey veins running up his forearm. Shocking. Sexy. Too fucking good looking for his own good.

"Let's get you settled in first, honey." Eliza says shooing me along the corridor. On the walls are the standard posters you'd see in a practice, one with a hotline number to call for abused children, one for drugs and addictions and then there's a picture of Logan standing in the middle of a group of kids all wearing baseball gear.

"Cute, right?" Eliza says. "He does so much for the community. He runs the little league. You should come watch on Saturday, my it's adorable seeing all those kids running around and then Dr Logan in his kit. Now that's a nice sight if ever I saw one." He does? Wow. I'm impressed he can find the time with running *the only* practice here in Willowbrook and the spill over folk from Coppertown. I merely nod. There's no way I'm going to watch Logan dressed in tight pants and top with those muscles on display not to mention anything else that might show it's form. No damn way.

Eliza opens the door at the end of the hallway next to the one that says, Nurse on it. Light floods through and hits the pale wood floor. The desk is much like Logan's, square, antique and with a leather inlay of dark green. The carvings on it are spectacular, I go to it and run my hands along it.

"Thank you, Eliza." I place my Mulberry bag down on the desk and move round to take a seat.

"Oh, hey you're the new doc, right." I am taken back by the most beautiful girl I've seen in a long while with her baby pink spiky hair, a nose ring and flower tattoos on both her arms. She's wearing pink scrubs. "Sadie. I'm the nurse. Glad to meet you."

I extend my hand to meet hers. "Pleased to meet you too, Sadie. I'm looking forward to working with you all." I lie, well maybe with her and Eliza but not with Logan. I know, I know. I've got to let it go, but I just can't – not right now in any case.

"I hear you two had a thing going on back when you were kids. Any chance you'll start dating him again? He's hot, right? Needs a good woman that one." She winks as she leans against my door frame. Wow, she's a bit of a firecracker this one.

"Enough, Sadie." Eliza says and nudges her away from the frame. "Kids eh? She'll be busy this morning. We have the pregnancy clinic so she'll be out of your hair for a good few hours." Eliza chuckles. I nod.

"Right then, Dr Bennett. I'll let you settle in. Logan will be right in to show you around." Eliza leaves me to it as I sit down in the large chair and swivel round to face the window that looks out to a beautiful garden full of shrubs and trees already getting set for Fall.

I hear him cough and swivel back round to the face the door. My breath hitches as I drink him in, leaning against the door frame, one arm slightly lifted against it. I can see the bulge of his bicep, his head is cocked to one side and I know I am in deep trouble.

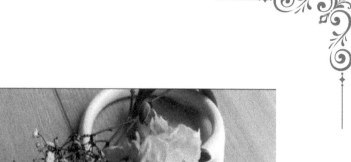

Chapter 34

L*ogan*
    Well, if it isn't a fine sight, to see Dr Sage Bennett sitting at what was my old desk before dad retired. Somewhere I've always wanted her to be. She looks right at home even though she has a strange look on her face and her

mouth is forming an O. I wink at her. She blows out and crosses her arms across her chest.

"What can I do for you?" She asks.

"Nothing, I just wanted to let you know your first patient has arrived. We have an electronic system if you go to your laptop and log in. Eliza has set you up with the password *glad to be back home*." She snorts. I try my best not to laugh since I was the one to suggest it.

"And who's bright idea was that?" She's looking so pointedly at me right now that I want to stride right on over to her and kiss her breath away. It'll wait, I know for sure I'm going to get my chance. I told you, I'm on a mission to get this fiery little lady to change her mind, not just about me but staying right here in Willowbrook. This is exactly where she belongs, Sage just hasn't come to realize it yet. She will, I have no doubt about that.

When you come to Willowbrook, it's kind of hard to leave. You only have to ask some of our locals. Summer Rogers came a few years ago having left a bad relationship behind in Denver and got herself a part-time job with Barbara in Bluebell café. It didn't take long before a romance bloomed between her and Dexter, our Major and that was that. They're now living happily together. There will be a wedding next Spring and we're all looking forward to celebrating this with them.

"When you're logged in just go to your calendar and you'll see what's booked in for you today. When you're ready to see your next patient just click on the appointment and it'll send a notification to Eliza and she'll show the next one to you."

"Very sophisticated for a small town practice. You're almost up into the twenty-first century. I thought you'd still be doing the whole calling from your door system." I laugh. She frowns. Oh boy, it's going to take some charming to get this woman to see what's right in front of her cute button nose.

"Lindsey, is a seventeen year old who wants to go on the pill. She'll be here with her mother. We had a conversation about a week ago but I requested she come back with her ma."

"Sure, no problem. Sounds pretty straight forward." She stares at me and I give her another wink. Next thing I know, she's hurled a pen at me.

"That's not very nice, now then is it?"

"Just leave me alone. Besides, aren't you supposed to be on a different shift. *That was the arrangement*." Damn I love it when she's mad. It's such a turn-on. At this rate my hand is going to be giving me a lot of satisfaction, until I can get her back in my bed where she belongs.

"Just wanting to get you settled in and introduce you to some of the folk. We always take a coffee break at eleven, no patients until eleven-thirty. We close at four." I nod curtly and leave her to it.

"Shut the damn door." She calls after me as I am walking next door to my office. I turn back on my heels and close the door. She sure is a firecracker.

"Doctor Logan, can you sign off on this please." Eliza asks as she catches me about to sit down. "It's for the little league game this weekend. By the way, you are asking Sage to join right?"

"Of course. In fact why don't you let her know it's a practice event that we always go and offer our support and we'd love it for her to be around. If I'm honest, she's not really talking to me." Eliza raises her eyebrows.

"Trouble in paradise already? Tut, tut." She smirks. "Just you leave it to miss fix-it here, you two will be dating in no time."

"*Eliza*." I warn her. "Do not get involved. We're not looking to date do you understand?" Lord, I can't have Eliza meddling in my personal life, she is ever the romantic. I should have kept my big mouth closed. I sign the form for her, it's to order the new kit for our little ones. They grow so darn quick, it only seems a few weeks ago we ordered pants and jerseys for them. We've added custom baseball caps to the order and for adults to sell at the ball game. Every little bit helps to keep us afloat and since the practice or rather I, hold the team up financially as well as supporting them at all games and training with them, we rely on selling merchandise and fundraisers. Talking of which, we've got a fundraiser coming up in a couple of months' time.

"Say, Eliza how about we get Dr Bennett involved in the fundraiser. Let's bring it up at coffee break." She nods, her smile stretches across her entire face. I groan because I know this match-making look if ever I saw it.

My first patient of the day is Mr Willis, like I've said before he has nobody at home and relies on coming in to see me on a weekly basis. Today's topic it would appear is the weather and how it's playing with his arthritis. Actually, for an eighty-five year old he is sprightly. I've seen this man doing laps of the town and marching up and down Main street.

"As I was saying, doc. It's giving my hip a lot of pain. This change in the weather does play havoc." I nod and start writing him another prescription for an anti-inflammatory. "How's that young woman of yours?" He catches me by surprise as my eyes almost pop out of their socket.

"My young lady?"

"Yes, you know the one that got away. Sage." *Right.*

"She's working for us here now for a while. You know just until something new comes up for her in the city or another state."

He cocks his head to the side. "About time you did something about not letting her get away again." I shuffle some papers on my desk, I know I should be paperless but I am still one of those people who likes to make notes with a pen and paper. Naturally, I have to use the computer. Eliza would skin me alive if I didn't keep everything up-to-date electronically, but old habits die hard.

"Mr Willis, let's keep it to your arthritis shall we?" He shrugs in the chair in front of me and pulls his brown coat around him. It's not cold but the weather has started to change now we're entering into Fall.

"Just saying, is all." He mumbles. I smile at him.

"I've written you a prescription for some new medication, you can take four a day strictly within four hours apart. Good to see you're still taking exercise, I'm impressed to see you taking your walks. Now keep up the good work and if you need anything else be sure to give Eliza a call." He uses his cane to help him up, I move around my desk and give him a hand.

"Thanks doc. See you at Lazy Duke's tonight."

"For sure, and no drinking whiskey with these pills. Do you hear me?"

Old man Willis just raises his right hand and moves it as if to shift my words away. "Don't be so ridiculous young man. I'm still kicking around aren't I?" He makes me chuckle. What can I say?

A few patients later and it's already eleven. "Quick morning." I say to Eliza as I pass her in the corridor to enter our staff area which is more of a lounge with its two sofas and a square table in the middle. We have a kitchenette area with sink, microwave, small oven and hob and all the necessary cutlery and plates, cups that you would need in your own kitchen at home.

"Cakes. Delicious. Are these from Bluebell's?" I ask as I grab a chocolate muffin and make my coffee.

"Sure are doc." Eliza helps herself to a blonde muffin that looks like it's got blueberries in it and sits down next to me on the sofa. The door opens and Sage enters. Eliza shoots up as if she's just had a hot rod stuck up her ass and moves to the other sofa.

Sage makes her coffee and leans against the kitchen counter. So stubborn to the end. "Honey, come and sit over here with us." Eliza says. Sage doesn't move. I bet she'd rather cut her right arm off.

"Hey did I miss anything?" Sadie asks as she enters the staff area. "Wow, I'm already tired out. This morning's clinic was so busy. I tell you those James' had better slow down. They are on baby number four. That poor woman will never see her feet again, if they keep popping them out like that." I chuckle. It's true. Pete and Bethany James are intent on having a football team.

Sadie makes herself a coffee, places two muffins on her plate and heads over to where I am sitting on the sofa. "Not there." Screeches Eliza. I look at her as if she has lost the plot. I told you she was going to meddle. I groan and shoot her a warning look.

"Sage. C'mon will ya already." Sadie says from the other sofa where she sits next to Eliza. I can't help myself as I pat the sofa next to me.

"Come on, we need to talk about the baseball fundraiser. We'd like you to be on board." I tell her. Sage shoots me daggers as I continue to pat the sofa. "I don't bite." Okay, so if looks could kill, I'm telling you, I would be dead.

Reluctantly, she does make her way over and stiffly sits herself down placing one of the navy cushions between us. It takes all my power not to shift a bit closer to her. Just being this near to her is doing something crazy and weird to me. My heart is beating faster, my mouth is kinda dry and well I've got some weird shit going on in my stomach.

Eliza starts talking about the fundraiser whilst I keep stealing glances at Sage from the corner of my eye. Her skin is like velvet, creamy and perfect. I long to trace my fingers down her cheek, hook my hand behind her head and draw her in for a kiss on those perfect bee stung lips of hers. She senses me looking at her and shoots me a dirty look.

I'd like to be giving her some dirty looks, the kind that'll get her groaning and moaning my damn name.

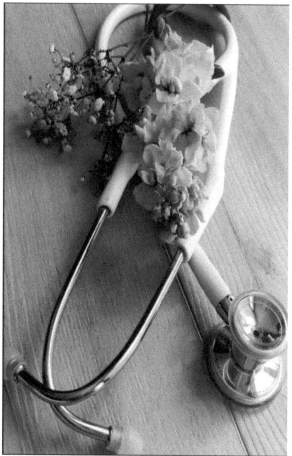

Chapter 35

S*age*
    "I am thinking," begins Eliza as she breaks off some muffin and pops it in her mouth. I watch as she chews then swallows it. I sip on my coffee from the mug in my hands, all too aware of the closeness of Logan. It's intense. The

sooner he starts the shift turns the better. Although, I am bewildered that I am feeling this pull towards him.

"You," she points at me, "and Logan can manage the cake stall together." I almost spurt my coffee out, Eliza wipes her hands on the red napkin on her lap, looking quite pleased with herself. What is she up to?

"Ooo, I think that sounds perfect." Sadie adds with a mischievous look 0n her face.

"I am sure I can manage a cake stall on my own." I blurt out.

"Nonsense, it'll take two of you. Trust me, Sage we get a lot of people who come to the fundraiser each year. It's a big thing here in Willowbrook, folk from all over come here and some of their kids play in the baseball team. Most of them arrive from Lewisburg, Hot Springs, Snowshoe, Summersville, Fayetteville, Oak Hill and Beckley." My eyebrows shoot up.

"Seriously? They're not all that close some of them."

"Oh, for sure, honey. It's a big event. We put on a band in fact, Logan you are playing this year at some point, right?" He nods.

"Absolutely, wouldn't miss it." He stretches his long, muscular arm across the back of the sofa. His fingers long and my filthy mind wanders to what they'd feel like sliding in and out of me. I squeeze my legs together, of course I already know how they'd feel. Too damn fucking good. I can feel myself blushing. Good Lord.

"That means then, you can't man a cake stall with me too. Sorted. Sadie can jump on if I get swamped."

"Of course I can. I'll be playing band after four when the stalls are beginning to wrap up and after we've had the parade." He says. Of course he would be.

"I'll be too busy with my craft stall." Sadie adds to the conversation.

"Wow, crafts what sort of things do you make?" I didn't figure Sadie for a crafting person.

"Patchwork quilts, cushions, macramé, picture frames. You name I make it. In fact I have an Etsy shop. I'll ping you the link for when you get a place here in Willowbrook." I'm not inclined to spit coffee out but with her comments about staying, renders another mouthful dangerously close to being spurted over myself.

I hear Logan chuckling and give him a sideways glare, narrowing my eyes. He holds his hands up in front of him in a *Whaaaat* kind of fashion.

"That sounds amazing, Sadie. Definitely send me the link and I'll take a look. Only it'll be gifts for my mom mainly since I have *no* intention of staying here in Willowbrook. This is just temporary."

She smiles, "we'll see. Only you know most folk that come here never leave, right?"

"So I keep being told. I used to live here and I managed to leave just fine. Right, I better get back to my patients."

"You don't have another patient for another hour. This isn't City State." Logan says with a grin across his face. "Just saying." I glare at him.

"Say, why don't we all meet up at Bluebell's later this evening go over more of the plans for the fundraiser?" Eliza asks. Don't these people have homes and families to go home to? I mean, don't get me wrong I love a good fundraiser and event as much as the next person, I grew up with them living here in a small town, but right now, I really need to try and keep my distance from Logan.

Aside from any traitorous happenings with my body and the way it's reacting to him, I have to consider that I *will* be leaving Willowbrook. There is no room for a new relationship in my life right now, not when I am going to move on again. Once was bad enough, the pain and hurt we went through, Miles leaving me is still raw. Why do I even want to entertain getting close to anyone again?

I mean, I could start to drop the *bitch* attitude. It was a decade ago, and Logan is trying that is when he's not damn well winking at me and causing me have palpitations, racing heart rate and swelling in my clit.

But.... Can I be friends again with Logan or will it get out of hand and I'll be back to where I was ten years ago?

Chapter 36

S *age*
     The day passed quickly, it felt good to be back consulting with
people and being there to help them. I even got to see Mrs Winters again.
She was my teacher at school when I was younger. I will always remember

how she encouraged me and would hold me back after school sometimes and do extra tuition.

Now in her late sixties she still looks as beautiful as she did back then, just her hair is now laced with some grey but those violet eyes of hers are still twinkling away. Mrs Winters came in because has a troublesome hip and we caught up on old times. It was wonderful to see her.

At four, I left the practice and made my way back to my folks where I've just entered the house. "And, how did it go?" Mom asks before I've even slipped my shoes off. Talk about eager beaver.

"It was okay, you know. Nice to see my old teacher again." I slip into my Ugg slippers and head into the kitchen. Dad is in his office I see pouring over papers, again. He needs to start to take it easy.

"And, being with Logan. Did it stir up old memories and feelings?"

"Mom, honestly. Stop right now. You know I'll be leaving soon again. There is nothing to report on the Logan front."

"I can wish though dear, can't I?" Mom adds coffee to the filter and puts the machine on.

"No point in day-dreaming about Logan and I getting back together, Mom. It's not going to happen." I don't bother to tell her that I've decided to make nice with Logan. That would just add fuel to the fire and she'd raise her hopes that her daughter is going to fall back in love with Logan and stay here in Willowbrook. Which I keep having to say, is *not* going to happen.

"Just mark my words, Sage, you will." She taps her nose. I sigh and roll my eyes. Not all mother's know best and on this score she is way off the mark. Even though I do still find him devilishly handsome. C'mon, I'm a woman not a dead woman. I can see what's in front of my nose and he is arresting and the way he's filled out to be a mighty fine man, hasn't gone unnoticed. I'm pretty sure he's got a woman or two tucked away somewhere that he goes to relieve himself and have fun with. Logan is definitely not a monk. He's a pure bred man of a man.

"Plans tonight?"

"I was hoping to stay in and rest my ankle. It's killing me. Eliza decided we should meet up at Bluebell's later to discuss the fundraiser that the practice is putting on." Mom places the coffee in front of me and I take a sip even though it's still hot. I take a cookie out of the barrel on the counter.

"That'll be nice, honey. Did you want to put me down for some baking. Logan's ma and I usually bake cakes for the cake stall? I can make some of my best-selling blueberry muffins with cream." Mom sits down next to me. This feels like old times, the two of us at the kitchen island, coffees in hand and chatting away. I'm going to have to admit that now I'm sitting here with her, I kinda missed it.

"Perfect, I'll let them know."

"Will Logan be there?" My mother is not a subtle woman that is for sure. I roll my eyes again.

"Of course, he owns the practice, *Mom*. I'm telling you nothing is going to happen between us."

"Ah, but I saw the way he was looking at you when he came over the other night. That man is still carrying a torch for you, honey. It's all over his face. You should give him another chance. He did nothing wrong. It was your choice to leave us all here in Willowbrook. We get that, you know your father and I, we really understand you wanted to chase your dream and I think Logan understands now too. At the time, it tore him apart and we were sad you left but time heals." Wow, that is some speech.

"I know, Mom. But even if I did start to have feelings for Logan again there is no point. You know, I want to go into a state hospital. Being here in a small town practice isn't my dream." I tell her and drink some more of my coffee and take another cookie from the barrel. My stomach gnarls - I'm hungry.

"There are benefits, darling of being in a small town. For a start everyone has got your back. The community is welcoming and we have so much to offer. That and you get to have a personal relationship with your patients, you see it through from the start to the end. You don't get that in one of those fancy big hospitals, do you?" She has a point, what can I say? Instead, I give her a hug and kiss her cheek.

"I'll eat at Bluebell's, Mom. Don't make dinner for me." I stand up and place my mug in the dishwasher.

AS I REMEMBER, BLUEBELL'S is busy for an evening. The diner is full of the older folk sitting at tables with blue clothes on them. It looks as if they're having some kind of function. The men are dressed with button down shirts on and ties, the women are in elegant dresses. Maybe it's someone's birthday. Barbara looks run off her feet. Some teenagers are sitting in one of the booths, they're looking at something on a kid's mobile and laughing. It takes me back to when Logan and I just to sit in a corner booth, only we'd be charged with hormones wanting to rip each other's clothes off. I better bury that memory right now before he turns up.

Talk of the devil, the door opens and in strides Logan. All six foot something of him. He's wearing a black t-shirt with his arms on display, I can make out the ropey veins in his forearms. He's always had sexy arms but now as a man they're really something else.

"Hi, just us I'm afraid." He says as he sits down opposite me, my mouth falls open and I am conscious I am gaping at him.

"*What*?" My voice is practically a screech.

"Eliza and Sadie couldn't make it."

"Why not?" I'm clearly not impressed.

"Eliza had to run an errand for her sister and Sadie got roped into babysitting for her niece, Linny. Her sister had to work a double shift as one of the girls went off sick in the factory." I have no idea what factory or where he is talking about since there isn't one here in Willowbrook.

"Great." I mutter. Barbara comes to our table with her pad in hand. She tucks a lock of hair behind her ear.

"What can I get you two lovebirds?" I don't even bother correcting her, everyone in this town is now going to think that Logan and I are back together.

"I'll have the chicken and mushroom sauce please, Babs." Logan briefly looks at the menu.

"And I'll have the steak with fries on the side, oh and some onion rings too please. Can I have a beer with that and one for Sage, too."

"Coming right up." She winks. Good grief.

"I bet Eliza is trying to match-make." I say and play with a napkin. His eyes are staring right at mine, I shift in my seat as I feel his gaze move to my lips, down my chest and rests on my tits. I knew I should have worn a top that wasn't quite so low cut. I fold my arms in front of my chest. He averts his gaze.

"Can't help a guy for looking, darlin."

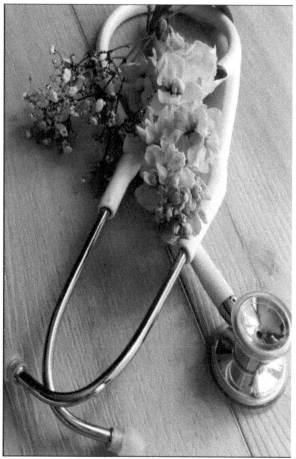

Chapter 37

L*ogan*

Okay, so that wasn't probably called for. I don't know what came over me, it's not usually how I am. Something happens to me when I get this close to Sage, there is no rational explanation, trust me I wish there was. Things would be a whole lot easier if I didn't still fancy the pants off her and find her so damn alluring and secondly, we have a history that I can't simply erase from my mind.

It was a disrespectful comment and I bite my bottom lip and mentally slap myself. "Sorry. I didn't mean it like that. You know me better."

"Then don't make stupid comments, jeez, Logan, we're grown-ups not hormonal teenagers anymore. Or haven't you noticed?"

"Oh, I've noticed alright, darlin'." There my mouth runs off with itself again. I need duct tape slapping on my lips. This isn't doing me any favors in trying to get on the right side of Sage and why do I want to be on the right side of her? Is it purely for professional reasons or is it more? Why am I even asking these dumb questions? Of course I know it's for more. I never really got this woman out of my head or my heart.

You can fall in love with someone else in life, you can be married, have the family and the whole nine yards, but when you know the one is *the* one you can't exactly do anything about it. Other than me stopping with the wise cracks.

Her eyebrows are raised, her eyes are fiery as hell. It's a turn on, that bit don't expect me to try and damper down because physically, well it's just not possible. We're all going to have to live with that. But... I do want to get past all this hostility on her side.

"Un-notice then, Logan. We've got to work together now and do this blasted fundraiser." She takes a sip of her coffee and waits for our order to arrive.

"I'm trying but it's hard, Sage. What do you want me to say? I can't help the way my damn body is reacting to you right now. I can't turn the clock back and pretend we never happened." I take a sip from my own hot brew.

Our platters arrive, Barbs is busy behind the counter with some kids who've just stormed in after football practice. I recognise some of them, the others I think judging by their kit, are from the opposing team. A school in Coppertown. I sure hope we won against them, it's good for our town morale.

Lisa, our waitress puts the plates down. She's just a kid herself, in high school. Her old man happens to my lawyer. Ben Johnson, a good guy. They arrived about five years ago. He said he was just passing through with his family to take care of his aunties estate but then they never left. Now his wife,

Denise an artist here in Willowbrook with her own studio and Ben have stayed ever since. I've watched Lisa grow up from a tiny child to the excellent student she is now.

"Thanks Lisa."

"Anything else, Dr Logan?" Her voice is gentle and southern. She's got that from her mother's side of the family. Denise comes from Carolina, Ben from New York. They met in college and apparently it was love at first sight. Not too different than for me and Sage all those moons ago.

"We're good thanks. Sage?"

"No, I'm all good too, thank you." Lisa heads to another table and takes an order from the couple sitting together holding hands. It's Riley Lucas and his girl, Emily. Cute couple. Been together for years too, now they're in high school and talking about getting engaged before they head separate ways for college. They look so young, so in love and it takes me back to the days when I'd sit here with Sage, holding hands, laughing at the same jokes, strumming my guitar whilst she studied and the kisses that we'd have. Boy, don't even get me started on those. I can't afford to be thinking of her rosy red lips on mine right now. Not sitting in front of her. I'll save it for when I'm on my own back home, preferably when I can head in my shower and rub myself. It's a dirty mind I've got thinking about Sage, even though I am trying not to.

"I take it, you know just about everyone and their uncle in Willowbrook, right?" She says as she places food in her mouth. I nod.

"Of course, you know what it's like living in a small town, Sage."

"Exactly, which is why I want to get out of here. There was a reason I left when I was younger, Logan. It had nothing to do with you. You understand that don't you." Whoa, this is the first time either one of us has brought up her leaving. And yes, I did think it had to do with me.

I thought Sage didn't love me enough to stay, I thought her heart had already left Willowbrook the moment she told me she was leaving. What else was I supposed to think? I was just a teenager. My whole world was Sage, she literally rocked my world and then some.

"To be honest, Sage. I thought it was about me, at least some of it. You just made the decision and that was that. You didn't discuss it with me. It was unfair, it hurt like crazy. It still damn hurts." I wipe my mouth with one of the blue napkins. She casts her eyes down, I can see that some kind of guilt or something has just washed over her. It's the last thing I mean for her to feel. Trust me. I want Sage to be happy, I want her to have the life she wants, the dreams fulfilled that are in her heart.

"It wasn't. You knew I had big dreams, Logan and I felt for sure you'd come with me. I didn't once think you wouldn't." Sorrow fills her eyes. Is this *the* Dr Sage Bennett, the same Dr Sage Bennett who came storming in here a few days ago and has been the ice queen from day one?

"Of course I knew you had big dreams, I never expected you to leave though. Perhaps I was way too young and too in love to think straight. I thought we had something so damn special that nothing would break it. Going to Michigan was one thing but not having anything to do with me after, that cut like a razor. You have to see that, Sage. And yet, here I am still damn wide open." I wish I'd kept that last bit to myself, as her mouth drops open and her eyes open wide like saucers. Holy fuck, that shouldn't have come out of my mouth. Now she knows how my heart still bleeds for her, how it continues to race every time I see her.

"Trust me, Logan I didn't do it to be a bitch. I just thought it'd be easier for us both and especially you."

"How the fuck did you figure that out?" I'm trying not to get mad as hell at her, only I am because she did to me exactly what I hear this Miles jerk has just done to her. How dare she sit there and tell me that it would have been easier. Is she fucking kidding me right now? I clench and unclench my fists under the table to hide my upset.

"Having a long-distance relationship wasn't for us, at least back then I didn't think it was. I wanted you to focus on your career, on your dad's practice on being the best doctor you could be. I didn't want you to feel obliged to stay with me, I wanted you to be free to find someone else knowing I wasn't ever coming back to Willowbrook." She sighs and rests her head in her hands.

"It wasn't your decision to make though, Sage was it?" She shakes her head and I want to put my hand out to touch her.

"What's happened has happened. We can't change that. But you need to know, Sage I would have waited for you for an eternity. You were my entire world back then. It took me a long time, years to get over losing you. Finally, yes I did meet my wife and we had wonderful years together until she passed away but who knows how our lives would have ended up, Sage. You didn't have the right."

She lifts her eyes to mine. "I know. I'm sorry. I'm truly sorry." I take her left hand in my right hand and stroke it gently, there isn't anything either one of us can do right now. We lost ten years together that could have been amazing, we could have kids by now, a family. Who knows but all I do know is that I have right now and holding her hand like this, is making my entire body zing. It's not just about my dick, it's about my heart and the swell it feels as I feel her small hand in my large hand, how I want to cradle her head into my shoulder and kiss her.

Sage removes her hand after a few seconds. Lisa comes back to the table seeing we are done eating and takes the plates. "Dessert for y'all?"

"Not for me, I'm so full I can't fit anything else in." Sage sages and I shake my head.

"I'll have another coffee please." I tell Lisa. Sage asks for one too.

"I guess we ought to discuss the fundraiser." She says. I'm not in the mood to discuss the fundraiser and I daresay Eliza knew this would happen by putting us both in close proximity to one another with a huge excuse. I've said what I had to say and then some, Sage has had her say and maybe, just maybe we can start to mend the bridges. If nothing more, at least we could become friends again.

I for sure have missed her and it'd be amazing if I could get this damn stubborn but oh so beautiful woman to want to finally stay here in Willowbrook where everyone loves her.

Chapter 38

S *age*
　　It's so weird that I am sitting across from Logan after all these years of feeling resentment, bitterness and anger. I couldn't understand back then why he would choose Willowbrook over me. Now, as I listen to him talk about his practice and the little leaguers, I can see that we were probably not

at that right time in our lives to have committed further. Sure, we both wanted to get engaged, married and have kids. To be honest, I still want all of that but I am also aware that being in my late thirties I could run out of time.

The thought of dating anyone right now fills me with angst. I gave up ten years of my life to Miles and for what? For him to decide he wanted a different track. At least when I left Willowbrook for Michigan I was young and Logan had time on his side to find someone new, to have a wonderful life with. Now we're both in our late thirties and if either one of us wants to have a family, then we have to start all over again. Only, I don't know if I'm ready to go there with anyone. My heart is firmly locked away and no man is breaking it through it and especially not Logan.

Although, as I watch him talking with such exuberance about the little leaguers it fills my heart and I can tell just how much he adores being their coach and taking care of them. He is animated, as his hands move about and he has that gorgeous grin on his face that shows his dimple off. It's so damn sexy, he hasn't lost his looks at all. If anything, this man has grown into himself. His broad shoulders have filled out, his biceps make me want to reach out and feel them, I need to get that in check.

"Do you want kids yourself?" I ask him as my second coffee arrives.

"Sure, of course. I long for a family but unfortunately when my wife passed, I've not found the right person to be with." He looks sad, it makes me want to reach out to him and stroke his hand and offer some comfort but I don't.

"What about you, Sage? Kids, no kids or are you too busy and focused on your career to want all of that?" His eyes are earnest, I know he thinks that my career means more to me than anything else, of course it does, but that doesn't mean that I don't have a biological clock ticking away.

"I do, yes." I say simply. He cocks his head to one side.

"I sense a *but* in there."

"I'm not sure I can be with anyone, after Miles told me he was moving to London, I kind of you know." I sigh and toy with the cup. "I don't think I can open my heart to anyone again. That and the thought of going on dates just makes me cringe."

Logan laughs. "I get that, absolutely. I don't think I could go out and do the rounds."

"How did you meet your wife?" I ask him, why am I even intrigued? I'll tell you why because a part of me is feeling jealous that she got to spend time with him, she got to see him grow into a man and spoon in bed with him. Oh, what on earth is wrong with me? It was all my choice, my decision. Nobody forced me to leave so why on earth am I feeling like this? Besides, I am also not a jealous person, I never have been not even when we were younger and all the girls wanted to buzz like bees around Logan.

He's always been one handsome fella, and back in school there were *those* girls, you know the type I mean, that didn't care he had a steady girl. They'd stop in the corridor and push their tits into his chest, they'd side up to him in the canteen even when I was sitting next to him and just be in his face. Sure, it drove me insane, it would anyone. Jealous though, never. I used to get a kick out of the fact that I had the most gorgeous man in school in love with me.

This, however, as I watch him talking, the fine lines around his sexy eyes, his five o'clock shadow, his super sharp jawline, that hair flopping in his eyes and those long, strong fingers around his beer bottle is sending my body into some kind of weird spin.

"She came to Willowbrook and we just got chatting. Funnily enough, here in Bluebells. I met her over on that table over there." Logan points to where the teenagers are sitting still engrossed in their mobiles. "The place was packed and she had nowhere to sit so she came and sat down by me and asked if I minded."

"And of course, you being the gentleman you are, couldn't say no." I finish for him. Ooh, was there a hint of bitchiness and envy there? Okay, okay. I admit it there was. I mutter sorry but he just gives me that darn sexy smile of his like, it's okay.

"Something like that. We got talking and then I saw her a couple of times afterwards. It just seemed we kept bumping into each other, the hardware store, Carol's bakery, Dan's the butcher and eventually I thought I'd ask her for her number and if she'd like to go on a date. The rest is history." He leans back and his chest expands, showing me just enough outline of his muscles through his tight tee. Mm, my heart is racing.

"Romantic." I say whilst all the while feeling envious even though I shouldn't be and what makes me feel even worse is that their love story ended tragically.

"No intention of going out into the field again soon, then?" I ask instead. He cocks his head and grins.

"There's only one woman for me, Sage." He winks. Is he talking about me? Lord, I don't think I can take this. Surely he isn't getting designs on me not after all this time.

"There's going to be a long wait." I tell him.

"That's fine, darlin'. I'm a very patient man."

Chapter 39

L *ogan*
"Hey brother." Daisy comes and plonks herself down next to me. I put my arm around her and pull her to me.

"Well lookie here, what you up to little sis?"

"Thought I'd come in for one of Deb's chicken and mushroom pies and cherry pie." She releases from my bear hug and looks adorable in her burgundy pinafore denim dress, her hair in plaits either side of her head and a floral blouse on. She looks like something out of Little House On The Prairie.

"Sage, how are you? Glad to see you both are patching stuff up. Will we be hearing wedding bells soon?" That gets her a dig in the ribs. "*What?*" Sage coughs, actually she almost splutters her coffee across the table. She takes a napkin from the centre of the table and dabs at her mouth. Her lips form a straight thin line. Oh hell, I know that look. It's the one that says *wtf?*

"Actually, Miss Nosey-Parker, we're here to discuss the little leaguers and the festival."

"Oh, right. Of course. Anyway, I'm just kidding but it sure would be nice to see you guys back together again. I mean you're single, Sage is single and there you go." My sister is ever the matchmaker. She simply cannot help herself.

Before I met my wife, Daisy hooked me up on a dating app. I was not aware of it until I began to get lots of likes and requests to meet up. Only then did she confess that she'd created a profile for me and had generated some interest. Honestly, I could have strangled her. My mother of course thought it was the perfect solution to a Sage Bennett cause of my broken heart. Needless to say, I didn't go on any of the meets and forced my little sister to message everyone back explaining what was going on and that I was off the market.

Love in my book just has to happen. It can be the smallest of smiles, the way a woman's hair falls, the gaiety of her step, that smile that extends to her eyes.

"Don't get your hopes up, Daisy. We're working together now and this is strictly professional." Sage's tone is curt. Daisy shrugs and holds her hands up. I know how much she'd love for Sage and I to get back together, hell I'm pretty damn sure the whole town would love for us to be a couple again. I know I want this in the time but Sage, well she's got that whole *I've got to get out of Willowbrook* thing going on. Still.

"And, how is the Marshall this fine evening?" I ask Daisy which causes her to blush furiously.

"He's fine, I guess."

"Daisy, why don't you just ask him on a date, already?" She blushes even more. "I mean, you guys have had the hots for each other since you were teenagers. Honestly, it's not like you to drag your heels now then is it." I have succeeded in shifting the focus from Sage and myself to her.

"Yeah, Daisy what's going on with you and Marshal D? Even I recall you fancying the pants off him when we were in school. Did he never get married or has he been waiting for you for all these years?" Sage chuckles, it makes me grin. She does have a point. These two need their heads butting together.

"Shoot me if I know. Maybe he's just shy." Daisy offers. Sage laughs out loud. It's sexy, throaty and feminine at the same time.

"There is nothing shy about Deacon, Daisy. That man has got more front than anyone I know. I'd say it's because he is sweet on you. It's been years he has had an eye on you." Sage says. Daisy shrugs again.

"Can I get you anything, honey?" Barb asks as she comes to our table.

"I'll have the bill please." I say and Daisy places her order for the chicken and mushroom pie followed by cherry pie. "I'll have some cherry pie to go please, Barb."

"Coming right up." She hurries away, it's busy in here tonight and from what I see, she only has the one assistant in this evening.

"Sage, we can catch up on the festival arrangements later when we can actually get Eliza to turn up."

"Sure, no problem. I'm beat in any case and want to just go home and snuggle in bed with a book." That makes me smile because I have fond memories of Sage reading, if she wasn't studying she'd be losing herself in the magic world of her books and I'd play guitar. It makes me want to sigh and an image of what I'd like to happen again.

"Hector will be wondering where I've gone. He's probably going to be mad as hell that I wasn't in to give him his dinner on time." I chuckle. Sage smiles, I mean she actually gives me the briefest of smiles. No way.

"You want me to drive you?" I ask her as she stands up and places some cash down as a tip.

"No, I've got it thanks, Logan." The way my name sounds from her mouth makes me tingle. I feel warmth curse through my body, it's not her usual snippety tone, it's soft and gentle like it used to be. I sure am hoping that I can change this woman's mind before she gets a new position in a state hospital.

I'm a man on a mission and when I want something, I usually get it.

Chapter 40

S*age*
   It's been a long day, I'm ready for bed and my ankle is killing me. Damn thing. It'll take a few days to be right after I twisted it, maybe even a week. Such a drag.

As I lay on my bed with my head propped against my cushions, I rest it so it's elevated and close my eyes. I tried to write in my journal only thoughts of Logan wouldn't leave me alone and even now they're just filling my head. If I hadn't of decided to come back home, I'd not be in this situation right now. The thinking constantly about Logan is what I mean.

My phone vibrates. I placed it in silent not that I get many people calling me these days but working in a state hospital where it's a lot of pressure and constantly frantic, whirring machines, beeping at every angle – I would get into the habit of turning my phone onto vibrate only just for some peace. Miles on the other hand wouldn't and the interruptions to our evenings was borderline chronic. Some nights I felt like throwing the damn thing out of the window.

I pick up my mobile and can see it's from Hazel, my oldest friend. We used to be so close growing up always in and out of each other's houses, she was always my patient when I played doctor. It brings a smile to my face.

"Gosh, you're a hard woman to pin down and why haven't you hooked up with me yet?" Straight in. Guilt takes over, I am a shitty ass friend.

"I've been sort of busy."

"How so? I heard you went walking up the mountain and had to be rescued. It's a small town. Oh, by the way, I also hear you have been canoodling with Logan in Bluebells." Her voice is almost accusatory, but I know she's kidding with me.

"I'm sorry. I just feel like it's been non-stop since I got back. I did get airlifted off what a drama. So embarrassing." Hazel chuckles. I can imagine her head full of curls bouncing and her brown eyes soft and gentle. "By the way I *was not* canoodling with Logan. Jeez, the folk in this town." I sigh and rearrange my foot on the cushions that are supporting it. What I need is an ice pack.

"Rumour has it, you're both back together only I'm guessing they're working overtime in the rumour mill, right?" I groan.

"Absolutely they are."

"So, you're not tempted then, I mean have you seen him? If I wasn't married I'd be lusting after Logan. Hell, I do lust after him. Johnny thinks it's funny." That's her husband by the way. They've been together for a long time and then some. Since high school days, slow burn romance but eventually they got their heads together and made it happen.

I laugh, she is right Logan is a fine man. He's tall, broad shouldered and extremely well defined. I guess from all the log cutting he has to do for firewood for the cabin and his outdoors lifestyle. Just thinking about him sends a tingle up my body. I can't be having that.

"He is handsome." I say.

"Girl, what planet exactly are you on? That man is model material, he's got better abs than a hockey player. Is there no spark between you both anymore?" Her voice is soft as she asks and I am betting Hazel is another person here in Willowbrook who'd loving nothing more than to see Logan and I back together again. And would it be so bad? *Whoa stop right there. Of course it would be. You have a medical career you are chasing not a small village practice placement.*

"Of course it would be. Okay, I'm not going to lie he's gorgeous. Fucking gorgeous I can hardly take my eyes off him. But as for getting back together, be serious. I'm going for another job in a state hospital as soon as I can get an offer."

"Damn shame, Sage. We all miss you here especially me." That pulls on my heart. She's my oldest and best friend. We've been through so much together. Her mother dying when Hazel was just fourteen, boys, teenage drama and angst. Her father going off the rails after her mother died and Hazel and her brother having to manage and fend for themselves. Thankfully, her dad went to rehab and managed to overcome his addictions but it doesn't change the fact that for a couple of years growing up those two kids were all they had. It's sad to think what they had to go through.

"I know you do. But I'm just not cut out for this small town, honey. You know I never was. Everyone is in your face, they all gossip and talk about your business." I shudder.

"Honey, they all care. Here you're not just another face with no name. The community in Willowbrook is amazing. We've always got each other's backs. We support our local businesses, we have more festivals than any town I know." This is true I know that but maybe I want to remain a nameless face in a big city.

"How are Johnny and the kids?" I ask instead to change track. The less we talk about me and how I am actually feeling about Logan and all those old feelings stirring up the better. I've only got to get through a few weeks or couple of months at most until something surely turns up for me in a large hospital.

"There you go, changing the topic. They're fine. Johnny has just had a promotion so he's now VP of the local bank branch. It's exciting for us but I don't think we'll move out to a bigger house or anything. We love our little abode." It's a cute cottage style property tucked down Briar lane with a pond behind it.

"Don't blame you, honey. I love your house." I feel suddenly a sense of something, I can't quite put my finger on it. Is it envy? Loss? Either way, I think I'm wondering why I can't have the little cottage with the husband and the kids. Am I lonely? Is it my age? Hitting nearly forty does make you wonder about a lot of shit. I tell myself to get a grip, it's the career I want not the house with the white picket fence. Or is it?

Holy fuck, my mind is playing tricks on me now. I told you coming back to Willowbrook is not good for my mind. I hear some shrieking in the background.

"Gotta fly, Sage. My kids have started war on each other." I chuckle.

"Catch you later. Let's meet up for a coffee when you have some time." I tell her.

"Perfect. I'll text you. Between working, the kids and the house I am spread thin but for you Sage, always. Oh by the way, there's a new yoga class started up in town. I know how much you used to love yoga. If you fancy coming it's at eight on Thursday."

"I'll check it out and meet you there, then we can go for a coffee afterwards." I hear Lina screaming at her brother.

"That's it kids." Hazel shouts at them. "Speak soon, honey." She hangs up and I look at my phone. Maybe having kids should be permanently off my agenda.

It was good to talk to my best friend, I sure have missed her and definitely I'll try the yoga class. I can be careful with my ankle. Reaching for my book on the bedside I make myself more comfortable and start to read. It's fucking useless.

Five pages in and I haven't even absorbed a word. Why? Because I can't get the sight of Logan's eyes, his chiselled jaw and his smoking hot body off my mind. I place the book over my face and groan. That man is going to be the death of me for sure.

Chapter 41

*L*ogan

Hector bounces around like a crazy dog as we get ready for our morning run. It's much cooler this morning and fall is now in full force. It won't be long until Thanksgiving and I am looking forward to spending time with my folks and having the big dinner, watching cheesy movies, the whole nine yards.

Pop and I will catch a few hockey games or catch up on the sports in general. He's more a football fan but my love is hockey. I don't bother with a lead for Hector, he knows the trails that surround my cabin.

Opening the door, I feel the crisp morning air but damn if the sunrise isn't something spectacular to look at this morning with the pinkish red coming through the darker sky. There's just something amazing about this time of year. Hector bounds out and wags his tail, he cocks his leg against a tree and then runs in front as I close the door behind me. I don't lock it. Nobody ever comes up this way.

I allow my mind to think of Sage and last night. It felt good to finally talk, not have the hostility or bitterness of our past between us. I feel good, you know like we could get back on track. All I need to do is try to win her over, only this woman is intent on moving away. Again. I shake my head as I run. It's a much slower pace today, I'm not out to break any speed records. Not anymore.

Maybe when I was younger for sure. Having been a cross country runner in school, I loved the miles, the pace and always being the winner. Nowadays, hitting nearly forty I'm more about the fresh air, the scenery and it sure is beautiful here in West Virginia. I'd never want to live anywhere else. Oh, okay maybe Colorado would be stunning too but here is home, my business is here, my family are here and my friends are here. I'm content the only thing that is missing is a woman in my life who I can snuggle up to at night with in bed, keep her safe, protected and love her.

One day for sure, I'd love to have a family a kid of my own. I adore my nephews and nieces they bring so much joy to not just me but our family. My mom sure likes being a grandma and she's damn good at it too. Those kids love her so much and it always makes me smile when I see her with them. Pop loves it too, I can tell. The way he plays with them, takes them on mystery tours in his car and at Christmas he's the best. He bundles them up in their coats, scarves and hats and trundles around Willowbrook with them pretending to look for Father Christmas. When he brings them back to the house, the tree magically has presents underneath it. The kids must know by now that Santa doesn't exist, but they still have lit up faces and huge smiles.

It'll be sad I guess when they grow up some more and it will no longer have the magic about it. But, when I have a kid, I am hoping my old man will still be around and he can do the same for it.

Hector bounds up to me and jumps up, his hind legs on the ground. I ruffle the fur on the top of his head, right now he has his adorable curls going on. "Hey boy. What's up? I'm coming. Just a bit slow this morning is all." He's happy with that, snuffles my hand and dashes off again scampering in the leaves and sniffing nearly every tree and bush he comes across.

Before long, I've covered two miles and it's time to turn round and make my way back home. I've got to open the practice as Eliza is late in this morning, something about a dentist appointment. Sadie doesn't have a key to open up but I am thinking I ought to really organize one for her.

I reach the large Northern Red oak tree that I use as my marker on my shorter runs, tap it with my left hand then circle round it. Hector runs ahead all the while his tail wagging. He's my best friend and I feel a burst in my heart of the love I feel for this furry friend of mine. I have considered studding him so I could have a couple of pups, conscious that man's best friend is with us only for a limited time. Maybe I will.

We reach the cabin and I place one leg behind me and begin my lunges, I usually do twenty on each side then do some squats, a hundred of them. Hector paws at the door so I stop to open it for him, he dives straight in and heads to his food bowl. Then comes back out.

"Okay, buddy. I'm coming to fill it up." We go back in together, I open his cupboard and fill his bowl with the dry food and give him some fresh water. A frission of excitement passes through my body as I think about seeing Sage in less than an hour's time. I know I said we'd do shifts to avoid each other but at the moment we have too many patients who want morning appointments for me to start passing them all over to Sage. Besides, since we managed to act like actual adults last night, I think this could work out. I hope so. My plan as you know, is to get closer to her and somehow convince her that Willowbrook is where she belongs.

And, she does belong here. Her family and friends are here, everyone loves Sage. I know I have a huge grin on my face and I know she's changed and that just because we were sweethearts back in the day, that I could not be the man she is after now. Only, I did see the way she looks at me and that's got to mean something, right?

Hector wolfs down his food and I take myself to my bedroom and head for the shower, allowing the warm water to stream over my body. Just thinking about Sage makes me hard. I take myself in my hand for relief all the while thinking about her kissable lips, the way her skins radiates, the glint in her eyes when I've caught her checking me out and that body of hers, man what I wouldn't do to feel Sage one more time.

Chapter 42

S *age*
  It's a Friday and I sure am looking forward to the weekend, I want to search for more roles online and start to look for somewhere small I can rent here in Willowbrook in the meantime. I can't stay with my folks forever, I mean don't get me wrong I love them to bits. Mom and dad don't interfere

with me when I get in from the practice, we all eat together and watch some tv, then generally I come upstairs and write in my journal or catch up with my friends from New York.

They're mostly busy nowadays and traveling around, so they don't in all honesty have too much time for me. A few days have passed since I sat with Logan at Bluebell's and even though we've been working in the same place the last few days, he has been pretty good at staying out of my face.

We've been busy and now the weather has started to get a bit cooler more and more people are coming in with virus symptoms and the such like. Poor Sadie has been rushed off her feet with vaccines and jabs. She is off for the weekend with her fella, they're visiting Colorado for a long break which means that I will be heading up the moms and toddlers clinic on Monday. I am actually looking forward to it.

I try not to think that had things with Miles and I worked out, I'd be looking at having a kid or two of my own. Possibly. Was it really ever on the agenda or were we just to super busy to even contemplate a family? And why now am I thinking about it? My hormones more than likely. Yet, as I lay on my bed I am wondering what it would be like to be a mom, have that bundle of specialness in your arms and kissing the man who created it with you.

Am I fucking longing for a family scene? What the hell is going on? No way. I am Dr Sage Bennett, I am a career woman and a very busy one. I do not have time to start changing diapers and looking after a baby. It's Logan and seeing him again, this is all his damn fault. When we were dating back when I was seventeen, I used to day dream of him being a dad, our kid being swung up high in his arms, playing football together. It was intense but not as intense as wanting to chase my medical career.

But I've done that. I got to top of my field and I made it to where I wanted to go, maybe it's time for something new.

I lay on my double bed, the same one I've had since I was around fifteen and place a hand to my head to check if in fact I have a temperature. Because, you know, all these weird thoughts are way off mark for me. Yet, why am I still thinking about him? The way the creases appear around his eyes when he was looking and smiling at me and that damn wink he has going on with his dimple. Okay, seriously I think I'm coming down with something.

My phone beeps. Good maybe it's Hazel and we're going to catch up. We did go to yoga yesterday by the way. I almost forgot to mention it. There I was in my downward dog position ready to go into half-moon when the door opened and in came. You guessed it, Logan.

Now, I can take a man who is supremely fit and get a little, shall we say, lustful but boy, *that* man is a whole different kettle of fish. He placed his mat down, you got it. Right next to mine. Hazel on the other side chuckled, I had to throw her daggers.

His legs in his shorts were so damn fine, muscular but not too heavy like a weight lifter and when he went into downward dog, his tee rode over his body slightly and I caught a look at his abs. Is an eight pack a thing, only that is what Logan has got going on? I swear I almost collapsed from panting so badly and my mouth was literally salivating. When did Logan become such a hunk of a man?

There I was in my position with my head to the left taking in his firm triceps and the way his ropey forearms contracted when he got into position. Actually, I got slightly wet looking at him, anybody would. In fact the other ladies on the other side couldn't take their eyes off him either.

"I had no idea you did yoga." I said after the class.

"I don't but a little bird told me you'd be here." He winked. I blushed and felt a warm rush all the way up my body. I turned and glared at Hazel.

"*What?*" Was all she had to say and shrugged her shoulders. "Gotta dash, something I forgot to do." And with that my bestie was out of the yoga studio leaving Logan and I face to face, with just a hand distance between us. I could feel the heat coming of his body and I'm not surprised since he is so scorching hot. I couldn't say anything, his broad shoulders, his stubble on that perfect jaw of his and those damn eyes had me beholden to him.

"You want to grab a coffee or something at Bluebell's?" I was so dry mouthed, I could hardly speak.

"No, that's fine. To be honest I'm kinda tired and my ankle is still real sore. You know what I'm going home to ice it and will see you in the morning at the practice." I rolled my mat up and turned away from him, boy did I need to get out of there quickly before I said yes. I can't say yes, I can't get involved. I. Am. Leaving. Soon.

"If you need any help with that ankle or anything else that's a throbbing, you know how to reach me, darlin.'" Honestly, did he really say that? I was throbbing, it was insane. Fucking insane.

So, here I am now on my bed thinking of Logan and his hotness which is making me one hot mess and it's very difficult not to get my vibe out and give myself a good seeing to. Only, with my folks downstairs, well I kinda feel a bit awkward about it. There you go, until I get a new job out of this town, I really do need somewhere else I can stay.

I glance at my mobile, it's not my bestie or one of my other girlfriends, it's Eliza.

Hey honey, sorry to bother you. We have an emergency. One of the Johnson's kids has got something in their eye. Can you go down to the practice and see what's going on for him?

Sure of course, np. Be there in fifteen.

Thanks, honey.

I quickly get myself together, not bothering to change out of my grey sweats or my NYC jersey and slip on my Nikes and head out of the room, down the stairs and out the front door. My folks are wrapped up in some celebrity show or other and don't even notice.

Within a few minutes I am at the practice. Weird, why is Logan's car here too? Surely, it only needs one of us.

I try the door and it is open, I have a key now in any case. I enter, the light are all on as it's dark outside being seven p.m. "Hello." I call out. I don't see Mr or Mrs Johnson or their kid in the practice waiting room.

"Oh, hi. Are you okay?" Logan comes out of his office.

"Are you with the Johnson kid?"

"What? No, what kid?"

"Right. So you know nothing about one of their kids having something in their eye?"

"That's correct. Hold on a minute. Did Eliza call you?"

"Yes." I reply.

"She messaged me to say she'd forgotten to turn the lights out after we all left today, that's the reason I'm over here."

"If she is trying to match make us, I swear I'm going to let her know just what I think on Monday." I say. Logan chuckles.

"Well, now you're here. Let's go and grab a bite to eat. You hungry?" Actually, I am since I didn't eat dinner with my folks earlier. I deliberate, what harm can a bite to eat do?

Chapter 43

L*ogan*
    She looks like a rabbit caught on the road with headlights in its eyes, not sure which way to run. I let out a huge sigh of relief when she finally gives in and says she'll come and grab a bite to eat with me. Only, I have no intention of taking her just to Bluebell's or the Rib Eye Shack. No, I want to

treat Sage to something more special. It's the least I can do for her helping me out here at the practice and for being part of the fundraiser/festival we're hosting in a few weeks.

Which reminds me, we still have so much to do. Sadie will be on the craft stall, Sage's mom and mine will be managing the cookie stand and I'll be getting the band together to play on the main stage, I need to speak to Abe we need some kegs too and god, there is just heaps still to do. Thank goodness for Eliza who always manages to pull it all together. I thank my lucky stars for the day she walked into my life and needed a job.

"I can drive us." I tell her, knowing that ankle has sure got to be sore still.

"How about I just drive behind you? Much easier that way if you piss me off I can run out on you." Is she kidding? I raise my eyebrows.

"Why would that even happen? Wow, you have such a low opinion of me right now. I wasn't the one who left remember, you knew I had responsibilities." I say for like the umpteenth time.

"We've covered this already, Logan. Let's not get back into it. We're supposed to be putting it all behind us and besides, I am hungry and you know how I get." She tells me as she slings on her baby-blue pea coat. The colour brings out her eyes and sets off her hair. I want to go and grab her by the collar and bring her lips to mine.

"Don't I just. I recall you getting hangry on more than one occasion, you're almost like a volcano when you get going. C'mon then, darlin' let's go."

"Will you stop with the darlin'. You know I am not your darlin.'" She ties the belt around her waist and throws her brown Mulberry bag across her shoulder.

"Sorry, old habits die hard." I take my keys out of my pocket and start to walk towards the door.

"Try harder." She always has to have the last word, I turn and give her my lopsided smile, knowing full well she has a thing for my dimples and my wink. I see her blush. Gottcha.

I make my way to my truck and she to her car. "Where are we going in any case? The Rib shack or Bluebells? Only, I don't fancy going to Bluebells, we've had enough of nosey town folk already."

"Just follow me, we're not going to either. I need to get away from everyone in my business too." I get in my truck as she nods.

The drive is peaceful there aren't many cars on the road right now, I marvel at the evening rolling in, the sky is a mysterious grey-pink, for sure tomorrow will be cooler again but with bright sunshine. The fall here in Willowbrook is beautiful. As I drive I'm listening to my playlist and *I guess I'm in Love* by Clinton Kane comes on. His words ring true, what can I say?

Oh, I'm obsessed
With the way your head is layin' on my chest
How you love the things I hate about myself
That no one knows, but with you, I see hope again
Oh, I'm a mess
When I overthink the little things in my head
You seem to always help me catch my breath
But then I lose it again
When I look at you, that's the end
And why do I get so nervous when I look into your eyes?
Butterflies can't stop me fallin' for you
And darlin', this is more than anything I felt before
You're everything that I want, but I didn't think I'd find
Someone who is worth the wait of all the years of my heartbreak
But I know now I found the one I love

I check my rearview mirror since I wouldn't put it pass my little darlin' to swoop in another direction and avoid having dinner with me. I've chosen a cute restaurant over in Coppertown where not many folks know us as having been a couple. For sure, some know me as their doctor they visit in Willowbrook. Generally, though when I come to Coppertown I am not invaded and I know that Sage and I will be able to dine in peace. At least, I hope so.

In front of me is the stunning view of Café Cimino Country Inn. I know Sage loves this place, it's where we went after prom when her folks treated all of us including my folks to a meal to celebrate end of school and the fact that Sage had been accepted to med school. With its two floors it looks like an old fashioned house, columns outside and a large wrap around deck. The lights are on and offer a stunning orange glow across the gardens out front adorned with shrubs and a water feature.

I park my truck and step out just as Sage pulls in next to me. "Wow, you're not thinking this is a date of any kind are you?" She asks suspiciously. I wish.

"Of course not, but we want to eat and we want to eat out of Willowbrook. Besides, I know how much this place means to you. I thought you'd like to have something good in your stomach."

"Thank you, Logan. I do love it here. Do you remember when we came after prom? Gosh, life was so exciting, school was out, I had just been accepted to med school." Her voice is breathless, like she has stepped back in time to a dream life. I try not to think what could have been if she'd not left us all here. I don't want the old wounds to open up and cut through my heart again. I'm only just starting to mend and to be honest, since that night, I haven't been back here either. It's a place that will always be in my heart special to just Sage and I.

"Let's get inside, it's getting fresh." I know my voice is full of emotion even though I try hard to not let on. Sage links her arm through mine, I don't let on either that she's just caused a warm sensation to run through my body or that I am blown away by her action. This isn't the same Sage I've been dealing with for the last few days. Maybe it's the place, the memories. Who knows, but I sure as hell am glad that she is on my arm right now.

I couldn't be prouder to have her by my side if I tried. I just hope this can be the start of rekindling our old flame.

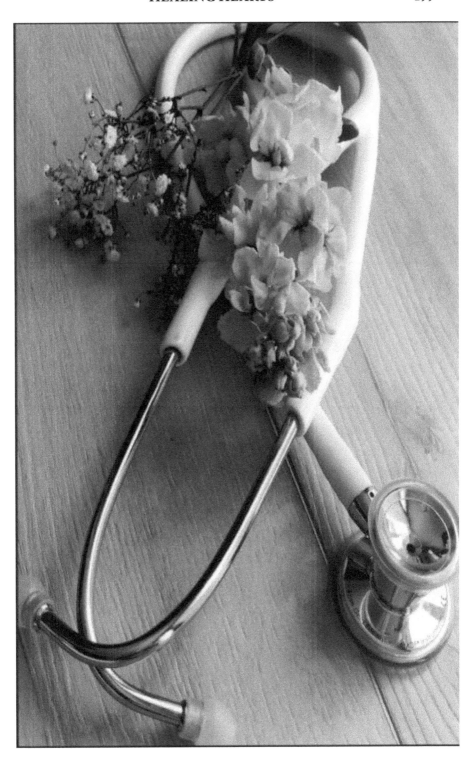

Chapter 44

S*age*
 Café Cimino is one of my favorite restaurants and just being back here takes me back all those years to sitting right next to Logan and holding hands under the starched white table cloths. Butterflies in my stomach then and of all things, right now. Jeez, what the hell is happening to me. I keep telling y'all this cannot go anywhere.

Although, I am liking being close to my folks and I do love all the trails and hikes around Willowbrook. Hell, I don't really mind all the town folk either, they're starting to warm to me again.

"Shall we?" Logan says as he guides my arm and sends an electric pulse shooting right though me even with a coat on. Wow. If there was anytime my body was defying me it is right now.

A smart young lad greets us at the entrance, wearing black pants, white button down shirt and an olive green waistcoat. "A table for two, in the name of Logan." That makes me smile because Logan has never used his surname, he always goes by Logan whereas I always go by Dr Sage Bennett. It's like he just needs the one name, no title, no airs and graces just down-to-earth Logan. I like it. Yeah, you know what I do.

I take in his broad shoulders, how smart he looks and his freshly shaved face. Not something I've seen since I've got back since he seems to prefer his stubble look. I reckon if he could get away with it and didn't have a practice to run, he'd stay up in that cabin of his with his dog and grow a beard down to his knees.

The lad takes us to a table tucked away in the corner, with floor to ceiling windows that look out on to the star lit terrace with mountain views. It's breath taking. "Thank you." Logan says and places his large hands on my shoulders.

"What *are* you doing?" I ask shocked.

"Calm down, just taking your coat." He chuckles. Of course he is, like he was going to start anything weird in public.

"Okay, thanks."

"Stop being so touchy. You really need to relax, Sage. I'm not here to devour you. We're just two people having dinner."

"Mm, only it's in one of *the* most romantic settings in West Virginia."

"Don't read too much into it. I know you're not interested and want to leave like a speeding bullet train, flying in and out to the next station." He takes my coat, the lad pulls out my chair for me then takes the coat from Logan.

"Can I get you the wine list?" He asks, I can see from his name badge that matches his waistcoat with gold italic letters, his name is Johnson.

"Yes please." I say since I need a drink, a hefty class of full bodied wine sounds a mighty fine idea right now. Am I nervous? Surely not? Then why am I tingling from head to foot, my body zinging like no tomorrow and butterflies in my stomach.

Logan sits directly opposite me, his warm eyes fixed on mine with a lopsided grin on his face, crinkling the skin around his eyes. Damn, he is so good looking, he is definitely one of those cinnamon roll type of guys.

"How are you finding it at the practice? Bit different to State right?" He takes the wine list from Johnson and studies it.

"It's different alright. Gosh they come in with the smallest of things, that a Panadol would fix." Logan chuckles.

"Some of them have no one at home, you need to remember that they see the practice as their daily outing. Take Mr Harper for example that poor man has no family here at all, he relies on the social centre and coming in to see me for reassurance, someone to moan at and get stuff off his chest."

I cock my head. "It's quiet, I'm so used to the rush of an emergency room, constant adrenaline, long hours on my feet. I felt like I was literally living in my scrubs." I tell him as I look at the wine list, Logan has now passed to me.

"What do you say to the Buccella Mica Cabernet Napa?" I ask him. He raises his eyebrows. Okay, so it comes with a hefty price tag but it's one of the best and I enjoy it's oaky notes.

"Sure, let's go with that." Johnson nods and leaves us to it. I study my menu to try avoiding Logan's eyes which don't seem to have stopped looking at me.

"Have I got something on my face, only you haven't stopped staring at me?" I ask him feeling myself blush.

"No ma'am, just enjoying looking at you after all these years. To be honest, darlin' I never thought I'd be sitting at a dinner with you after all these years. It's taking some getting used to." The way *darlin'* rolls off his tongue sends tingles up and down my spine in the best possible way.

Oh, God what harm would it really do if I could just melt a little bit and let the guard around my heart down? He's gorgeous, he's strong and protective, he'd be everything a woman could ever want so why don't I just give in to my body's reaction?

"You know we'd all love it if you stayed here in Willowbrook. The patients love you, Sadie is in awe of you and Eliza has taken you under her wing like a second daughter." All of this is true and I haven't the response because I've come to like all of them too. I really have.

"Tell me about your wife." I blurt out. Do I even want to know about someone so precious to him? I'm already jealous even though I have absolutely no right to be. None at all.

"She was beautiful, caring, smart, funny. All the things a man can dream of. We had a wonderful life together until..." He breaks off and takes a sip of his wine. I shouldn't have asked. I shouldn't have brought her up, I can tell how much it still hurts him. It's only been about a year, of course it's going to hurt him.

"Sorry, I shouldn't have asked." I mirror Logan and drink from my wine glass.

"Don't be sorry, Sage. It's painful of course it is, when you lose someone it always hurts, over time we just become more tolerant to it. But that hole, that never goes away. I've thrown myself into the practice and Hector, some refurb on my man's old cabin and you know anything I can think of to take my mind off losing her. But, it is time to move on." His eyes are directly on mine, I don't shift my eyes, his eyes hold mine and I feel like I'm melting into a pool under his attentive gaze. I know his words are directed at me, it's me he wants to move on with.

Only, oh God. Can I do this? Should I do this?

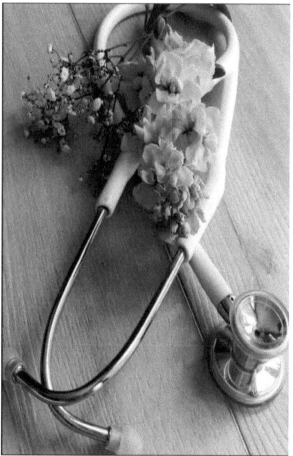

Chapter 45

L*ogan*
    I can't stop looking at Sage, she is a vision with her hair curled around her shoulders and the way her delicate fingers grace her wine glass. "I'm so pleased you have come on board for a while, Sage. You know it means a lot to us." She nods and has the faintest of smiles on her face.

"Sure, of course. How could I not? Besides, I don't want to eat into my savings. It wasn't cheap living in Michigan, and Miles and I split everything down the middle." I inhale because that's definitely not how it would work if she lived or had lived with me. I'd be taking care of my darlin', there wouldn't be anything she'd need to want for and as for paying bills and the such like, that would be all on me.

"Do you want to talk about it, the break up?" I ask her as she raises her eyebrows, I'm bracing myself for a brush off. It's something I've gotten used to since she's been back in Willowbrook. She takes me by surprise.

"There isn't much to talk about to be honest. I thought we were going to be married, have a couple of kids maybe. You know the usual." She shrugs her shoulders but I know my girl and I can see the hurt in her eyes along with the disappointment.

"So, why did you guys breaks up?"

"He took a fellowship in London and didn't tell me until a few weeks before." Wow. What an absolute ass. How could anyone keep something so important and monumental from the person they've spent the last god knows how many years with? Instead, I remain silent.

Sage takes a large sip of her wine. I keep an eye on that since she has brought her car and there's no way I'm letting her drive back if she drinks more than one glass.

"We'd been together for ten years. Can you believe it, ten years? Then he just comes out with it, that he's moving to London." She pauses, toys with the stem of her glass and cocks her head. The light catches her beautiful eyes and I am drowning in them. Like always, like before. I could look into her eyes for the rest of my life and still wonder at their beauty. Like the sunrise at the beginning of each new day.

"That must have been pretty tough. I'm sorry to hear that, Sage." She shrugs.

"Maybe it just wasn't mean to be. I decided I didn't want to go all the way to London just to follow him and incidentally, in case you're wondering, no he didn't bother to ask me."

I cough because right now I think biting my tongue off is the best course of action. I'm so mad at that Miles jerk, that if he were here, I'd punch him right in the jaw. It's the least of what he deserves for treating someone like

Sage like that. I am bewildered how anyone would be willing to give Sage up. She's a tough act to follow and he'll never find anyone so loyal, so intelligent, so funny or as beautiful as my Sage. Okay, she isn't *my* Sage right now, but trust me, I am seriously working on it.

I get she has some trust issues right now, but I am a very patient man and Sage is worth the time and the fight that I've got on my hands to let her know that I am not that jerk and that she can trust me.

"You deserve better, Sage. You know you do. I'm only glad he wasn't the reason you left Willowbrook in the first place, that would for sure be a bitter pill to swallow."

"Absolutely. I guess it's one thing. Anyway, enough about my history. I'm kinda glad to be back, don't get me wrong I still feel a bit hemmed in, and everyone knowing all my business but there is definitely a certain charm about Willowbrook."

"Your folks must be over the moon and Ali." Her sister, I know is loving that her big sis is back in town. It was all she talked about for a few weeks before Sage arrived back. Sage smiles, her face lights up at the mention of her sister. They used to be inseparable that was until Sage and I got together and started dating, then we wanted time to ourselves without our respective sisters being in the way. Necking in a truck is best for just the two people involved not a sibling audience.

The waiter appears and takes our dinner plates away. "How was your salmon?" I ask her, knowing full well she'd go for that and I pride myself on remembering her favorite choice.

"It was delicious. Honestly, this is the best place for Salmon. How was your rack of ribs?"

"Out of this world, of course. Do you want dessert or do you still prefer to move straight to cheese and crackers?" I can't help smiling at her and giving her a wink, just you know, to let her know I haven't forgotten a damn thing. She actually smiles at me. Finally, a breakthrough, so it's tiny but it is a start.

"You remember." She says simply but, there is a twinkle in her eyes.

"But of course, you're a hard woman to forget, Sage Bennett." She blushes.

"Thanks." Her right hand is outstretched on the table as she plays with one of the green Damask napkins, do I risk it? Hell yeah. I stretch out my left hand so our fingertips are just touching. I can feel the warmth radiating from her, she doesn't retract. I allow my fingers to gently stroke hers.

"I missed you, Sage." I'm done beating around the bush. We didn't get off to the best start when she arrived back here in Willowbrook, but I sure am hell bent on intending that we end on the right not. I want this woman, my body craves her like some kind of drug. I've never gotten over, I thought I had but sitting this close to her again, I realize that no matter what happened between her leaving and this moment, I have missed her with my entire being. And I will walk on hot coals to get this woman back in my bed. Yes, siree.

"Thank you, Logan." It's simple but it's not some smart ass retort. There could hope here, I need that in my life right now.

"You want me to drive you back to your folks? You've had a couple of glasses. We can come back for your truck tomorrow morning. Or you can come for a night cap at the cabin." Now I know I'm really pushing my luck here, but you can't help a guy for trying, right?

I wait with abated breath for her to respond.

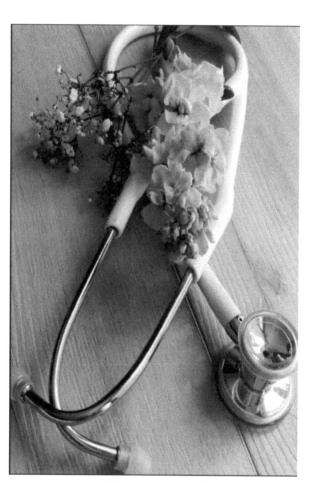

Chapter 46

S *age*
    Okay, so I'm not going to lie to myself or anyone else. He is definitely
doing it for me right now. I don't even want to try and fight it anymore, it has
been friggin exhausting and I think I like the idea of being held in those

strong arms again, to feel his fingertips on my skin again. What harm can it do?

Well, actually the way we left it all before – quite a lot of harm. Our hearts can get broken again and I don't think I'd recover from that so well. But he is charming, irresistible and I just can't help losing myself in his warm eyes holding that twinkle.

Before I properly engage my brain the words come out, "sure, I'll stay over at yours." He grins like he's the cat who got the canary. "Don't get any funny ideas. Let's just see what happens." There I had to get that in, even though my entire body is zinging right now and I just want to feel myself pushed up against his gorgeous broad chest.

"Hector sure is going to be surprised for me to have company." I'm relieved he has lightened the mood because it was getting heavy with the tension between us. Should we be doing this, picking up like we left off? Oh, god what if I tear his heart in two again? I'm so conflicted with all of this. I am going to blame my three-hundred and sixty degree turn on the wine.

The waiter approaches our table and asks us if we'd like anything else. "No thank you, we're good. Just the check please." Logan says as he reaches his hand across the table, our fingers make contact and the electricity that passes between us is just as it used to be. I'm in so much trouble right now but it's too late to pull out because my body would never forgive me and I am craving him right now. He's like some kind of drug that I am addicted to, god help me.

Logan leaves some cash on the table. Does anyone do that anymore? I mean pay with cash? I've not used cash since I can remember even when I go to Bluebells I just use contactless. I'd almost forgotten what real money looked like. "Did you tip?" I ask him. He raises his eyebrows like I've got two heads glued on me right now.

"Of course, what do you take me for?" Yeah it was a dumb question I guess. He comes to my chair and stands behind it as I move it backward just enough for him to take it and act all gentlemanly and help me up.

His hand is on the small of my back and I can feel his warmth radiate through me. That touch, it's already way too much but my body is on full Logan need mode right now and hell, I'm just going to oblige.

He guides me out of the restaurant and back to our cars in the parking area. "I'll drive, Sage. Like I said, you've had a couple of glasses. We'll come back in the morning for the your car." I guess that'll be okay since we're not in Willowbrook and nobody will know.

Although, I am betting my folks are going to give me the hundred and twenty questions when I get home tomorrow. I let him guide me to his truck and step in once he's opened the door for me. "You sure about this?" He asks. "You don't have to come back to mine." The way he says it really pulls at my heart the longing in his eyes.

"I know. I want to." I reach out my hand and stroke his cheek, his skin is soft and smooth. It's always been that way except more often than not since I've been back he has that sexy scruffle going on.

Logan nods and closes the door, I belt myself in as he makes his way to the driver's side, gets in, clunks himself in too and turns the engine over. "You have any country in this old thing?" He laughs.

"Of course I do. And less of the old thing. I'll have you know that Betsy and I are a thing. She's the love of my life." That makes me chuckle.

"A thing, eh? She's as old as the hills. You need a new truck."

"No way, she was my old man's and she's done me proud over the years. Besides, I didn't hear you complaining when we used to make out in it." Oo, that makes me blush.

"That was a long time ago, Logan. Get a new one, already."

"No way." He fiddles with the old fashioned dash and presses a button, a CD ejects. Before he begins to drive, Logan reaches in for the glove compartment and takes out a stack of cds. "Take your pick, darlin." And at the sight of some of these old ones, I catch my breath and can feel instant tears pricking at my eyes.

"Have you kept all of our music?" Oh. My. God. He has. Every single album we've written together is here in my hands. "I don't know what to say, Logan." My voice trails off as I shift through them until I find the one I'm looking for.

"Here put this one on." I tell him as I hand it to him whilst I put the others back in the compartment.

"I knew you'd choose that one." He winks at me and my heart melts and I literally pool. He places it in the car stereo, turns the dial for the volume and hits play.

His voice comes out, strong, sexy and the lyrics make me want to cry they're so poignant, so beautiful and so everything we once were.

I'll be standing right here waiting for you darlin'.

I'll never leave this spot, my eyes will always be looking, as I stand here.

Waiting for you.

I don't want you to go, but I know you have a dream to follow.

You've got my heart, always and forever.

There'll never be another who I'll love quite like I love you, the way your hair falls and that smile on your face.

You are my drug, my addiction, my everything and when you go my darlin' don't you fret, because I'll be standing here waiting for you.....

I remember him singing this to me at The Lazy Duke on the night before I hot footed it to Michigan. I almost didn't leave, I wanted to run up to the stage and straight into his arms and never be let go. My heart broke so much, it was in pieces, shattered to oblivion. As he sang, his eyes never left mine, he was my soulmate, my life, my breath.

Lost in my memories, the touch of his hand on mine as he drives, brings me back to the now. I squeeze his hand and look at his profile. Logan turns his face towards me and winks. Damnit, he gets me every time.

"Don't run away again please, darlin'. I don't think my heart will take it a second time." My breath catches, the lump in my throat is so big, I can't even swallow. How am I going to do this? What am I doing sitting in his truck going to his cabin when I'm going to be leaving again soon?

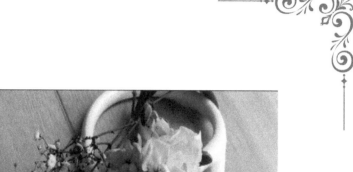

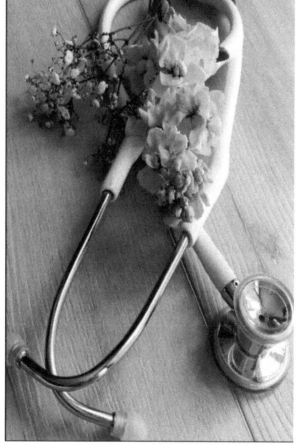

Chapter 47

L*ogan*

    Am I nervous? You bet I am. To be honest, I have no idea what we're doing here. I can't think of anything else except holding her in my arms again, feeling those soft lips on mine and running my hands through her long hair. I feel myself twitch in my jeans. Not good.

Okay, we can behave like adults, like ex-lovers, surely? I don't want to push her away, not again but maybe I can convince her somehow that here is where she belongs, with me, with her family, her sister, and the folk of Willowbrook.

"You know I'm going to leave here again Logan. It's just not the place for me, we've been over this. Why don't we just take this slowly and see where it heads. Besides, we're adults now. I am pretty sure we can go into this with open eyes, we're both adults." Damn, she is going to break my heart all over again if I let her.

Sage is too irresistible to leave alone, I've missed her. The way she smells, her cute laugh and the way her nose wrinkles when she does. So many adorable things about Sage I have missed over the years.

We pull up at the cabin, I had left a couple of lights on inside and a glow emanates from the cabin giving it a lived-in, homely look. It always makes me smile; I absolutely love this place. It's peaceful and inspirational. Sometimes I take photos, I've never really done anything with them except for hang a few on the walls. One day, maybe I'll send them into a magazine and see what happens there. But my passion is taking care of people being a doctor then second is chilling on stage with my band and playing my guitar.

I step out of the truck and go round to open the door for Sage. Gingerly she takes my hand. Electricity shoots up my hand and arm, my heart prangs. Yep, she still has the same effect on me she always has. Her head is lifted, and she is **actually** wearing the faintest of smiles. I'm betting she felt it too.

As she steps down from the truck, I close the door behind her and slip an arm around her waist, Sage doesn't pull away and relief floods me. She is right we just need to take it real slow; I am just completely taken aback by the three-hundred-and-sixty-degree turnaround. Our past is too hard to fight, I can't fight it that's for sure. I don't want to fight it. I never want to forget; all those years I have tried to suppress it to cover my pain and hurt.

"Thanks." She says as she leans into me some more. I can feel the warmth of her body through her coat even though the evening air is now much cooler now the sun has gone in and we're already way into the fall.

"Wow, it's so much prettier than I recall. And the lights just showcase it so beautifully."

"It's taken a lot of work and then some, but I'm pleased with it now. I'm pretty much off grid, everything is solar with only grid as back up which thankfully I've not had to use since I've lived up here." We get to the door, and I release my hold on her to insert the key in the lock. As soon as I open the door, Hector comes bounding up to me and stands on his back legs, his front on my stomach.

"Whoa, hey boy. Have you been good?" I know he has been, he's always such a good boy and was an easy dog to train from the off.

"Oh my gosh, look at his tail, it's so friggin adorable, it looks like it's going to wag right off." Sage chuckles, it's throaty and sexy. I ruffle Hector's curls on top of his head. He tries to lick my hand.

"Down, c'mon down you get." He does as he is told without needing to command him a second time. "Out you go." Hector sniffs at Sage's hand and she strokes his head. He obviously remembers her from the mountain. Satisfied all is in order, Hector bounces out the door and finds his favorite tree and cocks his leg then comes dashing back in almost knocking Sage flying.

"Hey, steady on." I tell him. Hector sits awaiting his treats for being such a good fella. "Come on in, sorry about Hector. He gets so excited when I've left him for a couple of hours." Sage moves in and I can see her appraising the space taking in the high vaulted ceiling with beams exposed, the open plan lounge with open fireplace, kitchen, and diner.

"This is impressive, Logan. It must have taken years." I nod as I place my keys in the blue ceramic bowl on the antique pine dresser by the front door and slide off my loafers. The wood floor is warm beneath my feet, where I have run underfloor heating. Sage follows suit and slips her shoes off, I take her coat from her and hang it on the hooks on the back of the heavy distressed oak door.

"Oh, don't worry about him. He's adorable. You always did like this breed, Airedale Terrier, right?" I like that she hasn't forgotten. There must be so many things she recalls, I'd love to hear them.

"Correct. You remembered." I say simply as I guide her to the kitchen where she takes a seat on one of the high stools by the granite island.

"Red or white wine?" She cocks her head to one side.

"Do you have a spare room, or will I be getting a taxi back?" Well blow me down, is this how they do it in the city, all upfront only here in Willowbrook we kinda just see what happens. "Red." She replies before I get a chance to say anything, I need to pick my jaw up off the floor.

I cough, "whichever you are most comfortable with. Only, you may prefer my room, darlin.'" She leans over and swats my hand playfully.

"Yeah, we'll see Logan." Oh, we will definitely see, by the time I get close enough to her, Dr Sage Bennett is going to be begging me to take her to new orgasmic heights and not wondering about a spare room or a damn taxi.

Chapter 48

S*age*
I watch as he places his full glass down on the distressed pine square table in front of the fireplace. It has gotten cooler, Logan crouches down in front of the fireplace. Damn if that butt isn't sexy, I don't know what his and the way his jeans tighten on those superior thighs of his. He's definitely like

those book boyfriends you just can't get enough of. Logan's physique is incredible, he has certainly filled out since we were together. He's all muscle and it suits him.

"It's getting chillier now in the evenings, but I love this time of year." I say as he lights the firelighter, the flames instantly spring up all red and glorious, I do love a real fire.

Hector mooches close to Logan; nuzzles his leg and I watch as Logan tenderly strokes his dog's head and places a kiss on his nose. Oh my, it makes me swoon the softness of him towards the dog. It's adorable. Hector lays down, clearly enjoying the instant warmth of the fire as it starts to crackle and catches the logs nicely stacked.

"It's my favorite time of the year," he says warming his hands up in front of it. "The trees and their majestic color here in the fall are second to none. Then there's all the Thanksgiving celebrations followed by Christmas. So much going on, not to mention Halloween." Logan stands up and steps over Hector as he makes his way over to me on the sofa and sits down.

I can feel his body heat he's that close, do I shift up to be closer to him? I take a sip of the full-bodied wine instead. It eases nicely down my throat and has a woody note to it. Delicious, I do love a good bodied red wine. "I don't expect you get many kids up here for Halloween, or do you?" He chuckles and looks at me. His eyes are to die for, and I can feel myself being pulled into him, my body has shifted involuntarily and now we're so close our thighs are practically touching.

"Not really, but we do something at the practice, Eliza goes to town decorating it and Sadie loves it. Most of the kids come round after school before we close, and we hand out the sweets and fruits. I've been known to dress up for them." His lips are turned up.

"That I've got to see." The words naturally come out of my mouth before I even realize that perhaps I won't be in Willowbrook for Halloween and Thanksgiving. Only, it'd be fun, right? I never did Halloween with Miles, he said it wasn't right to encourage kids to eat way too many sweets and that it was wrong they were all allowed to roam around the streets in the dark. Seriously? Now I think about it he was a bit of a stick in the mud. Who doesn't love Halloween?

It used to be one of my favorite times of the year. Logan would dress up as Herman Munster, he looked ridiculous and funny at the same time. I'd always go as a black cat with a long tail, the ears, my face would be painted the whole nine yards. Of course, when I was much younger my mom would dress Ali and I up as cute pumpkins. It makes me smile.

"Memories?" He asks me, his right hand now on his thigh. If I just move my hand a fraction our fingertips will touch. I'm itching to touch him, just you know to feel the warmth of his fingers against mine. I know already electricity will shoot through me faster than you can say zip.

"Yeah, you know me too well, Logan. I was thinking of how we'd dress up and have a blast going round with the younger kids to chaperone them then head off to a party up at Henson's open field with a bonfire, toffee apples, warm cider and just hang out listening to music. You'd play your guitar, and we'd all sing and laugh. It was a good time."

He nods his head. "The best time. No cares in the world, no real responsibilities just getting our grades. It was fun, everything with you was fun, Sage." He looks almost sad, I know I ripped his heart out but I'm telling you, I ripped my own heart out too. His words get to me, my heart flutters and I almost lean over and press my lips to him.

I'd love to go forward with Logan and see how our lives play out, but I'm not sure I want to stay in Willowbrook. The place is too small for a now city girl like me. Isn't it?

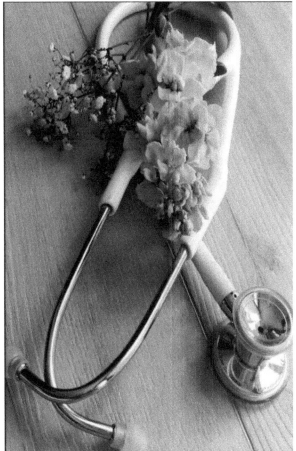

Chapter 49

L*ogan*

 The flames flicker gently, Hector is content, I can hear his faint snoring, it's a sound that gets me every damn time. And, sitting right beside me so close on the sofa is the girl of my dreams, the one I let get away. I can't hold back any longer, I must know.

As I move my head, I feel a smack against my forehead. "Holy shit." I say raising my head to where the smack took place.

"Oh my god. Are you okay?" Sage is laughing, she's laughing so much it fills my heart to see that amazing look on her. After so long.

"Yeah, what happened there. *Are you* okay?" I ask her and raise my hands to cradle her face.

Our eyes make contact, I can see her pupils are dilated and it dawns on me that she was leaning in for a kiss at about right the same time. No way.

Her lips are close to mine, I can smell the wine on her breath and chocolate from her dessert. Those lips are slightly parted. Gently, still cradling her face I lower my lips to hers. My heart feels like it's going to blow right out of my chest as I savour the softness of her plump lips, her tongue slides easily into my mouth and I feel as if I've gone back in time, sitting on the bed in my old bedroom, my guitar cast to the side as we locked in an embrace that neither of us ever found easy to pull away from, only coming up for air.

I allow my tongue to slide into her warm mouth, damn it's sending all sorts of signals around my body as I pull her head closer in, brushing the side of her face with my thumb. Sage groans into my mouth, the same groan I know so well.

Somebody wake me up right now, if this is a dream to be honest, I never want it to end. I feel as if I am floating, she's here, really here in front of me, her lips against mine, our tongues dancing their familiar dance like we've never been separated. My heart can't take it if she leaves me again.

Her breathing catches as I move my left hand down her arms to her waist and pull her closer into me. "Oh, God. Logan." She breathes into my mouth; I kiss her deeper and harder. She pushes her body against my chest and before I know it, I'm laying almost back on the sofa. With ease, Sage is laying over my body.

"What has taken us so long?" She asks, her mouth upturned. I'm telling you she looks like an angel right now only one with a glint in her eyes. Oh hell. I know that look, she wants me only. Okay, there is an only here so be ready.

Can I go ahead and let her into my bed again? Can I let her back into my heart? I don't think I can go through it all over again, I'm not built that way. Losing Sage the first time round almost killed me, then losing my wife took me to near obliteration. So, you can see why suddenly I'm nervous yet wanting her so damn much, that I ache, and my cock is urging to be released.

Do I throw all caution to the wind?

Her legs straddle me, and I feel her hands starting to unbutton my shirt, I feel like I am paralyzed. Part of my brain knows I should stop her to save my own heart but the rest of me, well let's just say I am a red bloodied man, and this isn't any woman, this is Sage Bennett.

"Take me to bed." Damn those words, okay I can't be that strong. Fuck it, I need her. I want her. She's here now with me and she wants me like she always used to.

In one swoop, I am off the sofa, her legs tightly wrapped around my waist, I cradle her ass so prevent her from slipping. Those slender arms of hers snake around my neck and those kisses she's placing up and down my neck are making my whole-body zing. I am on fire and she's going to get it tonight. Fuck my mind, fuck what's going to happen. I could still change her mind, right?

Hector doesn't stir, he's out for the count as I make my way to the heavy pine, bedroom door and kick it open with my right foot. "Oo, you beast you." She chuckles.

"I'll show you beast." It takes me all of four strides to reach my large mahogany bed, that I'll have you know I made myself including all the carvings of angels and cherubs.

"Wow, Logan. Did you make this?" She asks me, her eyes so wide they're like saucers right now. I nod. "It's stunning, you were always good with your hands."

"I'm gonna show you just how good I am with these hands." She blushes. Cute. Gently, I lay my girl down on the bed and kick my shoes off before I slip hers off her feet. Her hair is sprawled out all over *my* pillows and I love the sight of her laying there waiting for me to undress her, one piece of clothing at a time.

Her lips remain parted, and her breathing has increased, my heart is banging in my chest so hard it's going to drop right out. I undress her in slow motion, I want to take my time.

"Just take everything off, already." She's insistent, fiery, and damn sexy. I can sense her urgency and I'm betting that her clit is throbbing and aching to be touched right now.

"Don't be so impatient." I tell her as I lower myself next to her almost naked body, just laying here right by my side in the prettiest pale blue sheer lace bra and panties is making so damn hard. She's a sight that would make any man think they're about to come in their pants like a hormonal teenager.

"Are you sure about this, darlin'?"

"Yes, I'm very sure." Her breathy voice is so low I can only just hear her. Tonight, I'm going to make her all mine, she's not going to want to go anywhere once she's experienced me again.

Chapter 50

S*age*
    God his body, it's something out of a GQ centrefold. The muscles on him, he is so ripped as I allow my fingers to trace his veins up from his wrist to his biceps that even without doing bench presses are neatly formed. He

smells woody and of wine, it's delicious and I can't wait to kiss him as my mouth hungrily locks onto his.

Our tongues dance once again, I am transported back in time to his bedroom where we first laid together as a couple, innocent and fresh for each other. My first love.

My heart is pounding so fast he must be able to feel it, my breath catches as he moves his head away and starts to place fluttering kisses down my neck, to my collar bone whilst one hand latches onto my breast, his fingers caressing my nipple.

I can feel that familiar ache of longing between my legs, I am so ready for Logan right this second and whilst I want him urgently, I know he is going to take his time. As he latches on to my budding nipples with his mouth and I groan loudly.

"I want you so bad." I tell him as I try not to pant with lust.

"In good time, darlin." He licks my nipple then the other one and teases them taking them into his mouth and gently biting on them. I grab his free hand and try to push his fingers down further to my wet pussy, but he isn't having any of it. God, I need him it's driving me insane.

His cock is so erect against my leg surely, he must be aching too, I bet his balls are tight and high. Easily I move myself just enough to be able to grab him with one hand and fuck, he feels heavenly so rigid and turned on by being with me.

I move my hand up and down whilst maintaining a firm grip on his cock. "Darlin' that feels so good. So damn good." His breath is warm as he begins to move down my stomach leaving a trail of kisses behind. I can feel that sexy feeling of his few days old stubble as he reaches the top of my panties and starts to rub me between my legs through the flimsy fabric.

My hand is no longer able to reach him, damn it. He felt so good.

I'm soaking I can feel how wet I am, it's been ages since I have even had sex let alone with someone like Logan the master of seduction caressing my body, bringing me so close as his thumb massages my swollen clit.

The heat soars through my body as his long runs along my slit through my panties and a finger pushes the slight fabric to the side, and Oh. My. God. As his finger slides inside me, I can feel my pussy grab it. She's greedy for sure.

My hips buck as he finally allows me the grace of his warm tongue and mouth onto my pussy, I'm so ready to shower him with my juices but hold on because I want this release to be with Logan whilst he's deep inside me. Only, I am struggling to hold back because it feels so fucking good.

His tongue delves into me, it runs up and down my slit, his thumb all the while massaging my swollen and aching clit. "You want two fingers, darlin'?" I nod and gasp.

"Yes. Everything. Give me everything." I hear him chuckle the vibration against my pussy turns me on even more. He licks faster, massages my clit faster and bits down on it gently. I am soaring so high, it's as if I am on some kind of drug. My eyes start to roll to the back of my head.

"Damn darlin', you taste so fucking good. I've missed your pussy so much." He slides another finger inside me, and I feel like I'm dying and going to heaven, am I floating with three inside me? He works me so well, just like he knows how to.

Our bodies know each other intimately and our mouths are made for each other as he works his magic, bringing me even closer to the edge. I place my hands on his head and fist his hair, "fuck me, damnit."

"Grab the headboard baby and get ready." His voice is husky just the sound of it makes me whimper, his commanding tone and what I know I'm about to get are making me putty in his hands.

I reach up and behind to grab the headboard as he slowly moves his fingers out of my pussy and comes over me, using one hand he places it under my head and cradles it.

"You're so damn beautiful, Sage. The most beautiful woman I know." His soft and gentle eyes are so heavily dilated they're almost black, his lips brush mine and his tongue teases my lips.

"Now be a good girl and open those legs nice and wide." I moan, he's got a dirty mouth on him when he wants to and I fucking love it. His hips fit perfectly to mine, and I can feel the tip of his raging cock against my clit. Fuck me, I'm going to come before he even enters me. I hold on, I bite my lip and squeeze my eyes because I do not want to miss us riding the wave together. But fuck me, it's not easy.

Gently and real slow he begins to enter me; I feel myself open to accommodate him and with my wetness he slides right in as if we've never been parted, he feels amazing as he begins to rock forward and back. I go to put my arms around him to touch his broad back.

"Get those hands back on the fucking headboard. Do as you're told, darlin'. You want this don't you?" Of course, I do, more than I've wanted any man in my life.

As instructed, I grab the headboard, he removes his hand from under my head and grabs my left wrist with his right wrist. I can feel the pressure but not enough to hurt me and it's such a huge turn-on, I can't even tell you what I'm feeling right now.

Logan's stride begins to pick up, he starts to move faster, as I find myself screaming out as my eyes roll back, my head drops to the side and his warm mouth finds my neck.

"You're mine, darlin'. You're so fucking beautiful, and so damn tight and wet." Oh God, I am moaning and screaming, the wave begins from the pit of my stomach, the heat intensifies throughout my body and his strokes are so fast as if he's running a hundred-meter spring, my legs wrap around his waist and hang on for life.

"I'm coming for you, only you, darlin'." I hear him scream out my name as we explode together the climax so intense, I can't release my legs from around his waist.

My entire body is quivering he has fucking wrecked me.

Chapter 51

ogan

L   We're laying side by side, one arms is under her head as she snuggles into me, it's familiar, warm, and exactly as I remember her. Our bodies fit so perfectly, they know each other from years of being together, the familiar smell of her shampoo, the touch of her velvet skin, the way her right leg is flung over both my legs and her gentle hand on my chest in the same spot it always was, the very same spot where it belongs now, tomorrow, and forever.

"Did we just really do that?" She says, I chuckle.

"We did indeed. I hope you don't regret it." I hope not because for me it was the most amazing feeling in the world and my heart is swollen and overflowing for Sage right now. If I'm honest, a part of me never stopped loving this woman. She is perfection, smart, funny, honest, stubborn to the core and damn beautiful. Everything.

"No, of course not. I knew what I was doing." She sighs and runs her hand across my chest. It feels so good to hold her in my arms again, I never thought this would ever be the case again and yet here she is, naked and in my bed, all folded around me. What more could I want?

"But you do know I'm going to leave. This can't go anywhere." This is what I thought she'd say and despite her words my heart isn't sinking to my feet. No way.

"We'll see about that darlin'. I'm going to make you realize just what you'd be missing."

"Oh, really. Well, you know I've got a profession and that I want a fellowship. I'm not going to get that here, Logan." She sure is a straight talker.

"You may just change your mind." I kiss the top of her head. I feel her chest rising and falling against my side as she snuggles in. I hope you guys are all rooting for me because there is no way I want Sage to leave me again.

"I don't think so, this is just fun. We both need someone right now, so don't get yourself any funny ideas. You hear me?"

"I hear you darlin'. Doesn't mean I gotta listen to you." For that I get a playful slap to the chest. I take her wrist and bring her hand to my mouth and kiss her fingers one at a time. I know this woman, she wouldn't have slept with me simply for fun, she has more depth, more integrity and she's not a hook up kind of woman. Somewhere in her heart, I know she has feelings for me. Otherwise, she would not have slept me. That much I do know about Dr Sage Bennett.

"You hungry?" I ask her because I am starving after giving her three orgasms, I think I'm due some energy source of some kind.

"Absolutely, I am."

"Great, let's go see what's in the kitchen. I know I've got cheese, crackers, pickles, and some sliced chicken breast."

"Sounds perfect, let's do it." She unfolds from my body and already I miss her closeness and her warmth. I slip on my shirt and pull my jeans up my legs, Sage grabs one of my blue denim shirts I had laying on the back of a chair and buttons it up. I stop and swallow, damn she looks so good wearing my shirt.

If I wasn't in such need for some kind of sustenance, I'd be taking it off her in a jiffy and prising those fine legs of hers open once again and taking her to heights once again. My cock twitches, *not now I've gotta eat.*

As if she knows exactly what effect she's having on me, Sage flashes me a grin and cocks her head. "I thought we were getting food, you letch." She giggles. It's cute and girlie. Boy, have I missed her. I didn't realize just how much until right now. All the small things she does, the way she giggles, her eyes twinkling, that radiance she is wearing right now from her after-sex glow. Her hair all messed up.

I open the bedroom door for her, and she steps passed me. Hector raises his head from in front of the fire, I go towards him and pat him on the head and reach for another log from the basket close to him, the fire needs feeding. When the temperatures drop at night this time of year, it can get chilly up here in West Virginia. Flames spring up immediately, and Hector settles back down, satisfied with a fluff of the curls on his head, his tail wags as he places his head back down.

I can hear Sage in the kitchen opening cupboards and putting on the coffee machine. "Isn't it getting late for coffee?" I ask her. She shrugs her shoulders.

"Don't start that with me. It's never too late for coffee, besides I need you to drive me back to the restaurant for my car so I can get home." Oo, wow that stings. No way. I want her to stay with me for the night. I want to feel her snuggled into my body when I open my eyes first thing in the morning. She has got to be kidding me, right?

I cough and enter the kitchen area, resting one hand on the marble work top, with the other I place it around her waist and pull her close to me. "Don't be so damn difficult, darlin'. You're not going anywhere. You are staying right here with me in the cabin and when I wake up, you will be the first thing that I see in the morning. I want to feel you next to me, to see your beautiful face as the sun rises. Don't deny me that." Her mouth forms an O.

Is Dr Sage Bennett lost for words? That has got to be a first. EVER.

"Well, I suppose if you put it that way. But you know my folks aren't going to give over when I get home tomorrow morning. Especially not my mother. She'll have the wedding invitations out in a jiffy and that I cannot be doing with. You know how she gets. She's going to put two and two together and come up with a white wedding in the chapel off Main Street and..." I stop her by kissing her. She talks way too much.

"Ssh, you're an adult. Tell her you went off to Coppertown. Only, the truth about us seeing each other is going to come out sooner than later because I can't trust how I'm going to act around you. You're so damn beautiful that I can't keep my hands off you." I slap her butt and go past her so I can grab myself a glass from near the sink and pour myself some water. I'm parched.

"We agreed this was just for fun, so you're going to have to behave around me, Logan." Yeah, well we'll have to see about that. I give it a few weeks maximum before my girl decides and realizes that Willowbrook and I, are where her home is.

Chapter 52

S *age*
  Great, so now because of letting myself go a little last night, the wine and softening towards Logan, I have to go through my folk's front door and do the walk of shame. Fanfuckingtastic. Inhaling deeply, I slide my key into the front door.

Perhaps I can sneak off to my room and get showered quickly before heading back out to Bluebell's for a coffee and meet up with Hazel. We organized to meet, and I am looking forward to seeing her again after so long. Honestly, I feel totally crap as a best friend since I hardly ever get to see her when I've been back for visits.

"Is that you, Sage?" I hear mom's voice coming from the kitchen. Shit.

"Yeah, it's only me, Mom. Going up to my room to get showered and changed." I head for the stairs and nope, she is out in front of me quicker than Bolt off the starting blocks. Is she on some kind of uppers today only that was pretty quick?

"Not so fast young lady. Did you stay out all night?" She has upturned lips, and her eyes are scrutinizing me. I feel as if I'm back to being fifteen again. I shift uncomfortably just wanting to run up to my room. I know my messy bun on top my head is about to fall out, and I am still wearing the clothes I went out to dinner in last night.

"Er, yes." I go to place my hand on the handrail but mom's hand clasps over mine.

"Did you have a lovely time? Were you with Logan? Oh, gosh I am so happy. Finally. At last." Mom looks like the cat who just got the cream, seriously her face is lit up like Christmas.

"Mom, pleeease. Yes, to Logan. I'm not getting back with him or serious with him so you can forget about the whole white wedding business in the local chapel and inviting all your friends round." I huff.

"We'll see, Honey. I know that Logan and the way he looks at you still after all these years. He won't give up."

"That as it may be, Mom but you're forgetting a little detail here. I'm leaving soon."

"Oh, Honey. You say that now, but you'll change your mind once you realize that the love, he has for you and you have for him, that only happens once in a lifetime. You know that. Don't pass it up again, sweetheart. Not for work. When you can't work anymore one day or retire, you won't have anything else. Love is everything when it's the love of your life." Speech of speeches, right?

"Mom, my medical career is important to me. I want a fellowship and that's not happening here in Willowbrook, damn it." She is still smiling, that *mom knows best* look. She's very good at it and yes, I do still feel like a child standing here in front of her trying to escape up the stairs.

"Is that going to give you children and a community, Sage? Is it going to keep you warm at night, hug you when you're down and miserable, not to mention lonely in a big bed with no one by your side? Will it look into your eyes over a candlelit meal? Will it laugh with you at the funny things, be silent and watch a movie with you and just be there next to you whenever you need someone?"

"Mom, please stop." I run up the stairs and into my bedroom, closing the door behind me, resting my back against it. Tears sliding down my face. Jeez, all the emotions raging inside me are too much.

Everything my mom says is true, what will a fellowship give me? Logan has spoilt me for any other man out there. Having spent the night with him again, having been lifted to heights I'd forgotten, the way our hearts beat together, the tender kisses on my lips and neck, his strong hands roaming across my body and down to my core. I know he is *the only* man I want to be with.

It's like a rush through my body knowing that even with Miles, it wasn't a hundred percent right, it would have run its course in time, I have come to realize this now. Miles and his fellowship in London just came earlier than our natural expiration date.

I exhale, wow this is all way too much for me. I have a girlfriend date to get too. But last night has left me questioning so much right now. For a start my folks would be over the moon for me to stay, I could be with Logan, the man I have loved since I was a teenager, the same man I've been friends with since we were kids. Can I imagine myself working in the practice forever though? Will it be enough for my career aspirations, dealing with just the town folk? Gosh, I just don't know. I don't know.

I wipe my eyes with the back of my right hand and go to the en-suite and start running the shower water as I strip my attire off and step inside under the warm running water.

My head feels like it is spinning off my shoulders, I wish I had a fairy Godmother right now who could wave her magic wand and show me the way. The last thing I want to do is make a decision I could end up regretting.

If I stayed but felt unsatisfied with working at the practice, I could risk becoming bitter and frustrated, then take it out on Logan. Worse still, I could end up leaving after time. I shudder, that would rip Logan apart, it would destroy him, and he doesn't deserve that. He deserves all of me. Or I could love it here, love being there for the people of Willowbrook and Copper town, enjoy the festivals, the community, the knowledge that everyone has got each other's backs.

I rinse the shower gel off and reach for one of the fluffy white towels and dry myself off, tie it round me and go into the bedroom to my wardrobe where I pull out a pair of black jeans, a white tee, and a navy cardigan. It takes me about five minutes to get dressed, pull my hair into a ponytail, apply a dusting of bronzer, lipstick, and mascara. There I consider myself ready to meet my bestie.

She'll sort me out, she's always been brilliant at putting my life into perspective.

Chapter 53

L *ogan*
      "Come on, boy. Let's go." I put two fingers in my mouth and whistle for Hector to come and get in the truck. We're off to the practise for Saturday morning, it'll be fairly quiet then Eliza, Sadie, Sage, and I will be meeting at Bluebell's to discuss the fundraiser. On top of that I remind myself I need to

make time to sit down with Mrs Winters regarding the Fall festival. My mom will want to be involved again this year; she usually bakes the pies along with Sage's mom. It sure is busy.

I've got a spring in my step as I open the door for Hector, who bounces into the front and settles himself down with his two front feet dangling over the edge of the chair. I reach for the seatbelt and give it a good yank to snap it in and attach Hector's halt to it. He's such a good boy and lets me get on with it. I ruffle his head and go to the driver's side.

And yes, you can all guess why I have a spring in my step. Being with Sage last night was beyond my wildest dreams, especially after she came rocking back into Willowbrook being a stubborn Missy not to mention a grump.

I find myself whistling as I turn on the ignition, Hector nudges my hand as I grab the shift stick and reverse the truck away from the cabin. I sure am looking forward to seeing Sage today. I'm not going to lie, I do have a small amount of apprehension going on, what if she has decided last night was a mistake? What if it was just the wine, the atmosphere and maybe seeing what it would be like with me again? I shake my head; I need to knock that nonsense out of my mind and keep it at bay.

I want this woman with every fibre in my body, my heart wants her and okay, okay my dick can't get enough of her. Too much? Well, that's just the way it is. I'll do whatever it takes to make her mine again.

We pull up outside the surgery, Eliza's car is already outside, and Sadie is just walking up the few steps to the front door. She's got a four-pack tray of coffees and a bag of something from Bluebell's café in her hand.

Now I think about it, I'm hungry. It must have been the sex last night and ensuring my girl had a few orgasms, just to let her know what she has been missing.

"Hey, you." Sadie calls out. "I got you a smoked salmon and cream cheese bagel."

"Just what I need. Thanks, Sadie. Make sure you get some petty cash back from Eliza."

"Nah, don't worry about it. On me." She pushes the door open with her foot, the small bell on top rings out. Hector starts to murmur to be released from the halter. He's pretty good but he really prefers not to have a halter on him. I unclip him, open the door and he bounces straight out, cocks his leg on the tree out front of the practice and bounds up the steps, sits at the door and looks expectantly at me.

"Morning, Eliza. How are you this fine day?" I close the door behind me.

"Someone is nice and chipper, wouldn't happen to be anything to do with a certain young lady doctor, would it?" She chuckles.

"About that." I start to say.

"Can't talk now, have to call Mr Jacobs back." She pushes her glasses back on her nose and picks the phone up. I mutter something about, *yeah, right*. I know Eliza set Sage and I up, but I can't be fed up with her about it, look what an amazing evening we ended up having. If we hadn't been given a certain little nudge, last night would never have taken place.

Hector dashes round to Eliza's side of the counter, she reaches into her purse and pulls out some doggy treats. He takes one and lays down by her feet to chew on it. Traitor. But I love that everyone here in Willowbrook loves Hector as much as I do.

"Morning everyone." I turn as Sage comes through and I swear her face looks radiant this morning. Fresh and clear, her eyes have a sparkle in them, and that smile is wider than Julia Roberts' right now. Mm, I am thinking someone has the same happy step in their stride too.

"Good morning, darlin'. Looking forward to the day?" I ask as I lean against the reception desk, taking in her delectable shape, her legs encased in leggings which showcase those runner legs of hers, the same ones that were wrapped around me last night. I need to stop thinking about that otherwise Eliza and Sadie are going to be seeing my dick standing on charge.

It's pretty challenging, however, with her in those leggings, a tight sweater that gives me an amazing show of her perfect breasts and that small waist of hers. Is it getting hot in here, or is it me? Okay, it's me.

"Of course. What've we got this morning?"

Eliza turns to both of us and smiles. Sage narrows her eyes at her in a playful way. "I've got to have a word with you." She says.

"Oh, hell y'all look so cute."

"That as it may be, Eliza but you know the score. I'm out of here as soon as I get my position in State." Sage takes her coffee from the carton cupholder Sadie brought in and reaches in the bag for a bagel. "Mm, coconut latte. Divine." She has froth on her top lip, I reach over and run my finger along her lip. Sage smiles, damn this feels like old times. My heart literally skips a beat.

"We'll see, Dr Bennett." Eliza retorts. "Anyway, back to your question. You have young Crystal coming in about her cycle, she's having bad pains and wants to get some advice on what she can do or take. As you know she's a naturalist and not in for any heavy pain meds."

"Got it." Sage says and drinks more of the latte, then bites into the bagel. How I'd love to be that bagel right now, with her tongue twisting around mine.

"You've got Mr Jenkins, Dr Logan. He just needs a repeat prescription for his water tables. Sadie and I are clear so we're thinking of working on the festival plan for the stalls."

"Thanks, Eliza. Send Mr Jenkins in when he arrives. I'll be in my office. Hector, come on, boy." I pat my leg but he's not budging. Why would he when Eliza is the queen of dog treats this morning.

Sage follows me down the hall until she reaches her office door, then grabs my shirt taking me by surprise.

"What you doing tonight?" There is no mistaking the look in her gorgeous eyes.

"Whatever you'd like, darlin'." She does still want to see me. My body relaxes with relief. I can't tell you how relieved I do feel knowing that last night wasn't a one off for old time's sake.

"I'm thinking, *Dr Logan* you could take me to our spot in the mountain. We can take a blanket and a picnic basket, look at the stars laying on our backs, you know like we used to."

My heart is about to burst, I want to kiss her until the cows come home, only I spot Crystal coming through the door. It can wait until later.

Sage, me, the stars, and the moon. It's going to be a perfect night.

"You got it, beautiful." We separate and go into our own offices. I am going to make sure it's a night she can never forget. Told you, I'm on a mission to make her change her mind about leaving Willowbrook.

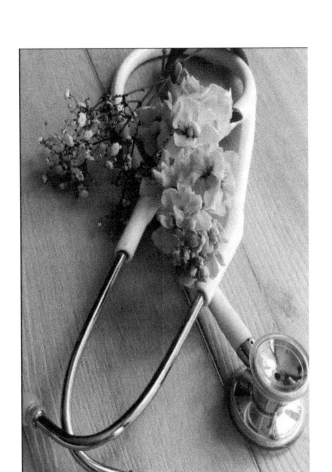

Chapter 54

S*age*
   I have no idea where my brazenness came from back at the surgery, like I have no idea what has gotten into me. That is, I guess what multiple orgasms do to a girl. Suddenly everything is seen through rose tinted

spectacles, I don't even mind that I'm going to be meeting with the gang later and my folks and Logan's folks at Bluebells to discuss the fundraiser.

You know what, I'm looking forward to it. Where this has all come from in such a short space of time is bewildering but I think I'll go with it.

I grab my jacket from the coat hook on the back of my office door and swing my bag over my shoulder. "Catch you ladies later." I say to Eliza and Sadie as I head out the door. They both look at me and Eliza winks. I am guessing she suspects that a certain someone, namely me, spent a lustful evening with a certain, swoony, devilishly handsome doctor last night. And boy was it hot. HOT. HOT.

Since we're all heading straight to Bluebell's I don't bother with my car, it's literally only down the road to Main Street. I spot my folks car outside the front and swing the door open, the bell chimes.

"Cooey. Over here." I hear my mom's voice and notice her waving. I wave back as I make my way towards her and dad. It's nice to see them both out together and dad not stuck in his office beavering away.

"How was your morning?" Mom asks, she has a permanent smile on her face it's the same one she was wearing this morning when she tried to cross examine me about being out at Logan's cabin last night. Good job mom never tried to be a lawyer; she'd not be great at it but as a counsellor she'd rock it.

"Hello, lovely." Dad says and squeezes my hand.

"Is Alli coming?" I ask them both as I sit down by mom, dad is on her right and Debs comes to our table.

"What can I get you folks? Nice to see you all together. My, it's been some time, right?" She can say that again, it's been an age since I sat here in Bluebells with my folks. What with being away in Michigan and practically hiding away at my folk's home whenever I returned to avoid bumping into Logan and not visiting very often in the first place.

I feel guilt knowing away in my gut, I have been a shitty ass daughter to say the least. Only coming down for the holidays and then staying for the briefest time. My folks deserved better than that.

"I'll have the steak and mushroom pie, fries on the side and green salad." Dad says patting his stomach. Mom raises an eyebrow, she tries her best to keep him on a healthy diet and low carbs, she has this mild obsession about his heart and cholesterol, not that it's high. I know his readings.

"Don't say a word, wifey." He says. Mom swats his hand playfully. Dad gives her a squeeze.

I swear, after forty years of marriage these two are like kids, I love the way they are together. It tugs on my heart; this is what I wanted once that was until I got grandiose ideas about a medical career in a state hospital. And when I met Miles, I thought we had it all sewn up, how wrong could I have been?

"Not saying anything, sweetheart. Debs, I'll have a green salad with onions on the side please not fried and the grilled chicken breast." Debs writes everything down on her lilac notepad and glances my way.

"I'll have what mom is having. Thanks, Debs."

"Great, it'll be with you shortly. I'll have someone bring you some fresh water over and what drinks would you all like?"

"Coffee for me." I say. Mom frowns, okay, okay so I have a caffeine problem which my mom worries about. Honestly, the amount of worrying she does, Mom ought to have multiple frown lines but she doesn't. Her skin is still peachy and radiant, and the only creases she has are those beautiful laughter lines around her eyes.

Mom and dad just ask for the water.

"We're going to be nine." I tell Debs. "Logan and his folks are on the way over, oh wait it could be ten if Daisy arrives too. Eliza is meeting us here with Sadie."

"No problem, Honey. Let me run you some more tables together. Are y'all discussing the fundraiser for the baseball team?" I'm surprised she knows but then I suppose it's an annual event here in Willowbrook a bit like the Thanksgiving and Christmas festivals. Oh, and then there is the Spring festival, the Easter parade, Homecoming event and. I'll stop there, if there is one thing Willowbrook is known for, it's the number of festivals and parades it has.

"Sure is." Dad says, "and I'll be making the float for the team to come through town on." Dad is pretty handy with his hands and his passion is carpentry. He loves working with wood and is pretty impressive. Mom has a beautiful dining room table and chairs all carved by my father's own hands.

Their matrimonial bed is also carved by him, it is something out of the world. All walnut with a high headboard and cherubs decorating it, birds, and vines. If he decided to change profession, he'd make a good living, but dad says, he wouldn't want to turn his passion into his bread and butter.

"I sure can't wait to see that, then." Debs says. "Okay you folks, let's get these tables organized and start bring you some food out."

"Thanks, Deb, Honey." Mom says. I notice how her hand is still in my dad's. It's so romantic. I want to have what they have one day. Only, chasing my profession may mean it never happens for me.

The door chime goes. As I turn, he takes my breath away with his broad shoulders, narrow hips, and muscular legs easily identifiable in tight jeans. With his cowboy hat on at an angle, Logan is so damn arresting. My breath hitches. Damn it, that man is going to be the death of me. I'm already pooling just looking at him. Am I salivating? Holy shit, you know what? I think I damn well am.

Chapter 55

L*ogan*

   "Hey everyone." I am trying not to focus on Sage's face, she looks pretty damn radiant this afternoon, even more so than when I saw her an hour ago at the practice and is she blushing? Oh yeah, she is.

"Well, hello Logan." Says her mom and yes she has a glint in her eye. Okay, so everyone around the table knows that Sage and I spent the night together last night. Not only because Sage had to go home early this morning and was caught by her mom, but you know, news travels fast in this town.

It wouldn't surprise me if everyone in Bluebell's knows right now. In fact, Debs comes towards me and nudges my elbow with her free arm, a coffee pot in the other hand. "I hear you had a visitor up in your cabin last night." She winks. I grin. Sage blushes a deeper shade of pink. It's cute.

"Did you now? I can't help the rumour mill around these parts but it's not what you think."

"That's a shame, Honey." Sage's mom says.

"Mom. Honestly." Sage blurts out. "Can we all just stick to topic please, the fundraiser. Have you seen Eliza and Sadie?" She asks me.

"On their way, Eliza is just heading over right now. Who is keeping the agenda?"

"Wow, that's pretty formal." Sage sages with raised eyebrows.

"We need to keep track, darlin' of who is doing what and also the spend against the budget for things like building the float, paying the band that kind of thing."

"You're playing, right?" Her father asks me. I nod.

"Yes, Sir. Me and the guys will be playing a set, we've also got a girl group over from Copper town who are just starting out and want to hit their own indie label. It's kind of exciting for them to play with us."

"I bet." He says. "Good to see you again, Logan." I like her father, we always got on, in fact he and I used to go on fishing trips frequently with my dad and we even had the odd camping trip, you know the guys only.

Ali arrives and takes a seat next to her mother and gives Sage a hug. "So, you were a dirty stop out I hear." She laughs. Sage playfully punches her in the arm.

"Oh. My. God. How many people know I stayed out late?"

"Late?" Ali raises her eyebrows. "I heard from Mom you were at Logan's cabin *all* night."

Sage folds her arms in front of her and gives an exasperated look, the one that says *I knew this would be all over town in a jiffy*. I stifle a chuckle because she looks so darn adorable right now.

We hear the diner's bell ring and glance towards the door. Sadie and Eliza enter, Eliza is carrying her trustee red folder that keeps all our records for the fundraiser. I keep telling her to put everything on a USB, but she won't have it.

"Hey everyone. Glad we're all here. Oh, wait one. Logan, where are your folks? I thought they were coming and what about Daisy?"

"I'll chase them up. Let me send them a group message. Deb, can we get more coffees please?" Deb nods from the counter and is straight over with the coffee pot.

Not long after our food is brought out to us, and we all start to dig in. My phone pings and I glance at the screen in front of me. It's my folks and Daisy.

Mom: *We're just eating at home first. Be there in twenty.*

Daisy: *At the Lazy Duke's having a quick beer with Marshal Deacon and the guys. Be there soon if I can drag myself away.* ☺ ☺

I relay the messages to everyone around the table and message Daisy back.

No need to come over if you're busy with M. Deacon. We can crack on without you. I'll put you down for one of the craft stalls in any case as usual. Give my regards to the Marshall.

Perfect, will do.

And, Daisy, why don't you just tell him you like him, like him and can he get his shit together and ask you out on a proper date? Or why don't you just ask him yourself?

Because, what if he doesn't like me like that?

Trust me, Sis. He does.

I'll think about it.

Okay, well don't think too long, he may get snapped up by someone else.

Shut up, Logan. Speak later.

"Everything okay?" Sage asks as she reaches for her coffee cup. I notice how her eyes sparkle and the way her hair falls over her shoulder. I am trying very hard *not* to think how she felt underneath me last night, or how good it felt with my head buried between her legs, tasting her nectar.

I can't have a bulge in my pants right now. Especially not with Eliza on my right and Sadie on my left.

"Yeah, all good. My folks will be here soon they're finishing up eating at home and Daisy is with Marshall Deacon."

"Those two, honestly why haven't they got it together already?" Sage says. She has a point, they've been dancing around each other for a very long time, I mean a few years. One day that man is going to see sense and do something about it.

"No idea but I think some meddling is needed." Eliza winks. Trust her, like she set Sage and I up. "My magic will work on them for sure." She continues as she opens her folder once our plates have been collected.

"Are we all ready?" She asks. Everyone nods and says yes.

"Okay, so I will take notes and minutes. Let's start with the stalls. I've got Daisy on crafts, Sadie on crafts stall two. Sage, you and your ma are on the cake stall, correct?" Eliza is being very officious.

"Absolutely," Sage's mom says. "We'd love to." Sage raises her eyebrows, it makes me chuckle because right now, I am thinking the last thing she wants to do is be involved in the fundraiser but she's part of the practice right now so it's kind of compulsory.

I am hoping she'll learn just how amazing our community is, how we stick together and that what we have here in Willowbrook is unlike anything else she'll find in a big city where she will just blend in again as another number. A nameless person in the throngs of people in the streets.

I steal a few glances at her, she gives me the faintest smile. It makes my heart sing, all I gotta do is convince her to stay.

How hard can that be?

Chapter 56

S*age*

We're drawing to a close on the meeting and boy have we covered a lot. We have got Mrs Winters the schoolteacher in charge of the bring a book and swap stall, Logan's and my mom are both going to run a cake stall. Daisy and Sadie on crafts. Debs has confirmed she will run her portable café outside with the help of a couple of the youngsters.

Mr Harrison from the hardware store has agreed to help dad built the float, no doubt they'll spend hours locked away in the garage back home. That brings a smile to my face.

Ali is going to be in charge of the stuffed toys stall with Mrs Greyson an elderly lady in the community who makes toys for the children's orphanage in Copper town and for the kids here in Willowbrook who may not be as fortunate as others. Her and Ali have been friends ever since Ali showed an interest in learning how to sew along with Daisy. They'll both have a blast, and it makes me feel so proud of my sister to be involved like this and with her old mentor from way back when.

Things are definitely shaping up that is for sure, and you know what, I am actually looking forward to the event.

There are still a few stalls that need to be firmed away, but Eliza assures us that they always go. Elkie who works in the salon will be setting up her face painting stall and I can't wait to see the kids running around with cute faces.

"You're smiling, Sage." Logan says with his head cocked. That brings everyone's heads swivelling round to me. Talk about putting me centre of attention.

"It's not a crime you know."

"You liking the idea of the fundraiser now? I reckon we may just get you to stay after all." He winks. Damn that wink, I've never known anyone who does it so frequently. Not that I'm complaining it makes me swoon for sure, I am a sucker for a man who has glinting sexy eyes, winks, *and* has dark tousled hair to his chin not to mention a few days' worth of stubble. So yeah, that covers Logan pretty much.

Well, we all knew I was going to be in trouble from the off, right?

"Oh, darling it'd be fabulous if you stayed. Why do you want to be so hell bent on getting out of Willowbrook? Look what you have around you. Friends and family who love you so much. A beautiful community of people. Everything on your doorstep and a man right over there who simply adores you."

I know my mouth is hanging open because trust my mom. There is no holding her back, I tell you once she's off she's like a greyhound out of the pen. Seriously, I could shrink under the table right now.

Alli grins, I shoot her a *do not start* look. She sticks her tongue out at me. Great, we're so adult like, yes, I do stick my tongue out at her too. This is very infantile.

Logan sits with his arms folded in front of his chest, I can see the veins popping in his forearms and recall just how they felt around me last night, the familiar smell of his woody fragrance and masculinity, his lips on mine and oh, God I have to squeeze my thighs together.

We all know where I'm ending up again tonight.

"Mom, you know I want to progress further. There's nothing wrong with the practice or working with Logan, Eliza, and Sadie. In fact, I am loving it, more than I thought I would. Honestly, I also like being back home. Not going to admit at first, I was not enamoured but I was nursing a broken heart."

"Yeah, that jerk." Ali butts in. "I could kill, Miles the selfish prick." She can say that again, but you know who am I to say mean things, especially as this is exactly what I did to Logan back then. It makes me feel like shit knowing that I broke his heart in pieces literally. But he wasn't the only one whose heart hurt, mine felt like it was bleeding, I never thought it would ever be fixed. My head was a mess, it was a job to even focus on my studies and every second of every minute of every hour of every day, I wanted to come back home to be close to him, but I had a dream and that pulled me so hard in the other direction.

Now though, looking at him with that grin on his face and the way those eyes are dancing for me, I swear I could lose myself in them forever. With my folks sitting round the table here, his folks who arrived not long ago, our sisters, Eliza, Sadie. Well, yeah it feels like home. It's comfortable, it's warm and I swear I may even be getting those vibes, you know the ones that make you feel like home isn't so bad after all.

My folks begin to get up and put their coats on, Ali follows and Logan's folks.

"I'll get the check; we can put it on the practice." Logan says.

"Are you sure, honey?" His mom asks. He nods. Some things never change, he has always been a generous and thoughtful man, and it shines through not just now but the way he is across the fundraising and wants to do what he can for the younger generation to be able to have a baseball field, the games and to be part of something bigger.

It makes my heart swell, and my breath catches in my mouth. *I cannot fall back in love with Logan. I must not fall back in love with Logan.* I just can't.

"Let's catch up over drinks back at ours." His mom says to my mom. They've been friends since forever, ever since Logan and I were kids. Mom nods, and dad helps her with his coat. He's such a gent, I love how close they still are after all these years. It's heartwarming and I want this with somebody, but I don't think it can be Logan as much as my body wants it to be and my heart, because I still have a career I want to follow.

This is a crap situation, I'm right back where I started ten years ago only, I'm wiser now, older, I should have a better head on my shoulders.

Do I let my heart rule my head or my head rule my heart?

Oh, shit. What a damn mess this is right now.

Logan has that look in his eyes, the look that is asking *are you coming back to mine?* And am I?

He's pretty irresistible and I did enjoy being with him again last night. It was like stepping back in time, I felt like I belonged there, and this is the danger zone area. I know that if I continue to see Logan my heart that's already catapulted back in time is just not going to allow me to pursue my dream.

Or maybe this will become my new dream. God, I'm torn up inside. My head wants one thing, but my heart and my body are aching for him.

Chapter 57

L*ogan*
  I loiter to wait for Sage to come out, she's just saying her goodbyes to Ali and her folks. Mine are going over to hers for drinks. And yes, I am waiting to catch Sage to see if she wants to come over to mine and spend time

with me, grab a pizza from Jefferson's on the way and chill out in front of the fire with Hector.

She comes out, a smile on her face. Ali gives her a hug then she turns to her mom and gives her a hug. My folks' wave at me.

"Catch you both later." I say as I open the door to my truck. Sage makes her way over to me.

"Well, that went well. I'm quite looking forward to the fundraiser now. It feels good to be part of something."

"That's a step in the right direction. I told you; you'd get to like it back here again."

"I never didn't like it, Logan. I just wanted to try something else first. Besides, it's only short-term."

"You keep telling me that, darlin'. But I have a feeling things will change." You'll see." It makes me chuckle when she huffs at me and flicks her hair over her shoulders. Yeah, it's her defiant action.

"Logan, you need to get real and know that I am not staying."

"You want to come over to mine? We can grab a pizza and chill at mine afterwards with the fire on, a movie, some beers. What do you think?" She cocks her head to the side and looks me in the eye. I can tell she thinks it's a good idea, because she's also carrying the faintest of smiles.

"Yeah, why not. I'll meet you at Jefferson's."

"Perfect follow me." I tell her as I step into my truck. I watch as she makes her way to the practice to collect her car and wait patiently for her.

A few minutes later she is behind me and flashes her lights to let me know to pull out of the diner's car park.

I swing a right and head up Main Street to the end past the hardware store, pharmacy, butchers, the grocery store and the corner bookshop and café. Applying the handbrake, I check my rear view and can see Sage fixing her lipstick. Cute. Adorable. So unnecessary, she is beautiful just as she is.

I swing the door open and step outside my truck just as she comes out of her car. "Still cheese and pineapple?" I ask her. "With stuffed crust and onion rings and garlic bread?" I walk towards her and place my hand on the lower part of her back. She still moulds well into my hand. It's a warm and familiar feeling. One I want to experience a whole lot more.

"You got it, no changes. And what about you? Still shredded beef with olives." She chuckles. Sage never did get how I could eat olives with shredded beef, hell even I don't know how I do, but I love it.

"The very same." We head to the door to the pizza parlour and open it.

"Hey, Dr Logan. How's it going?" Jefferson who has been running the place for the last twenty years glances up as up from the dough he is kneading.

"Jefferson. All good thanks."

"The usual. And for you Miss Sage, do I take it your tastes haven't changed in all this time." Sure thing about Jefferson, is that he never misses anyone's tastes. That and Sage and I practically lived in this place growing up. It was one of our favorite things to do, grab a pizza and drive up to our spot higher in the mountains, listen to nature, look at the stars, have a night picnic with some lemonade, ah it was so blissful, so innocent and so damn perfect.

"Hey Mr Jefferson. Yes please, cheese and pineapple." Sage says and sits at one of the round wooden tables. He has six tables in the space all with pale blue iron chairs. It's quaint. On the walls are old photos of his family and how the place used to look all those years ago. It has that whole nostalgic vibe going on.

"I've kind of missed this place." She says as her hands rest on the table; I reach out to hold them in mine. Sage allows me to. I know we slept together last night and trust me it was the best feeling in the world to have her in my bed and wake up to her this morning. But this, well this feels so comfortable and so right but I am unsure of my boundaries with her right now. Does that make sense?

"Nobody makes pizza like Jefferson." I say and she nods.

"You've got that right, Logan. So," she starts. I hold my breath. I sure hope she isn't going to mention *again* about all this nonsense of her leaving Willowbrook again.

"What exactly are we doing here?" I know where she is coming from but decide to play it dumb.

"Ordering pizza." I give her my goofy grin; I know for a fact she loves it.

"Silly. You know what I'm talking about."

"Seems to me darlin' you're calling all the shots. You know already how I feel about you, Sage. You've always had my heart that hasn't changed. I want us to be permanent again to try for a second chance. I'm not really interested in a fling whilst you're between here and wherever the hell it is you want to be."

I wait for her to respond, trying not to hold my breath for too long.

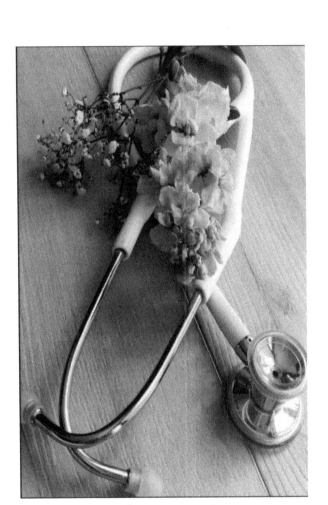

Chapter 58

S *age*
       Every fibre, it feels in my body, is on fire. All of my senses seem to have awakened, I feel like a heady teenager all over again. The way he winks at me, that goofy grin of his, the dimple, his shaggy hair to his chin, those irresistible eyes. It's all making me swoon and go gooey. That's right, *gooey* in

my *mid-thirties*. Hell, I know I'm not going to be able to resist him. And last night was out of this world.

It was like being back home with the man I should have stayed with. Oh, why did I have to be so headstrong, so determined, so... Damn it.

Mr Jefferson brings us our pizzas in the standard brown cardboard boxes with the company family logo on it. A chef's face with a chef's hat. Simple. "I'm guessing for takeout, correct?"

"Absolutely. Thanks Mr Jefferson." I say as Logan reaches in his pocket and pulls out some notes. I stand and my legs feel weak. Jeez this is getting insane. I'm a full-grown adult in charge of her body, aren't I? Only now I'm kind of wondering because really just looking at Logan, the way the veins pop on his arms, his muscular legs, and those narrow hips, they're enough to make any girl flush.

"Let's go." He places a hand on the small of my back, it's such a simple gesture yet goes straight to my clit. Yes girls, that's right. My clit is already in over-drive, and she is aching like a bitch on heat.

I don't hesitate and go to open the door, but he has beaten me to it. His momma brought him up with manners and it shows. "After you." He says with a crooked grin on his face. I want to reach up and touch the stubble on his jaw, the same jaw that is strong and sharp. Logan is one-hundred percent man and I mean that with a capital M, ladies.

I get in my car, yes after he's held the door open for me and put the key in the ignition. He goes to his truck and hops in with the pizza boxes. My stomach grumbles, I know we ate at Bluebell's, but I have a large appetite, God only knows where it goes, I must have hollow legs.

I follow his taillights as we drive the final few metres of Main Street then take a left at the T-junction. Either side are fields with breathtaking mountain views, trees of all colors as the season has now changed and we are into fall. It's beautiful here in West Virginia especially in the fall and it always was one of my favorite times of the year, second to Christmas.

Boy, does our town go nuts for Christmas. There are parades, stalls in the square on Main Street, houses decorate to the hilt and there is even *the best Christmas house* award each year. It's been a while since I actually went to the ceremonies for Christmas. To be honest, I'd simply come back from Michigan for Christmas eve night, stay for the following day then head back to work. It's long hours when you work in a state hospital and especially as part of the A&E team. It's rewarding but also can be harrowing. Some days I felt as if I would crack.

I keep my eyes on his truck as he follows the road round the bend then takes the dirt track to his right. It's densely populated with firs and conifers and our vehicles climb a small ascent until we come to the opening in front of his cabin.

I love the wood structure, it's so welcoming and homely. It must be amazing to come back here after a day at the practice, sit on the porch with Hector and let your legs stretch out with a bottle of beer in your hand and watch the sunset. I find myself sighing.

For real? Am I *actually* sighing over my imagination of something I don't even want? Or am I having a change of heart? Okay, WTF is going on with me right now?

Logan steps out of his truck with the pizzas in his left hand. Man has he got some sexy ass muscular legs on him, not to mention that tight ass of his. It's so perfect I want to bite it.

He strolls over to my car and opens the door for me to step out. Gracefully I swing my legs onto the ground and stand next to him. His head bows down and I can smell his musky aftershave, we're so close and those damn full lips of his have got me all hot and bothered, that and being so near to him again. He fuels my body, he's my magnet. I can't resist.

Stuff the consequences, right now all I want is Logan. Our lips greet each other, it's soft, delicate and I can feel his emotion through them. Our tongues find each other. He tastes faintly of garlic from earlier and coffee. Logan pulls away first, leaving me wanting more and more.

"C'mon darlin'. I've got a dog to let out and we've got some pizza to eat." Party pooper.

He strolls to the side of me, inserts his key in the lock and opens the door. A happy Hector comes running out and does circles around Logan's feet, sniffs at my shoes, and then goes promptly to the large tree close by and cocks his leg. Ada boy.

We step inside the cottage; I swear this is the largest front door I've ever come across as we both fit in side by side. The cottage is still warm from the fire he must have lit this morning to take the morning chill off. That and it's pretty weatherproof. It feels like stepping home, everything is comfortable and cozy from the sofa, the easy chair, his handmade wooden coffee table, to the kitchen area and the broad beams above us.

Logan makes his way to the kitchen in his boots, and I slide my shoes off and pad towards him in my fluffy Donald Duck socks. Don't dare say anything. They're my favorite comfort socks and I love anything Disney, always have always will. When you grow out of Disney, I swear you've just gotten old and miserable.

"You grab some plates from the cupboard while I stoke the fire. It's going to be a bit chillier this evening." He says as he makes his way to the lounge area and closes the door after Hector has come in.

"Hey big fella." I say as I run my fingers through Hector's mop of curly hair on top of his head. "Such a handsome guy." I say.

"You talking about me again, darlin'?" Logan chuckles.

"Give over. I'm talking about Hector. He's gorgeous."

"Yeah, he sure is. He's my best mate, aren't you buddy." Logan is done with the fireplace and comes to pat his buddy on the side. He reaches into a drawer and pulls out some kind of dog twizzle treat and passes it to Hector who is sitting waiting obediently, with his tail going nine to the dozen. I'm telling you, he is so adorable, like one big, fluffy teddy bear. I want a Hector.

Er, I'm not going to be able to have a dog if I go back to a state hospital, the hours will be intense and crazy. There'll be no room for a dog in my life. I dismiss the thought as quickly as it came to mind. I need to focus on my goals and not become distracted. Maybe I want to be distracted. "What are you thinking there, Sage? You've got a far away look on your face." Logan reaches for the plates and takes them to the sturdy, oak dining table. He's already got round plate mats on the table. From the pine dresser he takes some cutlery from one of the three drawers and sets the table.

Hector takes his treat and goes to lay in front of the fire that is now blazing with its orange flames. It gives off such a cozy vibe that I feel like I never want to leave. Oh. God. I am in such big trouble, here. BIG. TROUBLE.

"Oh, nothing." I can see from his raised eyebrows that he doesn't believe me. That's the problem when the heart throb in front of you, knows you better than you know yourself.

Chapter 59

L*ogan*

    We eat our pizza and Hector remains in front of the fireplace, he's such a good dog and never begs at the table. I glance at Sage and see how radiant she looks *and* cute with some cheese dripping on to her chin. Without thinking I remove it with my fingers.

"Thanks." She says.

"No problem. So, have you had an offer yet from any of the hospitals? I know you don't want to stay and I get that only I still think it's a real shame." She bites into her pizza and finishes the last slice off. I take a sip of my beer.

"I have had one but I've not mentioned it to my folks yet or Ali." She pauses and plays with the bottle of beer in front of her.

"You going to tell me which one?"

"Nashville." *Shit*. I almost choke on my beer and only just manage to swallow. Okay, so I was thinking she'd applied closer to home. You know like West Virginia State. That's a fantastic hospital for a start. Then there is Richmond or Cincinnati or even Lexington, to name a few that are a hell of a lot closer than Nashville.

"Are you okay?" She looks at me wide eyed. Am I? Am I hell, of course I'm not alright. My stomach feels weird like it's tightening and there's a fist in there ripping it out, that and my heart which has plummeted to my feet.

"I'm fine." I know I don't sound convincing how can I possibly? After last night and being with her, the way our bodies moulded together like they'd never been apart, the way she tasted, her lips on mine, the look in her eyes as she gazed into mine. I thought we were going to have a going on. How dumb can I be? I want to punch myself in the face damn it for being such a jackass.

"Are you sure, only you look like you're about to choke?"

"I'm perfectly fine." It comes out a little more abruptly than I wanted it to, but it's out there now. "Sorry, I didn't mean to snap. Nashville, eh? That's quite some distance. You sure do want to get out of Willowbrook."

"Actually, I'm not one hundred percent. It's the only offer I've had after so many applications and I did try some closer to mom, dad and Ali. Trust me, it's not originally what I wanted but they do have a good fellowship programme."

"You've got to do what you want to do, Sage. If it feels right, then go with it. I'm sure you'll be able to come home and visit and your folks will travel to see you. Sure, it's about a seven-hour flight or something."

She intercepts. "It's seven hours and forty minutes. It's a haul." I rake my hands through my tousled hair.

I push my chair back from the table and reach for her empty plate and take them to the sink and drop them in. They can wait until later. Now I'm unsure what to do. My instinct is to grab her and hold her body to mine, and inhale her fragrance, to feel her pressed up against me. My entire body is longing for her and so is my heart.

I wish I could turn it off but I can't. I've always loved Sage and I don't think that will ever change. *And* where do we go from here? This is only going to tear me apart. Again. If she decides to move half way across America.

"Where does this leave us?" I ask her. She stands and comes towards me as I lean with my butt against the sink, my hands resting on it to my sides. Sage slips her arms through the loop of mine and rests her hands on my lower back. Her face is tilted up, her lips are so kissable it's all I can do not to. I cave and lower my head and greet her lips with my own.

My heart is going to pay for this, I just know it is.

I'm praying that she decides not to leave, seriously I don't think I can take it again.

Our tongues find each other, I nip at her lower lip and suck on it. Sage groans and pushes her body closer into mine. I feel myself stir in my jeans, this woman is going to be the death of me.

I'm fighting hard with my head that keeps sending me warning signs and my body that she is setting on fire. My dick strains against my jeans, by reflex I push my hips forward knowing she can feel how rigid I am for her.

"There's nothing I can do to change your mind?" I ask as we pull apart from our kiss. Her breathing is fast, her breath catches and I can see by her pupils how much she wants me.

"Depends how good you're going to be at fucking me later." That makes me chuckle. She never was backward at coming forward.

"Well, I'll be sure to fuck you so you can't move Dr Sage Bennett."

"You better, Logan. I'm counting on it."

Without hesitation I swoop her up into my arms and stride to the stairs. I check that Hector is still comfortable and smile as I hear his gentle snoring. Sage rests her head on my shoulder and her arms around my neck. Then I take the stairs two at a time.

She's going to get it so much that she is never going to want to leave my bed again.

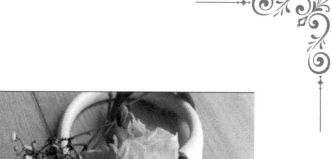

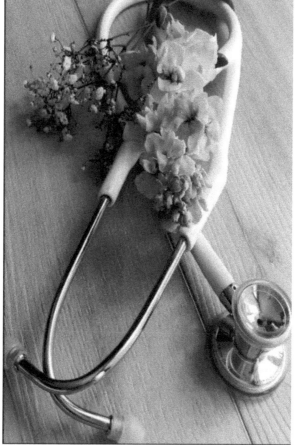

Chapter 60

S*age*
As he carries me into the bedroom, I can't help wonder why I ran off, why I left him behind here in Willowbrook with a broken heart. Why was my career more than what I'm feeling right now? The way his strong arms

hold me, my head on his chest inhaling his woody fragrance, it fills my senses and I feel like I've come home. Full circle.

I can't believe that I have wasted ten years, I mean seriously. TEN WHOLE YEARS. I kiss Logan's neck, feeling his scruff on the side of my face. He sure does have sexy scruff.

Logan lays me on the bed like I'm some kind of precious, breakable thing. It's gentle and takes my breath away. He's been doing a lot of that lately, you know, taking my breath away.

"Are you okay, darlin'?" He asks me. I nod as I lay on the soft bed my head on his fluffy pillows, I actually feel like I'm floating on a cloud. It's such a divine feeling, I never want to leave from here. *What did I just say? Holy shit.* It hits me like a thunderbolt, like I've been shot with lighting at the same time. It's true. I don't ever want to leave him not ever again. I'm suddenly filled with such emotion that even I'm taken aback. It's like nothing I've felt before with anyone, even more than what I had with him first time round. This is deep, real deep.

"Yes. I'm more than okay. Now get on this bed and show me what you've got." I say as I begin to wriggle out of my clothes. He bends down first and kisses me. It's long and lingering, pooling me and turning me to mush. There's no hurry as his tongue seeks mine. He tastes of wine and pizza, it's not a bad mix. Two of my favorite things.

I pull his top so he is closer to me and almost force him to join me on the bed. Logan pulls away just long enough to slip out of his boots and lay down right beside me.

I can feel the warmth of his body against mine as I wrap my arms around him and he holds me close. One hands he slips behind my head and cradles it, his gentle eyes looking into mine. It's intense and I know we've just both crossed the line.

You know, that line that has gone from casually having sex to deep, raw emotions that flood your body and have turned me into the queen of mush. Yeah, that's me right now. This man does things to my body no other man has ever managed before.

"I want you." I tell him in between kisses. He moves his head down to my neck and nips, bites playfully and kisses my neck. It's delicious and sends tingles up and down my spine.

"Don't be so impatient, Missy." He nips at my neck and I giggle.

"Stop damn teasing me, Logan."

"What you going to do about it darlin'?" I'll show him what I'm going to do about it, because right now my clit is throbbing and aching for him. Somehow, I manage to flip him over and straddle him. My hands on his broad chest. I slowly grab at his top and begin to move it up his flat, six pack torso. This man is a God, trust me he has abs he never had before, his V is on display. I trail my fingers down it and hear as he groans.

"You're going to be the death of me, Sage Bennett."

"Dr Sage Bennett." I say back and stick my tongue out at him. He pulls my head down and roughly forces his mouth on to mine. Oo, I like it.

His hand is on the back of my head and his other hand is on my ass as he slaps it. Ass slapping, mm, I think I like that too. It's new to me but his hand slapping me, well I'm telling you it feels fucking great.

I rock my hips forward and backward getting as much friction on his bulge through his pants and my clit as I can.

"You feel so good." He says, his voice is deep and husky. It pools me even more. My clit is aching so bad I need to get our clothes off.

We begin to unrobe ourselves, whilst kissing and grinding and both end up laughing. We're like teenagers, back to where we were all those years ago, when we'd fumble with our clothes and this reminds me of our first time together. How nervous we were, how much we were longing to be close.

"Take it slowly, darlin'. I'm so damn close, you're so sexy, you're driving me insane."

Teasingly, I move down his body until my mouth is on his engorged dick and let me tell you ladies, he is *big*. He's perfect. I fit nicely between his legs as I take his dick in my mouth and run my tongue along his swollen head, tasting his pre-cum. Oh yeah, he's close alright and so am I. Crikey, you'd thing I'd have some kind of control not being that teenager anymore but I haven't. I need this man so badly.

I take a firm grip of his dick and slide my hand up and down whilst flicking my tongue around his head. "Fuck me, that feels good, darlin'. Don't stop. Don't ever stop." I take him down the back of my throat and hear my gagging noises, he feels so good.

"Your mouth is made for my dick." His words turn me on even more if such a thing was possible, since I'm so wet right now. I continue to deep throat him and take my free hand to cup his balls. They're firm and tight, oh my god, I'm on the brink of coming. I need to hold on.

"Get on and ride me." He commands. I don't hesitate. Within seconds I'm sliding myself onto his dick, bit by bit until my pussy finds its way to accommodate his width and length. It hurts a little but the over whelming feeling of being so turned on overrides the slight discomfort.

I begin to rock forward and back, stimulating my nerve jangling clit and bite my lower lip as he teases my nipples with his mouth and his fingers, biting on them one after the other and rolling his thumb and finger around my taut nipples. I moan and throw my head back.

"Does that feel good, darlin´?"

"So good. I'm close, Logan. So close."

"Good, so am I. I fucking want to explode inside you."

With that he places his hands on my hips and begins to lift me up and down, I bounce harder and faster and oh my, I'm about to lose it. The wave starts from the pit of my stomach, my pussy tightens and grips him, I can feel him beginning to pulse as he thrusts harder until he is driving his dick inside me so furiously but fuck me, I am loving it.

I scream out his name as I come all over his dick, my eyes roll to the back of my head and I can even feel my toes curl.

I feel him pulsing and exploding inside me as his hands grip my hips so hard. We orgasm together and spent I fall forward on to him, my head on his shoulder, his arms now wrapped around me, holding me tight and with one hand, he rubs my back.

"I love you." I hear him say as he whispers it into my ear. Tears prick at my eyes. I wasted so much time, it makes my heart hurt that I left the one man who was always the love of my life behind.

"I love you too, Logan." I say between tears. He holds me tighter and kisses my head.

"It's okay, darlin'. It's going to be alright."

Will it be though? What if I go again? I'm so scared. So scared of so many things. Mainly of fucking this up. AGAIN.

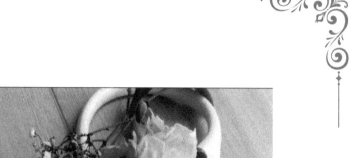

Chapter 61

L*ogan*
  Waking up with her next to me is my dream come true. Her hair is splayed across the pillows and she looks like an angel, she is *my* angel. I feel like I am floating on a cloud. Last night with Sage was like no other night, our hearts have become one again and we are now bonded once more. We

have come full circle it feels and I can tell you, I have waited it seems a lifetime.

I can't even begin to describe how I feel, it's like I am floating on a cloud, the sense of happiness and contentment fills me and my heart feels as if it is overflowing.

Carefully, I ease myself away from her side mindful not to wake her. I need to let Hector out who has managed to find his way into the bedroom and is snoring at the end of the bed. I check the time, it's still early only just six a.m. He stirs and his ears prick up, his tail waggs.

"C'mon boy." I whisper. Hector gets himself up and off the bed, I check to make sure we haven't woken Sage up, she's out cold. I'm not surprised, she must have had four orgasms last night and it was early hours of the morning when we finally fell asleep in one another's arms.

Will she stay? Will I be enough? Or will she go for a long distance realtionship? Only I'm not entirely sure how that could work out and if I am being absolutely honest with myself, it's not what I want. So here we are back where we started, her with her dreams and me wanting to be forever in Willowbrook, the small town I grew up in with the people who are my family and extended family.

Hector stretches on the rug in front of the bed then nuzzles my leg. I fluff his curls atop his head and quietly tiptoe out of the bedroom. We walk across the lounge area and I open the front door for him. The morning air is brisk, it's my favorite time of the year, the leaves are already turning color and there's a distinct fall smell in the air. I watch as Hector goes to his favorite tree, cocks his leg, kicks behind him with his hind legs then comes trotting in and past me, striahgt to the treat cupbord. He makes me smile, he and I we've been through a lot together.

Satisfied with his treats he chomps away whilst I put on coffee and wait for the machine to finish, I put some food in his metal bowl and give him fresh water. Hector comes and eats as I crouch down and wrap my arms around him. He's my comfort and right now I kind of need it.

Yes, we declared our love for each other, Sage and I last night and we didn't have brutal raw sex, it was a night filled of emotion, passion and deep seated love stemming from our childhood years. The way our bodies moved together as one, how we drifted over the crest of the waves of orgasm and lay spent in each other's arms. Yet, it was also the most poignant moment for me. Not knowing which way she will go scares me, it scared me more than it ever did when I was that eighteeen year old kid left behind watching her leave.

I don't think I can take another broken heart.

"Hey, you're up early." I hear her husky, sleepy voice behind me. I stand up, leaving Hector to finish his breakfast. Sage comes towards me, she looks so damn adorable in one of my pale blue shirts that comes down to her mid-thigh. Her hair cascading around her shoulders and some smudging under her eyes from her mascara. She has never looked more beautiful than she does right now in just the shirt and bare feet, with the cuffs hanging down practically covering her hands.

"Always up early darlin'." I say cheerfully not wanting to give away how scared in my heart I am. Sage walks towards me and places her arms around my waist. I wrap mine around her and inhale her fragrance, she is a mix of coconut shampoo and lingering Coco Chanel, her all time favorite fragrance. It's her signature note.

"You want some pancakes for breakfast, granola or toast and scrambled egg?" I ask my lips on her head. God, she feels so damn good, I never want to let her go. I keep saying that right? That's because I don't.

"Mm, let me see can I have all of the above. I am starving, someone worked an appetite up for me until the early hours of the morning." She giggles, it's adorable.

"Coming right up, m'lady." I release her and go pour her a mug of coffee and one for myself. Hector whines at the door.

"I'll let him out." Sage walks him to the door and opens it for him to scurry out. I never have to worry about him, he's not the kind of dog that will run away he's faithful as they come.

I start to take eggs out of the fridge, the pancake mix from the cupboard, some oragne juice and the bread for our toast. "Let me help you." She says as she comes to stand behind me as I mix the batter mix.

"I had an amazing evening, darlin." I say as I whisk away.

"I love a man who can make breakfast." She replies. "I love you, Logan." Her head rests on my back, my heart clenches and my stomach tightens. I want to be open to receive all the love she can give me, trust me I want every last single drop of what she can give, but I'm terrified as hell that she's going to get an offer other than the one in Vegas and she will be off again.

"I love you too, darlin'. To the moon and back. If I could reach up into that sky and give you the moon, I would. You're the other part of my heart, Sage."

"I know." She says quietly. Oh, God I hope my heart isn't about to be break again.

We chat about this and that, the practice, the fundraiser, Thanksgiving that's just around the corner and the holidays.

"Will you be here for Christmas?" I ask her as we sit down at the counter and eat. She places a couple of pancakes on to her plate, pours over some maple syrup and adds some blueberries.

"I'm not a hundred percent sure. I think I may still be here."

"I thought you might stay this time." I reply then take a long drink of my coffee.

"Logan, I want to. I feel like I've just found you all over again and this feeling, it's the most amazing feeling in the world. You make me feel alive, like I've just come back to life after a long sleep, but you know how much I want a fellowship." She sighs. "But it sure is pretty here."

"Sage, darlin' you need to know I can't do long distance and I don't want us to be back where we were ten years ago. We've been given a second chance here, and we should take it. How often does a love like this happen to anyone? It's rare, like a precious gem. You are rare. You make the sky brighter even when the sun shines, you are the other part of my beating heart, your smile lights up the room and your eyes make me drown in them. Life has no meaning if you're not by my side."

Her eyes are on mine. Somethings you know, have to be said. I'm not too manly to let my heart talk for me. If I'd have talked some more back ten years ago, then maybe she'd never have left in the first place and we'd have children by now.

I had and have dreams too.

"I don't know I can give you the commitment right now, but I do know I won't be taking the offer I've got. Maybe I can get something closer, like West Virgiinia State. That's only a couple of hours away and I could commute."

"I'd miss you at the practice for sure, however, that'd be amazing." I place my cutlery down and reach for her hand. She squeezes mine back. Inside I'm praying. In my dream I see us both running the family practice, with her carrying our baby inside her, and at weekends pottering around here by the cabin, laying down with the fire on and reading a good book, Hector by her feet. I see her holding our child, teaching it how to plant bulbs, how to read, seeing her being the most wonderful mother that I know she would be. Watching as she holds it's tiny hands as it takes its first steps.

"I know that look, Logan." Of course she does, she knows me inside out.

Only time will tell which way Dr Sage Bennett will go.

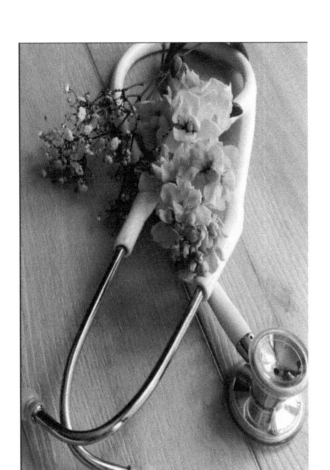

Chapter 62

S*age*
    I watch as he prepares us breakfast and can't keep my eyes of his body that should be illegal. Seriously, he's all ripped muscles and I am in love with those veins on his forearms as she whisks the batter mix for our pancakes. Not to mention his tight ass in his joggers. I forgot to mention that right

now, Logan isn't wearing anything on top and I can see how broad and muscular he is. I am salivating again and thinking about what his body does to me, is causing that familiar warmth to spread up from the pit of my stomach and ignite within my body.

"You checking my ass out, darlin'?" He turns and I can see the mischief in his eyes.

"Well, it is there right in front of me what can I say?"

"We need to eat and replenish our energy, I've got plenty more of last night for you and then some."

"You smooth talker you."

"I've not even begun, Dr Sage Bennett. When I'm finished with you all this talk about leaving me and Willowbrook will be a distant memory."

He could be right there, I'm already considering why move when I can be here with the man I love, the same man I've always really loved. Time only help put a bandaid on the scar but it never fixed it, it certainly didn't heal it and now we're here finally healing our hearts.

There is something warm and cozy about sitting at his island as he cooks and Hector comes back in from outside. I stand up and go close the door since the morning air is brisk.

"I've beent thinking." I say. He looks over his shoulder, his gorgeous eyes on mine. A woman could easily drown in those eyes of his.

"Shoot." He says then turns back to continue to whisk before pouring the mix into a pan on the stove.

"I don't know that I want to leave anymore."

He puts the pan down and comes to the island, placing both his hands on it. "Say that again." His voice is almost a whisper but I can detect the huskiness in it. I'm loving how his jaw his moving and the stubble he has from not shaving for a few days.

"I like it here, I never thought I'd say that but in all honesty, Logan I don't think I could leave you again." He doesn't say anything for a few seconds. I'm longing for him to say something, anything. I'm wearing my heart on my sleeve right now. It's killing me.

"You want to stay here in Willowbrook *and* with me?" Our eyes don't wander from the others. It's intense, I'm on fire because I know what I can have with Logan. Something I never could have had with Miles, something

I could never have from a fellowship in a different state or anywhere in the world.

What Logan can give me is warmth, security, arms around me every night, kisses that make me swoon, love making that takes me to a different planet. The way he loves me can't be found with another man, when you've found the one, you've found the one and now I finally know he is *the* only one for me.

Why I left before is now staggering but I am here I am with him and I don't want it to ever change. I don't want to lose what I have with Logan right now, what we can be together in our futures.

I nod, biting my lower lip as he rakes his hands through his hair. I know he wants to be excited and show it, but he is retraining himself, you know, just in case he hasn't quite heard what I am saying.

"That's right." I sit up straighter. Shit, I'm about to turn my entire universe upside down, actually he's been doing that ever since I slept with him again.

All those feelings came to the surface and I don't want to push them away. Another broken heart is not on my agenda and if I walk out his door and move again, I'll never heal. I'm not a young kid anymore, I'm a grown woman and I recognize how I feel and can clearly see what I want for my life now.

"To both. I don't want to leave *you*, Logan. I don't think I can. You see, I'm in love with you. Still."

"Baby," he says as he comes round from the other side of the island. "Say that again, it sounds so damn beautiful. I've waited the last ten years to hear you say those words again." He holds me to him, my head against his bare, muscular chest. I inhale his masculine body smell. I nuzzle my face into him and kiss his stomach.

"I love you, Logan damn it. I've tried my hardest not to, I've tried to ignore you when I first came back but I just can't."

He steps back and places one hand on my shoulder and with his other hand he tilts my face up slightly as his fingers rest gently under my chin.

"I love you too, Sage. I've never stopped loving you. I want the world to know you're mine. Damn I want our babies, I want to see your stomach swollen with our child, watch as you nurture it and blossom."

Tears sting my eyes, this is everything I want t0o. It's kind of weird how you can be on track for one thing with a single minded focus and then bam, just like that everything changes in an instant.

Maybe, I've been focusing too hard on being the top of my field to chase away the heartache I brought upon myself and the guilt for breaking Logan's heart too.

"I think it's a bit early for kids but yes, I want that too. I want to hold your child in my arms and look down at a baby mini-Logan."

"Our babies sure are going to be cute," he says smiling. "And if it's a girl, Lord help everyone. She's going to be feisty, sassy and have a mouth on her." He chuckles. I watch his Adam's apple bobbing up and down.

My heart is brimming and then some for the man in front of me. How you can love someone entirely like this, that makes you feel content comes once in a lifetime and I know how lucky I am to have been given a second chance. This is it. There is no going back.

"Do you know what a field day our mom's are going to have?" He says as he leans down and begins to kiss me, moving the hand from under my chin to the back of my head. I am swooning to the moon and back, I'm pooling into a puddle. My clit begins to throb with longing for him again. I am insatiable for Logan.

He is my new addiction.

"For sure," I say between kisses. "We're going to have to let them know to take it slowly." I giggle. He kisses me more deeply, our tongues find their familiar pattern again, he tastes of coffee. He tastes divine.

"It won't be long, Bennett and I'll be putting a ring on that finger. I'm not taking any chances with you walking back out of my life ever again."

"There's no chance of that, Logan. I'm all yours, now, tomorrow and forever."

Hector comes over and starts nuzzling his head against Logan's thigh. He manages to stroke the dog's head, it's as if he knows something amazing has just happened and wants to be a part of it.

We break away from each other. "I've got a breakfast to make, then I'm taking you straight back to bed, darlin'." I squeeze my thighs together at the thought of it and cock my head to one side.

"I can't wait." I stroke Hector's head as he sits by my side. He's the cutest dog ever.

We both watch as Logan makes the pancakes and places them on the plate beside him. My heart is stretched to the max just looking at him, the life I'm about to embark on with this man, the man I have loved since I was a kid.

True love exists, it's out there and second chances come but once in a lifetime and this is it for me. This glorious man, his dog and a cozy cab nestled in the woodland area of West Virginia.

I know I've come full circle and I'm well and truly home.

Epilogue

*T**hree months later***
Logan

Am I nervous? Oh my god, you had better believe it. Listen, I know that Sage is living with Hector and I up in the cabin and honestly, things could not be going any better, but still I am a ball of nervous wreck and energy.

In twenty minutes she'll be coming into Lazy Duke's with her family, my sister Daisy and my folks too.

We've got her here for just our regular Friday night out at Lazy Duke's. It's become something we do and it's always great to hang with our friends some old and some new like the Jenkinson's who moved into Willowbrook from Ohio last month.

Sage and I have been busy at the practice now we're taking on more patients from Copper Town and also from Ilks Creek not too many miles away. Things are going well and we've got the fundraiser for the baseball and the kids coming up in a few more weeks time then straight into the Thanksgiving Festival. For which my mom has already started baking and freezing. We all love the festival here in Willowcreek, it's a real special community that we have going on and I'm just so happy that Sage has found her feet here and there is no more talk of going to move somewhere else for her career.

In fact just the other day she told me that she can't even believe she ran off way back when and how could she have imagined she'd be as happy as she is right now. It fills my heart to hear her say that and then some.

"You guys almost ready" I shout across the small stage to my second guitarist and my drummer. Nick, on keyboard is already set up and waiting to go.

We've got five songs laid on for tonight and one that we're starting with for when Sage comes in with Daisy and our respective folks. They all know why they're here tonight it is only Sage who is in the dark.

My heart is fluttering, I feel like I can't catch my breath properly and oh shit, did I already say how damn nervous I am.?

"All set." My second guitarist, Simon tells me, who actually happens to be Abe's nephew. He's only a kid around eighteen but boy does he know how to strum the strings. He sure has got some talent and I can honestly see him going far if he decides to pursue his music career. He's not sure yet as he told me he really needs to have a degree under his belt, just in case things don't take off.

"Okay, I'm going to grab some beers but for you, Simon what do you want? Cola, Lemonade?"

"I'll have a coffee actually if that's good with you?"

"Sure, no problem. Back in five." I tell them as they are at their spots on the stage.

Abe gives me a nod and a wink. "Feeling scared, Bro?" He asks with a massive grin on his face.

"Is it that obvious?" I ask as I lean against the bar with my forearms resting on top.

"Just a little. You need to calm down, it's going to be absolutely fine."

Deacon Marshall who is sitting at his usual spot at the end of the bar nods his head at me. I'm wondering if Daisy mentioned it to him too, only you see you have to be careful with Daisy because she is *the* worst at keeping secrets.

I nod back as I place my order for three beers and a coffee with Abe. He pops the beers for me and places them on a tray and starts with the coffee at his all singing and dancing machine.

"On the house." He says.

"Thanks, Abe. I really appreciate that."

"You better get on up there, I can see Daisy and Sage heading this way."

I check behind me and sure enough I can see through the window that they're on the car park area with arms interlinked. My folks are behind with Sage's and seem to be chatting away animatedly.

Am I sweating? Shit. I think I am.

"Tell you what, get ready on stage, Logan and I'll have Becca bring the drinks over for when you're done."

"Thanks a lot. I owe you one." I head back to the stage and jump up at the front on to it.

"Guys, we've got to start with song one, they're already about to come through the door."

"Got you." Says Simon and they start.

We play our version of *When A Man Loves A Woman* sung originally by Percy Sledge, it happens to be Sage's all time favorite song even over the ones we have written together.

The door opens and my breath catches as I take her in, drinking every detail of her with my eyes. Her long slender legs encased in tight black jeans, a tight fitting navy jumper on top with her pea coat left open. She looks up at the stage as we begin playing and smiles and waves. My heart is brimming over, damn I love this woman to the moon and back, I'd die for her, I would literally give her my life and the air that I breath. I can't wave back as I'm on guitar but I do smile at her. She blushes. It's so damn cute the way that after these months she is still blushing like a teenager.

I watch as they head for the bar and order some drinks. She is about to sit down next to Daisy and we finish our song.

"Before we start the next song, can I just ask for Dr Sage Bennett to come to the stage please." Her head swivels round and she looks directly at me and pulls her eyebrows together.

It's as if the whole world has literally just stopped. Everyone is waiting and I mean everyone, since the bar is packed tonight, it's always packed out on a Friday for live music night.

"Me?" She screeches.

"Well, darlin' I don't know of any other Dr Sage Bennett in the house tonight." She is going a cute shade of red. "C'mon up don't be shy."

"I swear I'm going to kill you when I get you home tonight." She comes out with, there are a few chuckles. "I'm not singing, I've not sung for years." She says. Still as lippy as ever my woman. I love it but boy is she in for a shock. Finally, she is standing next to me, we're side by side. I can smell her favorite fragrance of the month, Daisy by Marc Jacobs. I give her a small kiss on the lips. We get a few whistles. My guys on stage begin to play a new track and I look at Sage and take her left hand in mine.

"What are you doing?" She almost hisses as she watches me go down on one knee and reach into my shirt pocket for the small velvet box I placed in there earlier.

I pull it out and release her hand to open the box. Sage's hands fly to her mouth and her eyes are wide open.

"Oh my god. Yes. Yes." She says.

"I haven't asked you yet, darlin'." I say but it is good to know that she wants to marry me too. That is some relief for sure.

"Sorry, yes. Ask me." There is laughter and some more whistling.

"Sage Bennet, ever since I can remember I have loved you. My heart has been yours for nearly all my life. You are the air that I breathe, the stars I see at night. I love you with every fiber of my body. You challenge me in so many ways and you've got a smart ass mouth, but I wouldn't change a damn thing about you. I'm so in love with you darlin' and I want to spend every day with you for the rest of our lives. What do you say?"

She's almost crying. I take the ring and put it on her finger on her left hand she has outstretched waiting.

I stand and her arms fly around my neck, she's pressed up so close to me that if she's not careful she's going to feel how aroused I am for her. The bar folk clap, whistle and cheer. "Logan, I will always love you, honor and respect you. I'm so sorry it took me so long to come full circle and be back in your arms." We kiss, it's deep and passionate until Abe calls out and tells us to get a room.

"To Sage and Logan." He shouts out and everyone raises their glasses or bottles.

"Now how about that song, darlin'?" I wink at her. She pushes me playfully and says no way.

"I'll catch up with you after the set, fiancée." I say loving how it feels rolling off my tongue.

"That you will, hubby to be." I watch as she steps off the stage still unable to comprehend how much I love this woman and how far we've come. Ten years, they were the longest ten damn years of my life.

But, we're here today, now claiming our love for one another and to spend our lives with each other until death do us part . I swear I'm never going to let her down. I will be the man she wants and needs, I'll protect

Dr Sage Logan and take care of her until I'm a very old man.

We've got our second chance, our hearts are finally healed and there is no greater love than what I feel for her. I am so excited for the rest of our lives to happen.

*****_The End_*****

About the Author

Kerry is a multi-genre author who was born in London and travelled extensively with her parents and sister. Her father was in the military and travelling was second nature to her.

Nowadays Kerry lives in Spain with her long-term partner, her four cats and her Chihuahua where she loves to spend time walking, biking and enjoying the mountain and sea views.

Kerry is an avid reader and when she's not creating plots, characters and making up places, you will find her enjoying a good read by some of her favourite authors.

One of her favourite pass times is rock-climbing and having scaled dizzying heights, she now settles for much shorter routes closer to home in the Prades Mountains.

Nothing delights her more than a good bar of chocolate and a nice cup of coffee, which she confesses to drinking far too much of.

Don't miss out!

Visit the website below and you can sign up to receive emails whenever Kerry Kennedy publishes a new book. There's no charge and no obligation.

https://books2read.com/r/B-A-SGNY-DEWVC

BOOKS 2 READ

Connecting independent readers to independent writers.

Did you love *Healing Hearts*? Then you should read *Meet Me In Casablanca* by Kerry Kennedy!

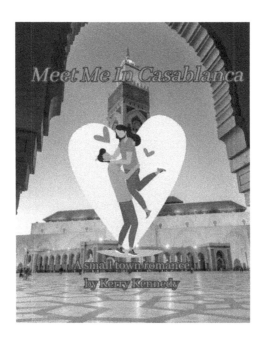

When Ellie's long-term boyfriend, Jordan, proposes to her, she is forced to confront the fact that her life has been on autopilot for far too long. Faced with the prospect of a future she never really wanted, Ellie decides to take a bold step and leave her small town behind to travel to Casablanca, Morocco.

In Casablanca, Ellie discovers a new world of sights, sounds, and experiences. She meets a handsome and charming man named Omar, who sweeps her off her feet with his passion and zest for life. As Ellie begins to explore this new life, she must confront her feelings for Jordan and the life she left behind.

Caught in a love triangle, Ellie must make a difficult decision about where her heart truly lies. Will she choose the comfort and security of her old life with Jordan, or the excitement and adventure of her new life with Omar?

Set against the backdrop of the exotic and vibrant city of Casablanca, this small town romance is a tale of love, self-discovery, and the courage to take risks.

Read more at https://linktr.ee/kerry_kennedy_author.

About the Author

Kerry is a multi genre author currently living in Spain and hailing from the UK. Five years ago she and her partner made a life decision to move to warmer climates and to be close to the mountains they climb.

An avid writer and reader, you will usually find her with a book in her hand.

Her pleasurable activities include rock climbing, hiking in the Prades mountains, biking along the trails of Catalonia with stunning mountain backdrops and of course drinking too much coffee.

She lives with her partner, four cats and her chihuahua.

Read more at https://linktr.ee/kerry_kennedy_author.

Milton Keynes UK
Ingram Content Group UK Ltd.
UKHW032039180324
439698UK00001B/170